PLAGUE

A *Just Cause Universe* Novel

Adrienne Dellwo

Local Hero Press Edition

Plague: A Just Cause Universe Novel
Published by Local Hero Press, LLC
http://localheropress.com

1st Printing
Local Hero Press: trade paperback, November 26, 2019
Printed in the United States of America

ISBN-13: 9781971445175

Cover art by Scott Story
Book design by Local Hero Press, LLC

Books by Local Hero Press

The *Just Cause Universe*

Just Cause
The Archmage
Day of the Destroyer
Deep Six
Jackrabbit
Champion
Castles
The Lion and the Five Deadly Serpents
Tusks
The Neighborhood Watch
Jackrabbit: Big In Japan
Arena
Hero Academy
The Path
Cinco de Mayo
Search and Rescue
Rooftops
Plague
Soldiers of Fortune
Just Cause Universe Compendium
Destroyer of Earth
Flint and Steel
The Club
Jackrabbit: Rinse and Repeat
Posse
Extinction Event
Rain Must Fall

Pariah of Verigo

Pariah's Moon
Pariah's War

Three Flavors of Tacos

The Guitarist
Making the Cut
The Scene Stealers

Collections

Airship Lies
High Contrast
The Good Fight
The Good Fight 3: Sidekicks
The Good Fight 4: Homefront
The Good Fight 5: The Golden Age
Muddy Creek Tales
Caped

Other Novels

Assassin
Blood on the Ice
Funeral Games
Hope and Undead Elvis
Horde
The Murder Squad (2026)
Roast Wyvern (and Other Recipes)
*Starf*cker*
Strings
The Oilman's Daughter
Troubleshooters

Nonfiction

Action! Writing Better Action Using Cinematic Techniques

Author Notes

How can I express adequate thanks to the people who supported me through the writing of this book? I leaned on my husband, Joe, and first born, Liam, for their expertise in weapons, tactics, and police procedure (not to mention making sure I ate now and then). My daughter, Naomi, unknowingly lent her voice to one character and her name to another. And thank you, Ian Thomas Healy, for inviting me to play in your oh-so-large and wondrous JCU sandbox. The first two books have been a blast and I'm looking forward to more!

Finally, to the great Stan Lee, who left us while I was in the early stages of writing Plague: Thank you for showing us the true power of storytelling and representation, and for inspiring countless artists to use their work to improve the world. My greatest goal as a writer is to make a worthy contribution to your legacy.

—Adrienne Dellwo
October 2019

CHAPTER ONE

Saturday, July 22, 2017
Bruderschaft Compound, North Idaho

Zeke Shepherd shot a nervous glance over his shoulder but saw nothing except the sheep, the dogs, the field, and the dense woods beyond. "You're friends with black people? With . . . nig—"

"Gah! Don't say that word!" Gabe shook his head, exasperated with the other boy. He leaned back against a tree. Even seated in the tall grass, Zeke towered over Gabe, who was small and slight for sixteen.

"Sorry, Gabe. You're friends with, uh, them?" Zeke kept his voice low even though no one was around to hear them. It didn't pay to be careless on the Bruderschaft compound. Saying the wrong thing could mean extra duties or beatings. Or worse.

Gabe sighed. "Of course, I'm friends with black people. And Hispanic people, and trans people, and Jewish people. I'm so accepting, I'm even friends with your stupid ass." His smirk let Zeke know he wasn't being mean.

It had taken Zeke a while to understand the newcomer. He'd never met anyone else like him. "But . . ." Zeke's head reeled, as it so often did when he talked to Gabe. Zeke had been born into Bruderschaft and had lived his whole life there, with his father and about a hundred and fifty of God's chosen people—all white, all Christian—but Gabe had only been there for a few months. Zeke shook his head, unable to fathom why Gabe would be friends with so many people who weren't like him. "But why?"

"Because they're *people,* dude. Just like *I'm* people."

"And they're . . . nice? Not criminals or terrorists or anything?"

"Damn but you're thick sometimes, Zeke." Gabe took a deep breath and ran his hands through what little hair had grown back since his father shaved it off. "Look at the people here. Forgetting for a minute they're a bunch of racist, nationalist, homophobes, some are nice and some are dicks, right?"

Zeke nodded.

His friend shrugged. "You thought there was something wrong with me at first and now you know I'm cool. It's the same with everyone, whether they're white or black, Christian or Muslim, gay or straight, super-powered or not. Some people in every group are cool, and some are assholes, and most are a mix of both."

"I'm trying to understand that, man, I really am. It's just . . ."

"Yeah, I know. Indoctrination from birth makes it tough. We need to get you away from this damn compound while you can still be salvaged."

Fear shot through Zeke's heart. As much as he'd begun to doubt some of what he'd been taught, he couldn't help but picture the outside world as a chaotic, violent, immoral place. How many times had his father told him he was far too weak for the world? The bell rang to signal the hour, and he leaped up. "Oh, crap! You'd better get back to the barn. It's getting late."

Gabe sighed again and stood up in no particular hurry. "I'm so damn sick of cows."

Zeke chuckled. "Should've thought of that while you were trying to get moved off dish duty. And chopping wood."

"I was sick of those, too. I'm sick of freaking duties altogether." Gabe brushed grass off his standard-issue canvas work pants. "Later, dude."

"See you at dinner." Zeke watched his friend walk away and rubbed a hand over his blond crew cut to wipe away the sweat. He picked up the tall walking stick that had once been his grandfather's. After five decades, the carved eagles and swastikas were all but worn away.

He couldn't see the main part of the compound from his vantage point because of the hill across the stream. The barns and silos were still in view, though, and he preferred to be where he couldn't see any buildings at all.

The flock had just about picked this field clean anyway, so he whistled at the dogs and headed north and a little west, farther away from the agricultural buildings and the farm fields beyond them. Despite the hill, Zeke knew he moved up past the schoolhouse, then parallel to the knot of houses and barracks they called the neighborhood. Northeast of the neighborhood stood the weapons and explosives depots. Up farther, through a knot of forest to where they'd clear-cut the trees a few years back, were the training grounds for the soldiers and soldiers-in-training. He didn't hear the drill sergeants barking orders, so he figured they were running stealth-training ops off in the woods.

He trudged up the gradual slope, not glancing back at the flock. They would follow him. They always did—he was the best shepherd in Bruderschaft. As he passed through the narrow spot between the stream and two large oaks outside the evergreen forest's edge, he gave a wide berth to the enormous wasp nest he'd seen the day before. No use looking for trouble.

Rustling hooves came up fast behind him and a cantankerous ewe ran past and clipped his leg. Two blue heelers, named Jimmy and Bob, followed right on her tail. As they nipped at her ankles to get her back in line, Zeke staggered sideways and his arms and walking stick flailed wildly. "Dang it, Eleanor," he yelled after the ewe. The stick smacked into something over his head. His intestines knotted with dread as furious wasps filled the air around him.

He swiped and knocked a few out of the air, but more took their place until a roiling mass of black and yellow bodies filled his vision. They bumped against him as if jostling to be the first to bury a stinger into his flesh.

"Get away from me!" Zeke threw his arms over his head and face and squeezed his eyes shut. "Stop!"

The frenzied buzzing diminished to a gentle hum. One insect bumped against his shoulder, then no more. He peeked out and his jaw dropped. The swirling cloud of wasps hovered in the air, two feet away.

They all stared at him with those alien, multi-faceted eyes; stared as if waiting for orders.

Chills raced up his arms. "G-go back to your damn nest," he whispered. They did. Every last one.

Saturday, July 22, 2017
Coeur d'Alene, Idaho

"Chloe, can you come down here, honey?" Chloe's dad, Phil, called up the stairs.

"Yeah, just a sec," Chloe shrugged her broad shoulders into a tank top with a low-cut back, and pulled her ponytail through a bright green scrunchie that matched the dyed streak of hair over her right ear.

She turned sideways a little as she left her bedroom so her dragonfly wings wouldn't smack against the door jamb and went to the top of the stairs. When she saw the grim expression on her dad's face, her good cheer vanished. "What's wrong?"

He motioned her to follow him and sat on the great room couch. Chloe's mom, Heather, met her at the bottom of the stairs and put a supportive hand on her shoulder. "Dad, mom, what's going on?" Chloe perched on a padded bench since her wings didn't mesh well with regular chairs.

Phil unfolded a newspaper and spread it out on the coffee table to reveal the picture on the front page—a stock photo of Chloe on one side and Zayden Lord's mugshot on the other. The headline above announced: *Exclusive: Local Hero Foiled Bombing*. Phil sighed. "We knew someone would eventually figure out it was you. Looks like *eventually* has arrived."

Chloe groaned. "Great, Round Two begins."

Round One had come after her wings sprouted during a televised gymnastics meet. It was the worst moment of her life. Competition judges determined her wings and extra back muscles gave her an unfair advantage. They kicked her off the gymnastics team that had been the center of her world since elementary school. Her points got thrown out, too, costing her team the chance to move to the next round. Her former teammates had harassed her the whole summer before she left for Hero Academy.

At the Academy, Chloe uncovered fellow student Zayden Lord's plan to blow up the school's auditorium and kill dozens of parahumans. When Zayden orchestrated distractions to draw the faculty and staff away from campus, it fell to Chloe and her friends to stop him.

Since then, the school and law enforcement had tried to keep the kids' identities under wraps, but they all knew it was just a matter of time. Chloe had hoped she'd at least have until Zayden's trial started in a few months.

"Shouldn't the paper have contacted me about this?" Chloe asked. Phil and Heather exchanged a look. Chloe raised her eyebrows. "What?"

Phil smirked. "After all the hounding after your wings came out, your mom wrote a strongly worded letter to the local media outlets, telling them to stay well away from you and not to contact us again."

"A perk of having an attorney for a mom, I guess." Chloe sighed and picked up the paper.

COEUR D'ALENE, ID—Local gymnast-turned-parahuman Chloe Wyld (15) was the Hero Academy student who unraveled a plot to blow up a building on the Denver campus and helped lead the group of students that prevented the explosion, according to multiple sources. It was last September when student Zayden Lord was arrested by Just Cause and placed into custody in the Deep Six parahuman prison in Montana pending trial. Hero Academy and law-enforcement agencies have declined to name the students involved in the effort to prevent the explosion. However, the *Coeur d'Alene Sentinel* has confirmed Wyld's involvement through several sources, including Lord's alleged co-conspirator Miguel Machado and a source at the school who asked to remain anonymous.

Wyld and Lord dated briefly, and Lord attempted to recruit Wyld to his cause, Machado said. Their relationship provided Wyld with the clues that would lead her to piece together enough of Lord's plan to stop it, he said.

Along with Wyld, Machado named numerous students who participated in the effort to stop Lord, including Charlie O'Neal (Meta Moth, 16), Lindsay Malone (Fireball, 14), and Justin Sharp (Corvid, 18), who recently was assigned to Just Cause Seattle.

Before entering the Academy, Lord is believed to have encountered Machado's older sister, Lucia Machado, in an online chatroom for parahumans who believe themselves superior to non-powered humans.

Lord recruited Lucia, who in turn recruited Miguel and his twin sister, Isabella, investigators say. The Machado sisters also are detained at Deep Six. Miguel has been cooperating with investigators from the beginning. It remains unknown whether he will face charges related to his alleged role in the plot.

The incident highlighted the small-but-growing parahuman supremacist movement, which has stoked fears of hate groups and led to an increase in protests, legislation, and hate crimes against parahumans, according to the FBI, Parahuman Resources Agency, and Just Cause.

Chloe was already so over it. She folded the paper and tossed it onto the coffee table with an eye roll. "I better let everyone know about this." She took out her phone and logged on to a group chat in Parable, Hero Academy's private social media site.

Get ready for a publicity storm, she posted. *Miguel gave our names to my local paper.* She went to the paper's website and copied the article link into another post. *Sorry guys.* Then she sent private messages to her boyfriend Charlie, and her BFF and Academy roommate Lindsay.

Charlie responded right away. *Damn. You ok?*

Don't really know yet. Not freaking but kinda anxious.

Big hugs to you hon. I know you hate this stuff.

She grinned. *Thanks. Hugs back. Still coming up for my birthday?*

Yep. Wouldn't miss it. Can't wait to see you.

Chloe didn't want to wait another week and a half to see him, but it would be awesome to have him and Lindsay there for her birthday—especially since she no longer had any close friends in town, thanks to the gymnastics incident. She still didn't like to think about it.

Lindsay messaged, saying her mom had already gotten a call from a cable news network but refused to talk to them. Her mother worked at Deep Six and became famous when she stopped a prison break almost single-handedly. *Time to get used to hero-style publicity, sister.*

Wish it could've waited until we were with Just Cause or something . . . but yeah, better get used to it. Sigh.

Saturday, July 22, 2017
Bruderschaft Compound, North Idaho

Gabe walked past the schoolhouse and toward the barracks, head down and hood up as if it made him invisible. He wished he *could* turn invisible, like a parahuman, to hide from the bullies and his parents. Because of the bullies, his and Zeke's friendship had begun right there outside the one-room schoolhouse.

Gabe's parents had dragged him to the Bruderschaft compound in their misguided attempt to make him straight. Days after they'd moved in, an older boy named Justice White and his buddies had decided Gabe needed a good beat-down. They were all proud soldiers-in-training, the highest thing most boys on the compound could aspire to be.

They hunted Gabe down, cornered him behind the schoolhouse, and Justice slammed a meaty fist into Gabe's cheek. The other boys jeered as pain exploded across Gabe's face and he crumpled to the ground. He balled himself up, anticipating more blows, but they never came.

"Hey, knock it off!" someone yelled. Gabe opened his eyes and saw the biggest boy on the compound standing there like a superhero, brandishing a heavy wooden walking stick. The kid's beet-red face and wide eyes revealed his own fear. "Five against one ain't exactly fair."

"What are you gonna do about it, pussy?" Justice turned away from Gabe to confront the larger boy. "All that size and you ain't nothin' but a coward."

"Looks to me like you're the cowards. Least, that's what my pa says about ganging up on younger kids." He took a step forward and the other boys squirmed, muttering and glancing toward their de facto leader.

"I ain't afraid of you, Shepherd," Justice glared at the big kid and then down at Gabe, who cowered at his feet. "You stay away from me, pervert, or I'll beat the gay right out of you." With that, Justice and his friends lumbered away.

Zeke knelt beside Gabe. "You okay?"

Gabe rubbed the knot on his cheek in lieu of an answer.

"I'm Zeke. You're John Beck's son, right?"

Gabe ran his hand over the stubble on his shorn scalp. "I'm Gabe, and this place sucks." Just like that, the two boys became friends.

Zeke didn't have any other friends on the compound. Gabe understood why. Somehow, despite indoctrination for all of his sixteen years, Zeke was a nice guy. Misinformed, but nice.

Zeke's size combined with the Shepherd family's status on the compound kept them both from being too tempting a target for the soldiers-in-training, or SITs, as Zeke called them. His father, Tom Shepherd, held a powerful position on the council, and he was a mean drunk who was even meaner sober. Everyone knew better than to cross Tom. If his bulging arms and reputation didn't scare you, his resting I'll-cut-you face would. Zeke, on the other hand, didn't seem to have a guileful bone in his body. He treated Gabe as an equal, which was a damn sight better than anyone else in Bruderschaft.

As he reached what they called the neighborhood, Gabe didn't see Justice or any SITs around the barracks and let out a relieved breath. They must still be out in the woods, playing soldier and pretending to shoot down the enemies of the Master Race. Still, he didn't risk using the main entrance of the barracks where he lived with his parents and twenty-some other people. He went through the back door, which was closer to his room and meant he didn't have to pass through the common area. He never knew who'd be in there.

Gabe detested the cinder-block monstrosity with its narrow hallway and communal showers. The elite families got houses, but Gabe's father had no status on the compound, so Gabe got a tiny closet adjacent to his parents' somewhat larger closet. All the furnishings were Bruderschaft issue—forty-year-old castoffs from Army surplus stores and defunct prisons.

No one locked their doors here. In fact, the doors didn't have locks. The council wanted everyone to know they had no privacy on the compound. Anyone could, at any time, walk into your room and do whatever they pleased. They could go through your stuff, storm in and beat you, or haul you off in the middle of the night. It all depended on what their leader, Barnabas, told them to do. From what Gabe had seen, no one questioned Barnabas's decisions. Not more than once, anyway.

Even with the door unlocked, the room was Gabe's oasis. He'd hung up a few posters of his favorite bands even though it didn't make his dad too happy. He'd asked why Gabe wasn't into sports, like a normal boy from out in the world. Gabe had looked him in the eye and said, "Probably due to the lack of a strong male role model during my formative years." That had gotten him cuffed on the ear. Since then, Gabe had made a concerted effort to be less of a smart ass. He didn't always succeed.

Gabe wedged his desk chair under the knob and slipped his tablet from the tan canvas jacket's inside pocket. It was too hot for the jacket, but he wore it anyway. He couldn't risk anyone finding the tablet or its charger, so he took them with him everywhere. He plopped down on the narrow bed and studied the Google Map images he'd compiled in preparation for the day he could run away from the little slice of hell that was Bruderschaft.

He would've fled already, but he had no money and nowhere to go. His sole ally in the outside world—Aunt Kim—hadn't responded to emails since he got here.

Aunt Kim was the family rebel and outcast because she'd gone to college but didn't go to church. Gabe and his mom, Sherry, had lived with her since he was a few months old. His father abandoned them when he wanted them to move to the compound but Sherry refused to leave Wisconsin. Removed from the constraints of an abusive husband and his fundamentalist religion, Sherry went wild. She drank. She took drugs. She brought home a parade of men to Kim's house. It all led to her arrest and eventual conviction on methamphetamine charges. She got ten years, leaving Gabe in his aunt's custody at nine years old.

Kim raised him to be his own person. Even coming out as gay was the least dramatic thing ever. She told him she'd suspected it for a while and took him out to dinner.

Behind bars, Sherry re-embraced religion, and her piety convinced the parole board to release her early. She surprised Gabe and Kim by showing up at their door. She and Kim had talked, then argued, then screamed at each other about Gabe until Sherry stormed out and Kim burst into tears. Gabe said he didn't want to go, and Kim said he didn't have to—she'd been more of a mother to him than Sherry had.

The problem was, she'd never done anything to make that *legal*.

The next day, Sherry took Gabe out of school and drove him—with his Pride t-shirt and blue hair—back to her hometown. She considered it a rescue, but Gabe knew it for what it was: *kidnapping*.

Jesus wasn't the only man Sherry re-embraced from prison. Gabe's father, John Beck, met them there, and right away he pinned Gabe down so Sherry could shave his head. Then they took away his phone and laptop and sent him to gay conversion therapy. Gabe also saw that for what it was: *psychological torture*. When he got out, they headed for Bruderschaft.

John didn't own a car because he didn't need (and wasn't allowed) one on the compound, so they took a bus from Milwaukee all the way to North Idaho. At a depot in Montana, as they changed buses, Gabe watched with envy as a woman played a game on a tablet. When she got up to chase her toddler, she tucked the plugged-in device down between the wall and the chair.

Gabe glanced around. John was in the restroom and Sherry stood at the vending machines, so he seized the opportunity and snagged the tablet just before their bus arrived. He'd never stolen anything before and felt horrible. He had to get in touch with Aunt Kim, though. She'd get him away from his parents. He knew it. Or thought he did.

He emailed her. She didn't reply. He tried again. Still nothing. After a half dozen different pleas for help had gone unanswered, he gave up. Looked like he could either stay or save himself.

So, he studied maps that showed skinny little roads winding through mountains so heavily forested you couldn't see ten feet in front of you most of the time. Maps with a few tiny dots representing farm communities in the area that traded—and sympathized —with Bruderschaft. The nearest town of any size was Coeur d'Alene, and it was more than forty miles away. That equated to fourteen-point-three hours on foot, Google Maps informed him. And that's assuming he didn't get lost in the woods, die of exposure, or get eaten by a wild animal.

The barrack's back door slammed closed, and Gabe heard his father's voice. As quick as he could, he tucked the tablet under his mattress and eased the chair out from under the doorknob. Best not to risk a beating.

CHAPTER TWO

Sunday, July 23, 2017
Bruderschaft Compound, North Idaho

All through Sunday-morning church services, Zeke prayed to God to make him normal.

The way Preacher Jethro James glared down his severe nose made Zeke feel like a little kid even though he towered above the old man.

Zeke struggled to keep the wasp incident out of his mind, but Preacher brought up the freak girl with the wings in Coeur d'Alene. A newspaper ran a story on her saying she'd been a girlfriend to the freak kid who thought freaks were superior to humans.

"A girl living right in the heart of our sacred land wants to rule over us all," Preacher said. "Her very existence blasphemes against God and it's our duty to remove blasphemers from God's sight."

Barnabas swaggered over to stand beside Preacher. "Bruderschaft is ready to take swift action if the little whore tries anything, and she will. She's an abomination and her mind is corrupt." Barnabas scanned their fearful faces. "How could it not be? Her mother's a damn feminist attorney, whoring herself out to defend illegals and social justice warriors and all those whiny women who don't want men to be men anymore. And her father! What a piece of work this guy is." He pointed at the congregation, but Zeke felt singled out. "He works for the corrupt school system that puts white kids in the same classroom as foreigners and freaks and teaches them lies about us all being the same. On top of that . . ." He paused, making sure everyone hung on his words. ". . . He coaches girls' sports. *Girls' sports*, as if that ain't the most ridiculous thing I ever heard."

Zeke stifled a laugh over the *most ridiculous thing* comment and made sure not to meet eyes with Gabe, who slouched two benches away. Zeke hadn't noticed until his friend pointed it out, but Barnabas managed to find a new *most ridiculous thing ever* several times a day. Gabe carried a small notebook, and Zeke knew *girls' sports* would be the next addition to his Official Most Ridiculous Things List.

Barnabas went on a rant about a feminist state senator who loved parahumans so much she wanted to cement their rights in the state constitution. "Women are too soft!" Sweat glistened on his brow as he shouted. "They don't belong in leadership. They should be home, raising their children to do God's work. Instead, she's gonna try to change the law of the land, to make everybody play nice. But we ain't gonna play nice with Senator Simmons, are we? Naw, we're gonna show her what happens to stupid, soft bitches like her when they try to pass laws in our state—*our state!*—giving freaks the same rights as God's chosen people." People in the congregation nodded back at him.

The word *freak* hit Zeke like a slap in the face. *I know I'm weak and unworthy, Lord, but please don't let me be a freak!* He understood now why Gabe hated *faggot* so much. He'd never considered how a label could hurt, but that was before the wasps. It had to be a . . . a test, right? God was always testing people, testing their faith. That must have been what happened. Wasps would never . . . do what they'd done on their own.

Zeke tuned out the rest of Preacher's sermon. He wanted out of the community room worse than ever.

Once services ended, Zeke grabbed his walking stick and escaped to the sheepfold, trying to shove the wasp incident from his mind. The dogs Jimmy and Bob yipped with excitement as he approached and ran to him for pets. At least the animals would never judge him or call him *freak*.

The flock moved in a big mass toward the gate as he approached. "Good morning, everyone." An older lamb ran along the fence next to him, bleating the whole way. Zeke laughed. "That's quite a story you got there, Abigail."

He opened the gate and headed out toward the field where they'd graze today. Eleanor charged ahead to walk at his ankle. He scratched her woolly head and watched Jimmy run ahead and circle back toward the flock. Jimmy barked, and Bob responded with the high-pitched yip common to heelers.

They reached the field and Zeke sat on a small hillock overlooking the flock. He left the herding to the dogs and let the clean morning air wash away Barnabas' venom. After a while, his eye fell on a large anthill crawling with its tiny black inhabitants. He watched their industriousness for a while and then scooted over beside it. *The wasps were a fluke or a test, right?* He hadn't been the reason they stopped swarming him.

He wasn't a freak.

Was he?

"All you ants, come on over here and line up." Their random meanders took on order in moments. Before long, rank after rank of ants stood in unnaturally neat rows, staring at him as if waiting for something. He realized they were, in fact, awaiting his orders. His stomach clenched and he tasted bile. *Why are they listening to me? How can they even understand me?*

He didn't know what to do next, so he sat there staring back at them.

Something nudged his back, and he turned to see Eleanor there, staring at him with black eyes shiny against her white face. "Hey there, girl. Go on and eat your fill."

With a bleat, she ambled off and resumed grazing.

Zeke looked from her to the ants, still in their lines, and back. *Is this why the sheep have always listened to me? And the dogs?*

His natural affinity for animals had landed him what he considered the sweetest job on the compound. He got to be out in the fresh air every day, which he liked just fine most days. It got cold at times, but he had warm clothes when he needed them. He'd rather be out there with sheep than stuck in school or soldier training. Zeke had never been comfortable handling guns. He didn't like the thought of hurting anyone, either. His pa said that made him weak, and Zeke didn't have any reason to question it. He'd been taught every white, Christian, American man had a duty to fight against the rising tide of foreigners, faggots, feminists, and freaks. Zeke tried to remind himself it was God's will for him to take up arms against his enemies, but he still couldn't stomach it. How could it be right to hurt Gabe?

Barnabas and Preacher said gays were evil sinners, whose very existence affronted God, but Gabe was the best friend Zeke had ever had. How could he be evil? He seemed so wise, as if he understood the world better than the kids raised in Bruderschaft. He just knew so darned much about so darned many things out in the world beyond the compound, it hurt Zeke's head to even think about it. Better to stay out of sight with the sheep, so his father and Barnabas didn't get reminders of his weakness too often.

Already weak, and now there's something else wrong with me. He brushed a beefy hand through the ranks of ants, killing scores and scattering the survivors. As he wiped the bodies on his canvas pants, a lump formed in his stomach. "Sorry," he muttered to the survivors. "Go back to what you was doing."

Freak. I'm a freak.

The ants who'd begun to regroup turned and dispersed, some heading back into the hill and others going off into the tall grass to forage. Or do whatever else ants did. Zeke had no idea.

He picked up his walking stick and called a command to Jimmy and Bob. They responded immediately to round up the stragglers. With precise coordination, they herded the flock after Zeke. They were bred for it and trained darn near from birth, but he never had to tell them twice.

"Hey, Jimmy," he called. The dog spun around to face him, his face the picture of canine alertness. "Go take a nap."

Jimmy cocked his head and looked as confused as Zeke had ever seen a dog look and then turned in circles like he was preparing to lie down.

"Never mind, Jimmy. Go back to work." With a yip, Jimmy turned back toward the flock. The dog spotted a lamb wandering off and ran after it.

Okay, kinda weird, but it could've been a coincidence.

Zeke meandered down to the stream and sat on a boulder. He scanned the bank. It didn't take him long to spot a little brown frog in the mud.

"Jump in the water." The frog leaped in with a splash. "Now come over here." It didn't react at first, then hopped from the stream and onto a rock—but farther away. He thought maybe it only worked on bugs when something occurred to him. *Maybe it couldn't hear me? 'Cause of the water?* He raised his voice. "Come here."

The frog turned to face him, splashed back into the water, and hopped out. It stared up at him, still and waiting, just as the insects had done. Zeke's hands shook with fear at the successful experiment. He couldn't be one of those freaks, like the girl in Coeur d'Alene everyone went nuts for just because she had bug wings. From the picture he'd seen in the paper, she was cute. He wondered if he could control *that* bug, too.

Zeke pictured her hovering over him and telling her to take off her clothes.

The fantasy made him feel guilty for thinking about a girl other than Naomi. Like him, she'd grown up on the compound, and they used to make believe they were married. Until he'd seen the picture of the dragonfly girl, Naomi was the prettiest girl he'd ever seen. He knew his father had been discussing their future with Naomi's pa. They weren't officially engaged yet, but he liked her and wanted to be worthy of such a good woman. Next year, he'd turn seventeen and could take a wife. As a councilman's son, he'd have his pick, and he never considered anyone but her. Naomi was beautiful, kind, and *pure*—not like the pass-around girls who slept in a different bed every night.

He wished Gabe were around to keep him company, but it wasn't even lunchtime yet. His friend's milk-barn duties would keep him busy until around two. *More time to figure things out . . . freak,* he told himself. But what next? He thought for a minute, then stood. "If you can hear my voice, come here now."

For a few seconds, he heard only the burbling of the brook and the breeze in the treetops. Then . . . rustling in the grass and splashing in the water. The frog reappeared at his feet, leading several more. Water skippers clustered along the stream's edge. Flies, wasps, and a few moths buzzed around him. A brown field mouse poked a twitching nose out of the grass. He saw a rabbit approach to a few feet away, and a skunk trundled toward him from the trees.

They did as he commanded. They all did.

Despite his fear of the *freak* label, he grinned to feel the power welling up inside him. All these creatures responded, just because he told them to. For the first time, he understood why men like Barnabas and Preacher liked to be in charge. This felt good.

A twig snapped behind him. "What the hell?"

He whirled to see Gabe staring at him wide-eyed. Fear erased the power high, and he gaped in terror. After a few seconds of frantic thought, he covered his mouth and murmured, "Go away!" The flying insects retreated, and the mouse disappeared. The other animals didn't move. "Go away," he said louder, unable to look away from Gabe's astonished gaze. The animals retreated with splashing and rustling. He had to justify his actions to Gabe somehow. "Y-you'll get us both in trouble if you're out here when you're supposed to be milking. You should go away."

"I said I was sick. Zeke, dude, what's going on?" Gabe's eyes darted back and forth as the last animals disappeared. "Why did you have bugs swarming your head and wild animals standing at attention?"

"Shhhh!" Zeke looked around to make sure they were alone. "No one else can know. Promise me you'll keep it a secret."

Gabe snorted. "Dude, who am I gonna tell? You're the only person I like here, and if I went to anyone with this, they'd just add 'liar' to my list of sins."

"There's a list of your sins?"

The wiry boy chuckled. "I don't mean a literal list. Just, you know, everyone has all these ideas about how horrible I am. Gay, lazy, disobedient, smart ass . . .. I'm sure there's more, but I can't think of them right now, you know, on account of you somehow controlling bugs and animals?"

"Shhhhhh!"

"No one's anywhere near us." Gabe sat on a fallen log and looked up at Zeke. "So, dude, again I ask, what the hell?"

Zeke gave a shaking sigh and recounted what happened with the wasps and his further experimentation. "But I can't be a freak. Everyone on the compound is tested for the Moo-whatchacallit gene . . ."

"Musashi gene."

"Whatever. Thing is, I can't be one of them."

Gabe ran a hand through his hair. "Okay, you can't say *one of them*. That's no better than *freak*."

"Why?"

"Setting yourself apart from *other* kinds of people makes it easy to hate them." Gabe paused and gave him a pointed look. "You remember that, right? Because it's one of the more important things I've tried to teach you."

Zeke nodded. "Yeah, yeah. Sorry. Anyway, my point is that I can't be a fr—a parahuman 'cause I ain't got the gene."

Gabe thought for a moment. "Maybe you're one of those people who have powers but not the gene. You know, the ones who say their powers come from God."

"Wait, what?" Zeke's eyes shot open wide. "That's a thing? For real?"

"I shouldn't be surprised you've never heard of that. If some powers come from God, it means you can't just blanket-hate everyone with powers."

A stunned Zeke stared down at his mud-covered boots. "God wouldn't pick me, though."

"Why not?"

He looked up, eyes watery. "I'm weak. God would never pick me. Not unless it's some kind of punishment."

Sunday, July 23, 2017
Pocatello, Idaho

Jeffrey watched as Idaho state Senator Nancy Simmons emerged from the back seat of her Lexus. He checked his posture and wished he had a lozenge for his parched throat. The dryness wasn't just because of the arid heat or the hotel's awkward perch atop a barren, wind-swept hill, but because he'd joined the senator's staff just two weeks ago and still found her terrifying. "Welcome to Pocatello, Senator."

Senator Simmons scoffed and looked at him over expensive but understated sunglasses. She was a handsome woman with dark hair cut into a professional swept-back style a focus group said made her look tough but approachable. An American flag pin sparkled on the lapel of her gray linen blazer. "I'd rather be dipped ins honey and rolled in fire ants."

A shocked Jeffrey looked over at Tamara, Simmons' executive assistant and his boss. She came around the car, looking professional behind glasses and muted lipstick. "Pocatello's the only place she hates worse than North Idaho." Tamara checked an alert on her phone as they hurried inside.

"So, she pretty much likes . . .Boise?"

Tamara shrugged. "Most of it, anyway."

Jeffrey, who'd arrived early to get them checked in, hurried to catch up to the senator so he could show her to her room.

Simmons stopped at the door Jeffrey held open and looked back at Tamara. "I thought I asked for the same suite as last time."

Tamara blanched. "You did, Senator, but . . .uh, there was a . . . problem with that room."

Simmons removed her sunglasses to regard her assistant with a steel gaze. "It's not like you to stammer, Tamara. What's going on?"

Tamara opened her mouth to answer and closed it again. Jeffrey cleared his throat. "I requested the change, Ma'am. I believe this room will be significantly safer for you."

The senator looked Jeffrey up and down. "Have you been promoted to my security detail?"

Security detail always struck him as an overblown way to describe the one guy who followed her around and the second guy who joined him on occasion, but Senator Simmons seemed to like it.

"I'm sorry to be presumptuous, Ma'am, but I . . ." His words backed up and Jeffrey understood why Tamara froze. This woman's glare induced heart palpitations.

The senator raised an eyebrow and turned back to Tamara. "Can either of you produce a coherent sentence?"

"I apologize, Senator." Tamara slipped back into professional mode. "Jeffrey has a special talent I believe will serve you well, but it's a bit unorthodox."

"What, is he a Feng Shui master? A foot masseuse? Spit it out."

"I'm a parahuman, Ma'am." Jeffrey winced at a teenager-like voice crack. "I, uh, I have an ability to see things. Like, visions. Precognitive."

The senator's eyebrows went up and her voice dripped with disdain. "You're a . . . psychic?"

"I know how it sounds," Tamara said, "but it's not wacky speaking-with-dead-people stuff or Tarot cards or anything. He's got the Musashi gene. Jeffrey can see the future."

Simmons tossed her purse onto the bed, sat in an armchair, and regarded Jeffrey as if he were a menu item she couldn't decide whether to order. "Just Cause? Champion?"

"No, Ma'am. I'm not interested in being a hero. Not like that, anyway. I want to be a public servant."

Simmons snorted. "Do you already know the election results? If so, I can save a lot of time and money."

Jeffrey couldn't hold back a nervous laugh. "No, Senator, I can't see that far ahead, and I can't control what I see. From time to time, I just catch glimpses. I call it *forecasting*. Events always happen the way I forecast unless I change something. They're usually related to danger."

Simmons motioned to the desk chair. "Sit."

Jeffrey did as he was told. Nervous sweat trickled down his sides.

"Give me an example."

He thought for a minute. "The first time I changed one, I was a sophomore in high school. For days, I kept seeing a bus flash by. It wasn't a normal school bus, though, it was bright pink. Then, one day as I was walking home with a friend, I forecasted her older brother whipping past us on a skateboard, losing his balance, and falling right into the pink bus's path. At first, I thought it was actually happening. Then the forecast ended, and I realized it hadn't happened yet—but I could hear the skateboard coming up behind us. I pulled my friend out of the way, so her brother didn't have to swerve, and he just kept going. Along came that bright pink bus, right on cue. Only it didn't hit him, it just drove past. I changed the future."

Simmons studied Jeffrey in silence until he wanted to shrink away to nothing. "Why pink?" she asked at last.

"Wh-what?"

"Why was the bus pink?"

"Oh. Um, I have no idea."

The senator burst out laughing. Tamara snickered and the tension drained from the room. "Interesting, Jeffrey, very interesting," Simmons said. "So why is this room safer than the one I requested?"

Jeffrey sobered. "Someone's going to shoot out the window of the other suite. Tonight, I think."

A flicker of concern flashed through Simmons' eyes. "If it's an assassination attempt, you should have notified my security detail . . ."

"No, Ma'am, it's not that," Jeffrey interrupted. "It's random. Some wanna-be gangbanger is going to fire a gun in the air, and the bullet is going to go through that window. What I forecast, it didn't kill you, but . . ." His eyes drifted to her left bicep. "The damaged to your arm looked severe."

She rubbed her arm, looking disturbed. "Well, if Tamara is convinced you're the real thing, that's good enough for me. Thank you for sparing me an injury, Jeffrey. I want you to report any future visions that concern me to Tamara."

"Yes, Ma'am, of course."

She gave a curt nod. "Tamara, keep this under wraps. The last thing I need is the media or my opponent getting wind of it. Jeffrey forecasts something, he tells you, and you handle it. Keep me out of it as much as possible." She smiled. "If I don't know about it, I can deny it later. Tamara, let's go over my schedule while I'm here, please."

Tamara made a *get-out-of-here* motion with her head and Jeffrey hurried out. He'd expected to feel relieved once the senator knew of his ability. Instead, he felt more defeated than ever. *If she's the best ally I've got in government, is there any real hope?* At least he had Tamara.

He went to the lobby coffee shop, then let himself into his room to wait for his boss and friend. He'd forecasted himself in the internship position, but he never would've made it there without that connection. He'd "come out" to her as para a few years earlier when she'd lead his political science study group.

When he realized he needed to be part of the senator's staff, he reached out to Tamara, afraid she might not remember him. Instead, she squealed and told him right then the position was his. "You're the reason I'm working for her, Jeffrey," she'd told him. "I think all the time about how hard it was for you to be openly para, even in a super liberal college environment. I want to help Senator Simmons make real change for you and everyone like you."

Tamara knocked on his door twenty minutes later. He opened the door and handed her a latte. "Sugar-free hazelnut, cold with no ice."

"Ah, you're a saint." She took a long drink.

"What's all that about not telling anyone?" Jeffrey asked. "She's such a big champion of parahuman rights —I'd think she'd be fine with it, or even vocal about me working for her."

"The senator's biggest fear, as a woman in politics, is looking weak or foolish. She thinks people who believe in psychics—her words, not mine, I know that's totally inaccurate—but anyway, she says those people come off as gullible." Tamara sipped the coffee and shrugged. "So anyway, she just wants to make sure you're legit before word gets out. Then she'll loosen up, I'm sure."

Jeffrey sighed. So much for her being an ally.

That's why you're here, he reminded himself. Someone had to make it easier for the next para who went into politics.

Sunday, June 23, 2017
Coeur d'Alene, Idaho

Chloe stared in dismay out the window at the myriad news vans, satellite trucks, reporters, and photographers in the park across the street. "So, there's nothing we can do to get rid of them?"

Heather shook her head. "Sorry, Fly Girl. As long as they're on public property, they have a right to be there. And they can legally get video of anything in full public view."

"Which means if I leave the house, I'm fair game."

"Yep."

Chloe plopped down on the bench and sighed. "I need to get out and fly before I go crazy! Think I could slip out the back and keep low enough to be out of sight until I hit the trees?"

"Probably." Heather took a long drink of coffee. "Tell you what, I'll up your odds. I'll go out there and give them a statement. That'll distract them for a few minutes."

Chloe rushed over and hugged her. "Thanks, mom! You're the best! I'm gonna go get ready." She raced upstairs.

"Don't hurry too much," her mom called. "I still need to do something with my hair and face."

"Better get on that, then!" Chloe dressed in a leotard cut low in the back for her wings, goggles, and a lightweight crash helmet. She buckled it beneath her chin as she headed downstairs. Heather grinned and went out the front door. The reporters swarmed, shouting questions, as photographers hoisted their cameras.

Chloe bolted out the back slider and took to the air. She flew just high enough to clear their six-foot back fence, crossed their back neighbor's yard, and hung a right. Staying low over the sidewalk, she relished the sun on her wings. As she zipped past house after house, she realized she hadn't been down this street in forever. She used to come this way all the time to get to her former BFF Jessi's house, back when they were teammates. Jessi had been a ringleader of the bullies who came after. Chloe considered veering off down a side street to avoid Jessi's house, but she wanted to fly over the pretty little pond at the end of the road. She kept going straight.

She regretted the decision when, too late, she spotted Jessi in the driveway. Jessi had spotted her first and snapped a picture. Chloe winced. Once that hit Twitter and Instagram, the press would be on her. With a scowl at Jessi, she turned and made a beeline for the dense, wooded hill just beyond their subdivision.

Chloe needed to stay low and out of sight, but that made for difficult flying. She dodged around trees, keeping a lookout for a clear path. Then, as she swerved around a lodgepole pine, she saw a small clearing ahead and grinned. She put on all the speed she dared and burst from the trees, startling a doe and speckled fawn, who fled into the thick underbrush. Chloe flew in an ascending spiral around the clearing, then dove and practiced reversing as she neared the ground. She reveled in her wings' maneuverability—none of the other winged flyers she knew could stop on a dime and hover, or make sharp turns, or even fly backward.

After a good workout, she retraced her route home. Just as she'd feared, the reporters and cameras awaited her at the base of the hill. *Can't avoid them, guess I'll give them a show.* No way did she want to stop and talk, but the Academy had taught her better than to try avoiding photos or video when they were inevitable. Evasion was bad optics.

She flew low over them and then arced up and smiled as she flew a few lazy circles. Several called her name and tried to yell questions when she came down low again, but she just waved and zipped up over a back neighbor's roof.

A young woman wearing a *Coeur d'Alene Sentinel* polo shirt stood in a neighbor's back yard with a camera pointed at her.

Annoyed, Chloe landed on the roof and pointed at the reporter. "You're trespassing."

"No, I'm not. Your neighbor's in my mom's quilting group and she gave me permission." She let the camera dangle from the neck strap and pulled out a narrow notebook and pen. "Jenna Holt from the *Sentinel.* Will you talk to me for just a minute?"

"You wrote the story about me." Chloe pulled her goggles down to hang around her throat. "I'll give you a quote, but first, I have some questions to ask—off the record." She flew down to land on the patio.

Holt tucked the notebook in a back pocket. "Did your mom teach you to say that or was it the Academy?"

"Both."

Chloe crossed her arms. "You thought it was cool to print all that stuff about me without confirming it? Even though I'm a minor?"

"Your mom's letter scared my boss pretty bad, so he wouldn't let me call you. I wanted to, though." Holt looked contrite. "I argued that you guys are kids and not really public figures yet, but he disagreed. After the tip came in, I did everything I could to confirm it—it took me a long time to track down Miguel Machado and find someone at the Academy who'd talk, but . . ." She shrugged.

"I don't suppose you'll tell me who that was."

"I have to protect my sources. I don't want to cost someone their job."

"But you're okay with siccing the vultures on me?"

Holt shrugged again. "You're big news around here. That's not our fault. It's just how it is. My advice? Hold a press conference and everyone will go away." She pulled out the notebook and flipped it open. "So . . . my turn to ask the questions yet?"

Chloe smirked. "I didn't say you could ask a question, I said I'd give you a quote."

"Oh, come on . . ." Holt threw her hands up in frustration.

"Are you ready?"

Holt's pen went to her notebook. "Ready."

"*Where we're going . . .*" Chloe raised her goggles into place. "*We don't need roads.*"

Holt blinked, pen frozen against the paper. "What?"

"Like I said, a quote. From one of my dad's favorite movies. You can attribute it to Doc Brown."

"Seriously? You're not gonna give me anything I can use?"

"What, I thought it'd make a great caption for your picture. Here's a bonus one for you, just to show there's no hard feelings over you lurking in my neighbor's yard so you could ambush me—*Hasta la vista, baby.*"

Giggling, Chloe zipped over the fence and saw her parents watching for her through the slider. Something was wrong.

Sunday, June 23, 2017
Bruderschaft Compound, North Idaho

"I think we can safely say that size matters." Gabe laughed at the innuendo.

Zeke blushed and chuckled. They'd spent the afternoon slipping around and experimenting with Zeke's powers. They'd learned he could control countless insects, or a horde of small creatures like squirrels, mice, and rabbits. He could control just a few medium-sized animals at a time, such as the dogs, but only a single cow. When it came to the sheep, though, they found if he controlled Eleanor, the brash and bossy ewe, the flock would follow her lead.

"I just don't get how they understand me," Zeke said. "Especially bugs and wild animals. How do they know English?"

Gabe thought for a few seconds and came up with a plan. "Let's test that. Tell the cow to moo. Like, a lot."

"Moo, Jenny, until I tell you to stop," Zeke ordered. The cow mooed.

"How is it you know the name of every animal on the compound when you can barely spell *sheep*?"

Zeke snorted and punched his shoulder.

"Okay, I deserved that." He rubbed at the spot and rolled his arm. "Now say *callete*."

Zeke screwed up his face. "Say what?"

"*Cay-uh-tay*," Gabe repeated.

The cow continued making a racket. Zeke scowled. "That sounds weird. What does it mean?"

Gabe rolled his eyes. "Just say it."

"I can't remember it. Say it again."

"Jesus, dude. *Callete.*"

Zeke sighed. "*Callete.*"

The cow mooed.

"Interesting." Gabe grinned. "*Callete* is Spanish for shut up."

Zeke gave him a shocked stare. "How do you know that?"

"I took Spanish last year in school."

Zeke's jaw dropped. "Your school taught you to talk foreign?"

"Unbelievable," Gabe whispered. "Real schools—out there in the world—all teach foreign languages."

"Oh. That's weird." He looked at the cow, which still mooed. He'd have felt bad if it were any other cow, but Jenny talked all the time, anyway. "So why did you have me talk Spanish at her?"

"To see if it understands your words or your intent."

"I don't get it."

"Of course, you don't." Gabe ran a hand over his stubble. "You didn't know what you were saying, so the cow didn't understand. I think the animals somehow know your intention, not your words."

"Maybe they only understand English."

"I don't think so, but let's test it. Say *callete* again." Gabe gestured toward the cow.

"Why? It didn't work."

"Because now you know what it means."

Zeke cocked his head. "Oh, yeah. I get it. Hey, Jenny, *callete*."

Jenny *callete*-ed. The boys cheered and high fived.

Sunday, June 23, 2017
Coeur d'Alene, Idaho

Chloe's hand shook as she gaped at the leaflet a reporter had given her mom. Someone had distributed them on windshields downtown. Phil put a comforting hand on her shoulder. "You okay, kiddo?"

The leaflet featured a Denver Instagrammer's snapshot of her flying over campus under a huge headline that screamed *Freaks Among Us!* Below the photo, it read:

This is God's Country, Our Country, and freaks like this girl aint welcome!
Let the whore know we dont want her and her kind hear! Drive them out!
No freaks No way!

"Guess I've got more reason to stay inside." Chloe collapsed onto a bench.

Heather put her arm around Chloe's shoulders. "Dad's friend Sam is on his way over."

"The cop?"

"It's *Detective* Abara." Phil eased the leaflet out of her hand. "He's head of the Hate Crimes Task Force."

The doorbell rang a few minutes later. Phil answered it and returned with one of the biggest non-parahumans Chloe had ever seen. He was black with a close-cropped hairstyle, six-and-a-half feet tall, and had shoulders so broad Chloe wondered if he had the same problem fitting through doorways that she did. He gave Heather a quick hug and offered Chloe a massive hand.

"Sam Abara. It's good to finally meet you, Chloe. Your dad brags about you every time we hit the links." He glanced in the direction of the park across the street where the media still camped out. "Sorry you're having to deal with them, and now this leaflet business."

"Thanks, Detective." Chloe blushed and sat on her bench. Abara perched on the edge of the couch and picked up the flier from the coffee table.

"Please, call me Sam. Has anyone from a hate group contacted you? Or have you had a run-in with them?"

She shook her head.

Abara nodded. "That's good. Most of the time, these groups are all bark and no bite—so long as you haven't directly crossed them. I'm sure the *Sentinel* article got them riled up. They like to take advantage of publicity to get attention turned to them."

"So, you don't think we have anything to worry about?" Heather asked.

"No, most likely not. Just to be safe, though, Chloe, don't go out alone. I'd suggest staying grounded for now. I'd hate for someone to see you and decide to . . . do something drastic."

"You mean like shoot at me?" The thought made Chloe shiver. "I mean, I guess I should get used to that. Facing danger is part of the superhero deal."

"Save it for when you're an adult and on the job," Abara said. "Don't risk a promising career—or your life —being careless."

Chloe sighed, miserable. "I'm going crazy in the house."

"Maybe we'll take a drive in a couple of days," her dad said, "go to Mount Spokane or someplace remote where you can stretch your wings."

She perked up. "Yeah, that'd be cool."

Abara examined the photo on the flier. "That's Justin Sharp in the background, right? Corvid?"

"You know who he is?" Chloe asked.

Sam nodded. "He caught my eye when he made headlines in Chicago a few years back. Seems like a good kid."

"Oh, yeah! Justin's great. We were in flight training together, and he was the head of Obvious Club, too."

"Obvious Club?"

"It's for those of us who are obvious paras. We tend to have a harder time . . ." She shrugged, realizing how stupid she sounded. "Well, I guess I don't need to tell you what it's like to stand out."

He gave a deep chuckle. "No, you don't."

"Did you hear Justin got into Just Cause Seattle?" she asked.

"I did. Good for him!" Abara grinned. "And good for you, figuring out Zayden Lord's plan. MetalBlade is a damn fine investigator and so are Icebreaker and Mustang Sally, but you bested them all on this one. I look forward to seeing where your career takes you."

"Thanks," Chloe muttered, face flushed. "It was just a hunch at first, but then I dug around and found some evidence."

"That's the way to do it." Abara stood, careful not to bump the ceiling fan. "I'll take this flier in and see if we can find out where it came from. Like I said, I doubt you're in any personal danger. But Chloe—trust your gut. If something seems off, it probably is." He slipped a business card from his pocket and handed it to her. "Put my number in your phone and feel free to call anytime."

Sunday, June 23, 2017
Pocatello, Idaho

"Idaho's reputation has long suffered due to hate groups," Senator Nancy Simmons told a banquet hall full of $100-per-plate democrats. A slideshow Jeffrey had created of superheroes with ties to Idaho played on a screen beside her. Most were obscure, and Jeffrey had done his best to hype the less-than-exceptional histories of Pale Rider, Steelhead, and Spudgun. The good part, with WyldWing, was just ahead. She'd already gained far more notoriety and seemed destined for Just Cause stardom. He hoped seeing her would help fire up the room as Simmons continued. "But we need to let them know—we need to let everyone know—hate groups do not have safe harbor in our great state!" She broke for applause. "Adding parahumans to the list of protected groups in Idaho's constitution will send our message loud and clear."

As the applause tapered off, a commotion came from the back of the room and Jeffrey stood to look. A security guard struggled against two men in faded jeans and red baseball caps who shouted as more security officers converged on them.

"No freaks in my state!" one bellowed.

"You keep 'em out or the Second Amendment will!" the other yelled.

Two hotel security guards rushed in to help the senator's security detail get the men out and they had it resolved in less than a minute.

Simmons appeared unruffled. "And that, my friends, is why we also need to increase funding for local schools, because education is our best weapon against intolerance!"

The crowd laughed and cheered.

The senator wrapped up the speech and went to greet her constituents. She shot Jeffery and icy look as she passed by.

"You couldn't have seen *that* coming?"

Sunday, June 23, 2017
Bruderschaft Compound, North Idaho

"Father in Heaven." Preacher Jethro James stood, head bowed, at the head table in the community room before supper. "We thank thee for our pure blood and white skin, for the truth we know in our hearts, and for our favored position at thy holy table. We thank thee for this land and its bounty, that we may strive to create a true Christian state, wiped clean of impure blood; wiped clean of those with impure thoughts and those who commit impure deeds; wiped clean of foreigners, faggots, feminists, and freaks, so those made in your true image may flourish and re-populate the earth. We, the Bruderschaft, ask this in thy holy name. Amen."

"Amen," the dutiful congregation repeated. Except for Gabe, who always mouthed *gay men* instead. When he first told Zeke about that particular joke, the blasphemy shocked Zeke and he'd asked if Gabe was a damned atheist.

"No, I believe in God," Gabe said, "but a really different God from the one these assholes preach. It's supposed to be about love and peace, not hate and murder."

"What do you mean murder?" Zeke asked. "No one here's murdering."

"Then why do they train soldiers and stockpile weapons?"

Zeke had blinked. "We gotta be ready. For the war."

"That's the thing, Zeke—no one is preparing for war except you guys. You know why that is? Because these assholes want to *start* the war, that's why."

Zeke hadn't believed it at the time, but then he started noticing things that bothered him. For starters, the secret meetings the men in charge—his pa included —held from time to time. They'd lock themselves in the bunker behind Barnabas' house for hours on end. Sometimes when they came out, they'd be angry like they'd been arguing or something. Nights like that, all their families knew to mind extra well rather than risk a beating. Zeke's pa would never tell him what the leaders discussed in there.

Gabe taught him a lot about the world and different kinds of people, but it confused him. He loved his pa. Feared him, sure, but still loved him. And he respected Preacher and Barnabas and the Christian soldiers. Someday, just like in the hymn, they'd go marching off to war, with the cross of Jesus going on before.

But Jesus didn't want war, according to the Biblical passages Gabe showed him. Preacher never mentioned those parts. So, what was the truth? Zeke didn't know, but he was no longer sure Preacher, or Barnabas, or any Bruderschaft elders spoke it.

Zeke stopped himself from ruminating on it all. He had bigger problems to consider—such as why he had parahuman powers. Was he a good Christian? A freak?

Or something else altogether? He debated whether to tell his pa or carry the secret to his grave. *What would happen to me if everyone found out?*

Zeke ate without tasting the food and headed back to his small house. The cleaning women had been through, he could tell by the smell of Pine-Sol and the tidiness—no gun magazines scattered around or ammo boxes sitting out, no beer cans littering the floor by the couch.

Zeke could also tell Naomi was on the crew because his unfinished homework sat on the coffee table. She already looked out for him, the way a good wife should, making sure he didn't forget anything important. He wished she was still around so he could thank her and smiled at the thought. Then his face fell as he wondered how she'd look at him if she knew he was a freak.

He sat in the brown recliner and picked up the history book with the Führer on the cover. It started with the lost tribes of Israel and traced the white race forward from there. They were studying World War I. Everyone else was looking forward to Hitler's rise and World War II, but Zeke wasn't sure anymore how he felt about all that. Gabe had him questioning everything. He wasn't used to thinking so hard and sometimes wished he'd never made friends with the newcomer. It was all so much easier before.

The front door opened and in strode his father, Tom, chewing on a toothpick. Zeke had inherited his large build and strong Aryan features, but somehow the face they shared looked a lot meaner on Tom. Maybe it was the deep, sun-baked creases. Maybe it was the narrowed eyes or the way his jaw always seemed clenched.

Except, for once, Tom had a smile on his face. Zeke saw why when Jemima Jones, Naomi's older sister, followed him in. No one had picked her for a wife, so she was stuck being a pass-around.

"Hey there, Zeke," she said.

"Hey, Jemima." His eyes flicked to her ample chest, then back to his book. He hoped his pa hadn't seen the glance. She was nineteen, just three years older than him, and it didn't seem right that she was here like this. Zeke gathered up his homework. He knew the drill.

"Son, I'm gonna need you to study in your room tonight."

"Yes, Sir." Zeke hurried into his room. He'd hear them just the same, but with him behind a closed door, both he and his pa had an easier time pretending he didn't know what was going on.

Zeke couldn't focus. Reading strained his brain enough without the moaning in the next room. He put the book aside and paced, but he felt too cooped up and climbed out the window.

Ain't it bad enough that my ma died? Now I gotta live with this?

After cancer sent his mother to sit at Jesus' feet, Tom had refused to take another wife. He could've had his pick, but he chose instead to entertain himself with the pass-around girls who kept the unmarried men happy. Sometimes they'd also "keep company" with the married men whose wives were in late pregnancy or had just had a baby, or the ones whose wives didn't lose the extra weight between babies. *Fat* wasn't an officially despised category, but with how the Bruderschaft men acted, it seemed like—when it came to women, at least—it should be the fifth *F*.

Zeke was pretty sure he had a younger half-brother from one of those girls, but no one ever talked about who fathered their children. Mercy White once asked the teacher if it wasn't a sin to have a baby without being married.

"Out in the world, yes, Mercy, it's a sin," Mrs. Clark answered. "But here, we do God's work, and with how them foreigners breed, He wants us to create every white child, every Christian soldier we can. The best way to raise an army is to have children and raise them to fight for their rightful place in this world and the next."

Zeke tried to convince himself he could take her at her word. As Barnabas's wife, if anyone would know a proper white woman's duties, it was her. Still, something about it seemed wrong. Everything about it seemed wrong if he was being honest.

He noticed light around the edges of Gabe's small window, so he tapped on the glass.

Gabe moved the curtain aside and peeked out. "Dude, what are you doing out so late?"

"Shhhh!" Zeke motioned for him to come outside and popped the screen. Gabe climbed out and they sneaked off into the deepening shadows between the neighborhood and the barns.

Once they were far enough away not to be overheard, Gabe turned to Zeke. "Okay, now will you tell me why you're out wandering around?"

Zeke shoved his hands in his pockets and shrugged. "Just didn't want to be at home."

Gabe looked worried. "Your dad didn't do anything, did he? Like, hit you or something?"

"What? No. Just . . ." Zeke kicked at a rock. "He's got company."

Realization dawned on Gabe's face. "Gotcha. Which one?"

"Jemima."

Gabe snorted. "Damn, that name kills me."

"Why?"

"Aunt Jemima? I suppose you've never seen it."

"Seen what?" Zeke's tone sounded harsher than he meant it, but he wasn't in the mood for Gabe being vague.

"Pancake syrup. Aunt Jemima's a brand I don't guess they'd ever buy here. 'Cause Aunt Jemima's black."

Zeke was taken aback. "They used a Bible name on a ni—on a black lady's . . . pancake syrup?"

"It's a Bible name?"

Zeke screwed up his face. "Duh!"

"What? Like I pay attention during sermons?" They both chuckled, then fell silent for a few moments. Gabe's face lit up. "Hey, let's see if we can find some bats or something for you to control."

A grin crossed Zeke's face. "Sounds good. Maybe I can get them to fly into my pa's bedroom or something."

Tom Shepherd drained the last drops of beer, crumpled the can in one hand, and tossed it on the bedroom floor with the others. He sat naked in the worn armchair and glared at the sleeping girl. The flesh was weak, and when he couldn't stand it any longer, he succumbed to sin. Barnabas and Preacher said God forgave Tom because of his good works, but he wasn't sure his good deeds made up for all the bad. He'd give Saint Peter a whole raft of sins to read from his book. Good thing they'd have eternity.

Guilt ate at him over the lot he'd given to Zeke. The boy had physical strength, but he wasn't tough. He wasn't smart. He wasn't good with a gun. He had no skill with soldiering or explosives, and he appeared to have given a girl his heart before ever giving one his other organ.

Guilt gave way to anger as he thought about his son befriending the damned Beck kid. Zeke had no future on the compound. Tom knew that for sure. He didn't belong in Bruderschaft. What could Tom do, though? He knew next to nothing about the world beyond the compound, and Zeke knew even less. How would they survive if they left? Where would they even go?

Tom's face grew hard, and he opened another beer. He was part of the inner circle, a Bruderschaft elder. He knew all the details of *Operation 88*, and Barnabas would protect his grand plan at all costs. If Tom tried to sneak away with Zeke, Barnabas would have them hunted down and killed. Tom may be a shit excuse for a man, but he loved his son. He couldn't risk it.

He drained the beer and bowed his head. Bruderschaft had them both trapped, and he couldn't see any way out of it.

CHAPTER THREE

Monday, July 24, 2017
Bruderschaft Compound

Zeke shifted in the too-small wooden chair and drummed his fingers on the desk, wishing Mrs. Clark would move on from math. The only numbers he needed to worry about were how many sheep he had out in the field and how many dogs he had to help herd them. School was a waste of time.

At least he just had to spend two days a week in class since he was old enough to have a permanent job assignment. They all knew how to read fine, so they just studied math, history, and the Bible with Mrs. Clark on Mondays. Tuesdays was weapons and tactics with Barnabas or another elder. He envied the girls, who finished formal schooling at 15 so they could focus on cooking and birthing babies and raising good Christian soldiers. Their husbands could tell them whatever else they needed to know.

At last, the noon bell rang out over the compound and the school day ended. Zeke and Gabe headed for the agricultural area. "I don't see why school has to be four hours long." Zeke frowned at the bruise on Gabe's cheek but said nothing. Gabe would never talk about it, anyway.

"Yeah, a whole eight hours a week, that's rough." Gabe snorted.

Gabe had told him kids out in the world went for six hours a day, five days a week. Zeke didn't believe there was enough to learn to spend so much time in school. Then again, he'd heard they taught fake "science," and lies about the government, and used mind control to make them obedient. He'd even heard those schools taught kids how to have sex and to hate God, and he guessed all that could take some time.

They walked out to the field to take charge of the sheep. Gabe frequently had early milk duty before school, so he had the afternoon to hang out with Zeke or read books he wasn't supposed to read on a fancy electronic tablet he wasn't supposed to have. The tablet was another of their shared secrets. Only the building they called *out-back* behind Barnabas's house had Internet access, and Gabe figured out if he sat below a window, he could load stuff onto the tablet now and then. Gabe said he'd even broken into out-back a few times, but Zeke wondered if he made that part up. That computer business didn't make any sense to Zeke, but Gabe seemed to understand a whole lot he didn't. It almost made Zeke wish he'd grown up out in the world.

Then he thought about all the weird stuff out there, the stuff he didn't understand, and that made him glad he hadn't.

Monday, July 24, 2017
Pocatello, Idaho

Jeffrey woke from a sound sleep to pounding on the door. He groaned and staggered across the room, pulling a t-shirt over his head. "Jus' a minute . . ." He squinted into the peephole and saw Tamara in the hotel hallway. He tried in vain to smooth down his bedhead before unfastening the chain and opening the door.

"What's wrong?" he asked.

Tamara pushed past him. "Shut the door, Jeffrey."

He did as she asked. "What's going on? Is the senator okay?"

She whirled to face him, arms crossed. "Did the gunshots wake you up?"

He rubbed his eyes and sat down on the foot of the bed. "Guess I slept through it."

Tamara sighed. "No, you didn't, because it didn't happen."

He sat up straight. "How's that possible?"

"You tell me. The senator thinks you're full of shit now. Plus, she didn't sleep well because the room you put her in is too close to the highway." Tamara sat beside him and buried her face in her hands. "I talked her out of firing you. You're welcome."

Jeffrey reeled. His forecasts had never been wrong before. It had never occurred to him they *could* be. He swallowed hard. "Thank you, Tamara. I'm sorry you had to do that."

"So, what happened? Why was your forecast wrong?"

"I don't know." He shrugged. "It was supposed to be random, so it still should've happened. It's not like I found the guy and took his gun away or anything."

Tamara peered at him. "Tell me exactly what you saw in your vision."

Jeffrey closed his eyes and pictured it. "It was like I floated in the air outside the window. I saw Simmons pull the curtains and turn off the light, but I could still see into the room. She sat on the bed to respond to a text, and I heard a car peel out and looked down. An old muscle car sped past and the passenger fired two shots out the open window. One went straight up, and the other went through the window and tore through her arm. Then the security guy ran into view and looked up at the shattered window."

Tamara cocked her head. "Where did the security guy come from?"

"The same direction as the car. Why?"

"That means the car would've passed him. Since you moved her to the other side of the hotel, he was stationed in a different spot."

"Why would that matter, though?"

Tamara shrugged. "Got me. It's a difference, though. Maybe the sequence of small changes somehow triggered the butterfly effect."

Jeffrey gave her a skeptical look. "Do you think the senator would buy that?"

She shook her head. "I'm not even gonna suggest it, not with the mood she's in. It's probably best if we don't mention it ever again."

Monday, July 24, 2017
Coeur d'Alene, Idaho

Chloe picked at her breakfast. She couldn't stand another day trapped in the house. "Mom, I think I should just talk to them and get it over with." Her dad had left for volleyball camp, and her mom took the day off to stay home with her. "Maybe that'll get them to go away."

Heather's brow furrowed over her coffee cup. "Are you sure, Chlo? You won't be big news forever. Something else is bound to draw them away before long."

"I know, but I want them gone now. How bad can it be to answer a few questions, especially if it'll get this over with?"

"The press can be pretty ruthless, and once a slip-up is out there, you have no control over what they do with it."

Chloe nodded. "Can we maybe pick one reporter to talk to, and then have them share the footage?"

"I'm not sure that's how it works, but I can ask someone. Who should we choose?"

"No clue." Chloe peeked through a crack in the curtains out at the smattering of news vans with their station logos. All three major networks still had people on the scene, as did the local stations. "At school, we watched a series on anti-parahuman political movements that was really good. Not scare-tactic-y at all. Let me figure out who did it." Chloe looked it up on her phone, then turned the screen so her mom could see his handsome, smiling face underneath the network logo. "Alexander Peters."

Heather nodded. "I'll go talk to someone. You wait here." She left the house.

Chloe watched as her mom crossed the street to the park. A few minutes later, she came back in with a producer in tow, introduced her as Amelia, and they settled in around the kitchen table.

Amelia smiled despite a sunburn and tired eyes. "It's so great to finally meet you, Chloe."

Chloe blushed. "So, do you think the network will agree to this?"

"We don't do it often, but it happens," Amelia said. "This Hero Academy story is huge, so it warrants special consideration. I'll call New York, and I'm guessing they'll fly Alex out right away." She took a sip of the coffee Heather put in front of her. "They'll probably ask that you allow us to air it first, though."

Chloe and Heather looked at each other and Chloe nodded. "I think that sounds fair. Mom?"

"Works for me." Heather turned back to Amelia. "Want to call in now?"

A huge grin crossed Amelia's face. "You guys have no idea how big a hero I'll be for this. Thank you so much!" She dialed as she stood up and wandered over to the great room window overlooking the park. "Ginny, it's Amelia. Chloe Wyld's agreed to talk to us first."

Monday, July 24, 2017
Bruderschaft Compound

Zeke and Gabe knelt on the ground, heads together, leaning over their latest experiment. They'd tested Zeke's control every way they could think of when it came to number, size, and species. From that, they moved on to investigating how far his control went. At the moment, Zeke had a tower of ants forming before him, one after the other climbing up to stand atop the others. Even though it was unnatural behavior for them, the ants complied with every command.

"What in the Lord's name is going on here?"

The boys whirled around and Zeke's eyes went wide when he realized Bruderschaft's resident tattletale Mercy White stared at them. He leaped to his feet. "Mercy! Wh-what are you doing here?"

Mercy ignored Zeke's question. "Just what are you and Gay-briel doing, I wonder?"

"Uh, nothing. Just looking at, uh, a bunch of ants." Zeke's mouth was so dry it surprised him he could choke the words out. "There's a big hill, and . . . uh, we was watching them gather food."

"Yeah, right." She sniffed as if something stank. "Maybe you should get back to minding the sheep, Ezekiel. I know what's really going on, and so does God." She made kissy noises with her lips, burst out laughing, and ran back toward the neighborhood.

Zeke's head slumped forward as she walked away.

"We're so screwed." Gabe's hand drifted to his bruised cheekbone. "If my dad hears anything . . ."

Zeke searched for any trace of the usual smart-ass Gabe swagger but found none of it. He didn't think he could handle this if Gabe lost it. "It's almost time to head in. Let's round up the sheep."

"I'll head back now, make sure a lot of people see me. Maybe we can discredit that lying little shit, or at least lessen the damage a little," Gabe said.

"Yeah, probably a good idea."

With a deep and trembling breath, Gabe started for home. Zeke trudged off, whistling for the dogs before he remembered he could just tell the flock to follow him.

Gabe walked around the barracks to the front door, where the cleaning women talked and laughed through their break.

"Hey, Naomi," he said, louder than he needed to. They weren't friends, but at least she wasn't awful to him.

Her smile faltered. "Oh, uh, hello, Gabriel."

He wiped sweat from his brow as the women's judgmental eyes bored into him. Then Justice White and his thug friends came around the corner and Gabe ducked inside the barracks.

Rather than rushing through, head lowered, Gabe lingered in the common area, saying "hi" to a few people along the way. He got blank stares in return, but at least they'd remember seeing him.

He slipped into his room, where he changed from work clothes into the black slacks and white shirt Bruderschaft required everyone to wear to dinner. He knew his dad would be back soon and the thought had him fighting tears. He assumed Mercy—with her ironic name—had gone right to the schoolteacher, Mrs. Clark, with a story about catching Gabe and Zeke up to no good. Mrs. Clark was Barnabas's wife, so word would travel straight to Barnabas, then the council, and then Gabe's dad. The gossip would spread fast, too.

Heavy footsteps came down the hall and he willed them to stop at any other room.

John Beck threw open the door and stormed in, glowering at his son.

Gabe stood, trying to keep the panic off his face. John punched him in the gut. Gabe doubled over with a loud grunt. He felt puke rise in his throat but managed to keep it down. His father grabbed him by the color and yanked him upright, so their faces were centimeters apart.

"Thought I'd made it clear if you humiliated me, I'd dig a hole for you out in the woods."

Gabe flinched as spittle flew from his dad's lips and landed on his face.

John sneered, his voice low and menacing. "It'd be so damned easy to make you disappear. No one here would blame me. So, keep pushing me, you sick little fag. See how much I'll stand before I take you for a walk at the business end of a shotgun." John let go and landed a punch that knocked Gabe's wind out. He fell backward onto his bed and curled up in a ball, trying to draw breath with lungs that struggled to work. He saw his mother in the doorway and had a moment of hope.

"Mom, please," he managed between gasps for air. "Help me."

Her eyes flitted away and she shut the door.

His dad slipped the belt from his trousers and wrapped the buckled end around one hand. "The least you can do is take your punishment like a man."

Zeke slipped into the house, afraid Tom would be waiting for him. The silent, empty house offered no comfort. It was just a matter of time.

He'd washed up and half changed into supper clothes when the front door burst open, the knob slamming into the wall behind it. "Ezekiel Matthew Shepherd!"

With his short-sleeved white shirt unbuttoned, he stepped from his room, head lowered. "Yes, Sir."

Tom stormed across the room and backhanded him across the face. "What the hell was you doing on your knees in a field with that filthy faggot?"

"It's not like that! We was just looking at some ants . . ."

His pa shoved him up against the wall. "Don't you lie to me, boy. The girl caught you, red-handed."

"I ain't lying! What do you think was up, both of us on our knees, a foot apart? I don't know much about gay stuff, but I'm pretty sure that ain't how it works, Pa."

"Why did you look all red-faced and guilty, then? Huh?" Tom pushed him aside and paced the small room. "I ain't having no faggot for a son, you hear me? You best stay away from him from now on."

Zeke bit back an argument and hung his head. "Yes, Sir."

Tom sat on the couch and leaned forward, head in his hands. "I'm glad your ma ain't here to see how you turned out."

"I'm sorry, Pa, but I promise I wasn't doing nothing . . . gay."

Tom flicked a hand and looked down at it. "What the hell?" He brushed something off and stared down at his work boots. Black spots crawled all over them. "Ants! God curse those lousy cleaning girls! Only dirty houses get ants." He stood up and stomped, brushing more of them off his hands and arms. "What are you waiting for, boy? Go get ant spray!"

Zeke sprinted for the equipment shed, grateful for an excuse to get away from his father's wrath. Something occurred to him halfway back to the house with the spray.

I never told the ants to go back to normal ant stuff. Dread grew in his gut as he realized they'd followed him home, awaiting orders. Just how much would they do for him?

When Zeke entered the community room, Gabe sat in a back corner with his chair facing the wall and a TV tray in front of him. Zeke felt everyone's eyes on him, judging him, and whispers spread across the room. He shot a sideways glance at the White table, where Mercy looked smug and proud. Her older brother Justice sneered at him.

His eyes met Naomi's and his stomach clenched with guilt at the fear and confusion on her face.

What did you do? she mouthed at him.

Zeke shook his head. *Nothing! I swear!*

A heavy hand landed on his shoulder. "It's the corner for you, boy." Barnabas dragged him to a chair he hadn't noticed in the front corner.

"Sir, can I speak to you privately? Please?" As intimidating as Barnabas was, Zeke would've groveled on his knees if he thought it would help.

Barnabas shoved him toward the corner. "What for? Sinners are liars, so if you think I'd listen to you . . . Well, that's about the most ridiculous thing I ever heard."

"But Sir, what Mercy said ain't true. We wasn't sinning, just looking at some ants."

"Shut up, boy, and serve your penance. Don't bring more shame on your pa than you already done."

Zeke sat and stared at the wall, anger rising at the injustice. The humiliation of everyone thinking *that* about him. He'd never kissed a girl, not even Naomi, but he knew he liked them. He wasn't some filthy faggot . . . Then it hit him—he was thinking those things about his best friend, the one person he could trust when it came to his powers. His *freak* powers. He sank deeper into misery.

The women served supper, starting with the men at the head table, then working their way back. He and Gabe would be the last ones served, and they'd get the smallest portions. Then they'd have to listen to Mercy be praised for reporting sin when she saw it.

"It's blazing hot in here," Barnabas told a serving woman. "Open the windows and let some air in."

A window slid up and a cool breeze circulated through the large room.

A wasp landed on Zeke's TV tray. *It'll do anything I want,* he thought with a thrill. "Go get the others and tell them to swarm in here," he whispered. The bug flew up and looked him in the eye before zipping out the window. He couldn't resist watching over his shoulder.

A minute later, Justice White happened to be walking past the window and glanced out, then did a double-take. "What the—?" A swarm of wasps blasted through the open window, smacking right into his face. He shrieked, backing up and waving his arms, and fell over a chair. His hand hit a plate and sent it spinning into the air and then crashing to the floor. Women and girls screamed. Men yelled. A bottleneck formed at the door as everyone tried to escape the furious swarm. Zeke watched the chaos with growing satisfaction.

Then Mr. Edwards screamed long and loud and Doc Jones ran toward him. Zeke felt bad, remembering Edwards was allergic. "Go away," he whispered, and the wasps flew back through the window as fast as they'd entered. He glanced toward Gabe's corner and his friend's battered face looked back with a satisfied smirk. He shot Zeke a quick thumbs-up, and Zeke smiled back. If Gabe had it right, Bruderschaft was full of bad people. To Zeke, the thought that bad people deserved punishment didn't sound like a ridiculous thing at all.

CHAPTER FOUR

Tuesday, July 25, 2017
Coeur d'Alene, Idaho

"Alex Peters. Pleasure to meet you, Chloe." He shook her hand.

Chloe couldn't help but notice he was super cute in person, even though he was kind of old, like over thirty. His awesome smile, perfect TV hair, and smooth voice made her melt. "Um, hi," was all she could manage.

They sat in the great room, where Amelia and the photographer had rearranged furniture to maximize the lighting and background of the shots. Chloe's bench stood on an angle before the fireplace, where the camera wouldn't see any windows behind her. A lighting crew had arrived two hours before the scheduled interview time and still tinkered with stands and gels and reflectors. Alex Peters had a mic on his lapel just like the one clipped to her uniform and attached to a black box tucked behind her. Another long, skinny microphone on a tall stand hung above them.

Chloe almost said no when they asked her to wear the blue and yellow Hero Academy uniform. Then she decided it would take away the stress of figuring out what to wear.

Heather Wyld stood back in the kitchen, where she could hear everything from off camera. She'd warned

Amelia if questions got hostile or too intrusive, she'd end it right there.

"Okay, Chloe, first things first." Alex took the seat across from her. "Will you say the name of your town for me? I want to make sure I pronounce it correctly."

"Oh, yeah. Core-duh-lane."

He repeated it a few times. "I've never been in this area before. It's beautiful."

"Alex, keep talking so I can check your levels," the audio guy said.

Alex gave him a nod and turned back to Chloe. "I've always wondered what it's like to be a Hero Academy student. What's your favorite part?"

"I really love training. There's an aerial obstacle course in the gym that's pretty cool, but I spend a lot of time flying outside, too."

He chuckled. "I didn't expect that answer. I should have, though, given your gymnastics background. I've covered enough Olympics to know how competitive athletes are."

Chloe laughed. "Yeah, Sally's always telling me not to overdo it."

"Sally?" he asked. "As in, the legendary Mustang Sally? You talk about her more like she's a friend than an idol or teacher."

"She's kind of all of those things, wrapped into one."

They continued chatting until Amelia told them everything was ready.

Alex grinned at her, which made her stomach flutter. "We're just going to keep talking like we have been, you have no reason to be nervous."

Yeah, right! Chloe nodded and swallowed hard.

"Miss Wyld," he said, his tone remaining conversational. "Zayden Lord was pretty famous before he started at Hero Academy. Tell me your first impression of him."

"Um, he seemed really nice. Humble, like, not full of himself at all." She paused and took a deep breath. "The other girls noticed he kept trying to start conversations with me, and he watched me a lot."

"And how did you feel about the attention?"

Chloe squirmed. She tried not to think about those early days with Zayden. "It was . . . nice." *Stop saying 'nice,' you sound like an idiot!* "I mean, I guess it was really flattering. He complimented me a lot and made me feel special. Some of the other girls were jealous. Especially Izzy." She regretted that as soon as she said it.

"By Izzy, I assume you mean Isabella Machado?"

"Yeah. I was worried she'd be upset with me. She seemed super nice at first, so I didn't want that."

"Before long, I understand you and Zayden became a couple."

Her heart sped up as she found the topic even more upsetting than expected. "After a few days of hanging out together a lot, he asked me to be his girlfriend and I said yes. It didn't last very long, though."

"Tell me why it ended."

Chloe fought to contain a rising panic. "I, uh . . . I'm sorry, I don't really want to talk about it. Is that okay?" She looked from Alex to Amelia.

Amelia nodded. "That's fine, Chloe. We can move on."

"Did I just mess up the whole thing?"

"No, not at all," Alex told her. "This isn't live. We do a lot of editing, so we'll just take this part out."

She breathed a sigh of relief. "Okay, good."

"We don't need to get into specifics, but can you talk about it in general? That way there's a flow to the story that makes sense."

"Uh, yeah. I guess I can do that." She glanced at her mom, who looked concerned. Chloe nodded to let her know she was okay.

Alex crossed his legs and folded his hands over one knee. "Can you give me any indication of why things didn't last between you and Zayden?"

"I guess . . . it was just the way he acted sometimes. He'd go from nice to sort of cold and aggro really suddenly, and I started getting creepy vibes. I just didn't want to be around him anymore."

Alex nodded. "But the time you spent with him gave you clues that other people didn't see."

"I thought I was being paranoid at first, but it turned out I was right." She went into the weird flashes of memory—Zayden's brother Dax's memories—that she'd seen any time he touched her.

Alex leaned forward, gaze intense. "Why do you think he paid so much attention to you?"

"He wanted to recruit me. That was it, the whole time, but he was subtle about it. I'd gotten some anonymous emails that sounded like hate-group propaganda that I eventually found out came from him. He finally just came out and asked me to come over to his side, while we fought on the roof of Heroes Hall. I guess he thought a flyer would be good for his team."

It still stung that the whole thing had just been a big manipulation, and that he'd never really liked her at all. She hoped it didn't show. She didn't want anyone thinking she was hung up on the jerk.

Alex asked follow-up questions about how she'd pieced things together and the roles various people assumed during the battle to stop him. "So, in the end, it was his own brother who truly defeated him. Despite his disabilities."

She smiled, thinking about Dax. "Yeah, Dax was amazing. He's so sweet and just . . . pure. I can't believe anyone ever thought he'd hurt people. It just boggles my mind. Without Dax, I never would've had the visions. I never would've pieced it together. A lot of people would have died."

"You mentioned hate-group propaganda. You've grown up in an area that's been a hotbed of racist and anti-parahuman organizations, and I understand you've even been targeted yourself. How do you feel about him trying to recruit you into something like that?"

Chloe sipped from a glass of water. "It makes me sick to my stomach. All that stuff around here, it used to be a lot worse, but I grew up seeing their leaflets on windshields and stuff. And now that they put me on a leaflet . . . it's kinda scary. I don't like knowing there are people in my town who are like that."

"Hate groups have been bolder of late, in response to the current political climate as well as because of Zayden's para-supremacist agenda." He paused for her to respond, but she just nodded, not knowing what to say. "Chloe, what would you say to people who believe there's something wrong with parahumans, or that parahumans feel superior to those of us without powers?"

"I guess I'd say . . . we're just like everybody else. All the parahumans I know—well, except for Zayden and Izzy and Lucia—they want to help people. My friends at the Academy proved that when they put themselves at risk to stop Zayden. Just Cause and the Champions prove that every day. People think it's some glamorous life, like actors and rock stars and stuff, but really, it's a lot of hard work, and it's scary, and people you care about get hurt and killed. Then there's the media attention . . . Sorry, but it's not fun at all. I hated it after my wings first came out, and I hate it now. I'm only doing this interview because I got sick of hiding inside my house. Heroes are way more like police or firefighters than celebrities. We all need to pull together for everyone's sake, not fight against each other."

Alex smiled and gave her a slow nod. "Well said. Nice job, Chloe." He looked up at Amelia. "I'm happy. You happy?"

Amelia grinned. "I'm happy."

Tuesday, July 25, 2017
Bruderschaft Compound, North Idaho

"Ezekiel, the sheep!" Mrs. Callahan from the barns ran breathlessly into the school. "We need your help!"

"What can possibly be so urgent, Faith?" Mrs. Clark asked.

"No time to explain. Ezekiel, now!" Mrs. Callahan turned and raced back out the door.

Zeke ran out and skidded to a halt when he saw what was wrong.

Sheep ran wild. A full-on stampede headed for the school at top speed with Eleanor at its point. Zeke almost yelled for them to go back to their fold, then realized but how that might look. It needed to look natural. *The dogs!* "Where are Jimmy and Bob?" he yelled to Mrs. Callahan as she wrangled a rowdy group of lambs.

"Trying to round up the ones that went the other way."

He nodded and headed for the large group, whistling and calling for them. On the sly, he also told a few at a time to head home when they came close enough to hear his mutters. The first ones turned and headed back the right way. He headed for a few strays meandering toward the neighborhood and got them redirected.

Mercy and the other kids who tended the flock most mornings turned up with the dogs, but by then Zeke had most of the animals under control. With Jimmy and Bob's help, they rounded up the last few and saw them back to the fold.

Once the gate was shut, Mercy shot Zeke a smug look. She made a kissy noise, spun on her heel, and walked away. The other kids laughed, surrounding her like a queen's fawning courtiers.

Zeke bent over, hands on his thighs, to catch his breath. "How'd they get out?"

Mrs. Callahan, looking bedraggled and exhausted, pointed to a spot in the fence where three men worked to fix some downed posts and chicken wire. "They knocked down the fence and just ran wild. I've never seen sheep act like that before. I've no idea what got into them."

"That fence was solid," Zeke said. "I checked it over just a few days ago. It had to take some doing for them to knock it down."

Faith Callahan gave a curt nod nodded. "I've checked it too, and Barnabas inspected all the fences not two weeks ago. Unless someone messed with it, those sheep worked to get out."

One of Mercy's followers, a younger boy, had stopped to scratch Bob's ears. "They was going crazy, just like the wasps at dinner last night."

No, it couldn't be. Could it? Zeke tried to remember the exact instructions he'd given the wasp. When he'd told it to "get the others," he'd meant the other wasps. Had it somehow communicated his orders to other creatures? It would explain the strange behavior. They had headed toward the neighborhood, to swarm like the wasps had. They must have worked at that fence for hours to get it down. *Dang. I gotta be more careful.*

Tuesday, July 25, 2017
Coeur d'Alene, Idaho

Alex shook Chloe's hand and thanked her as the crew packed up the equipment and cleared it out of the Wylds' living room. "Our editors are working overtime to get the footage out as soon as possible. It'll hit our cable channel and the website within the hour, and then it'll go to everyone else."

A beaming Amelia hugged her and her mom, darted out the front door, returned for the clipboard she'd left on the coffee table, then hurried out again.

Chloe breathed a sigh of relief. "I'm glad that's over with."

"Yeah but be prepared—you're going to be on every news channel and social media, too." Heather put an arm around her. "I wish I could shield you from all this, Fly Girl, but I guess when you're a real-life hero, this is what you have to deal with."

"I just hope I don't end up an embarrassing meme"

"You did great, Chlo. I'm proud of you." She kissed Chloe on the head. "Let's eat, and then we can head out to Mount Spokane, so you can stretch your wings."

Chloe squealed and hugged her. "Thanks, mom!"

Heather's phone rang. "It's dad, probably wanting to know how it went." She tapped the screen and turned away. "Hi, babe. Yeah, they've all cleared out."

Chloe messaged Charlie and Lindsay while she ate and posted on Parable to let everyone know the media storm was coming. Mrs. Jordan, the Academy's Dean of Students, had already posted some guidelines for dealing with the media.

Girl, I'm glad I'm in the middle of nowhere, Lindsay messaged. *I'm not important enough for them to come all the way out here.* Lindsay lived in a tiny town in central Montana, where the Deep Six parahuman prison was located, deep underground.

Two Reno stations and a Vegas reporter are coming this afternoon, and I already talked to BuzzFeed and a couple of newspapers on the phone, Charlie replied. *I haven't returned TMZ's messages yet.*

Ew, Lindsay typed. *Better you don't.*

Sorry, guys, Chloe thumbed in.

It's totally not your fault, Lindsay sent back. *No worries, sister!*

It was gonna come out sooner or later, Charlie said.

Gotta go. I actually get to go fly! I've never gone this long without it before. Well, at least not since I COULD fly, lol. Ttyl Then she switched over to a private message and sent a heart and a kiss emoji to Charlie. He responded with a kiss and a wink. Chloe grinned at the phone, then sprinted up the stairs to get into flying clothes. As she headed back downstairs, her phone beeped and she wondered what Charlie had forgotten to say.

It wasn't him, though. She cocked her head in surprise at the displayed name—Justin Sharp, who she'd been in flight training with and now interned with Just Cause Seattle. He was cool and all, but they'd never been friends. *Hey, Speed. Saw your interview. You did good.* He'd given her the nickname after their flight instructor proclaimed her an aerial speedster compared to the other winged fliers.

Thanks, Corvid! She swiped. *Congrats on the Seattle post!*

Thanks. How you holding up under the pressure?

Sigh. It's hard but I'm doing ok.

Good to hear. Duty calls but I'm here if you need to vent. Remember that, k?

She sent him a thumbs up.

"Charlie or Lindsay?" Heather asked.

Chloe laughed. "Neither, actually. It was Justin."

"The one with the bird wings? I didn't realize you were close to him."

Chloe grabbed some protein shakes from the fridge and stuck them into her bag along with an ice pack. She'd need them to refuel after flying. "I'm not. We hadn't talked since he graduated. I think he took his position as Obvious Club leader pretty seriously, though."

The house phone rang. Heather answered and wandered off down the hall, making Chloe concerned about who was on the other end. They'd just gotten rid of the media camp across the street—they didn't need any more excitement.

Her mom returned a few minutes later, keys in hand. "That was the mayor."

Chloe gave her a blank stare. "Wait, what?"

"He wants you, Charlie, and Lindsay to be in the Diversity Day Parade. You think they'd participate?"

"Cool!" Chloe grinned. "I'll ask them."

Tuesday, July 25, 2017
Bruderschaft Compound, North Idaho

Zeke wished he'd taken longer to get the sheep rounded up. He'd been too focused on not revealing his powers to recognize an opportunity to get out of class.

"We're going to cut our tactics lesson a little short today so we can talk about current events," Mrs. Clark said. "You all know about the wicked para-supremacist Zayden Lord and his Mexican accomplices. Barnabas told us all the other night that the filthy inhuman thing in Coeur d'Alene was his whore."

They all nodded. Zeke wondered where this was going and felt dirty, as if all that girl's sins were his because they were both paras. *Freaks.*

The teacher continued. "Now, the whore has spoken to the lying media. I want to play you a few clips of what she had to say—about us." A concerned murmur rose up around the room as Mrs. Clark turned on the TV and put in a disc. A still frame of Chloe Wyld filled the screen. Zeke thought she looked pretty and a little nervous. He didn't blame her. The video played, and the girl nodded while the reporter spoke off screen.

"You've grown up in an area that's been a hotbed of racist and anti-parahuman organizations. How do you feel about that?"

"It makes me sick to my stomach. All that stuff around here, it used to be a lot worse, but now that they put me on a leaflet . . . it's kinda scary. I don't like knowing there are people in my town who are like that."

A handsome reporter came on screen. "Hate groups have been bolder of late, in response to the current political climate as well as because of Zayden's para-supremacist agenda. Chloe, what would you say to people who believe there's something wrong with parahumans, or that parahumans feel superior to those of us without powers?"

Chloe came back on screen, looking thoughtful.

"I guess I'd say . . ."

The video cut back to the reporter, who nodded while Chloe's voice continued.

" . . . heroes are way more . . . than celebrities. We all need to pull together, not fight against each other."

Mrs. Clark turned off the DVD player. "There you hear it, straight from the whore's mouth. She believes parahumans are superior and need to band together—against real humans like you and me. And she especially hates God's chosen people, Bruderschaft and our brother organizations. So now we know who the freaks will come for first. The stupid girl leaked their agenda, and we'll be better able to prepare because of it. Just watch, they won't let her speak in public again."

Zeke trudged out to the field after class, feeling doubly dejected over being a freak and knowing people like him wanted to destroy his community. He wished he could talk to Gabe, but they both knew they shouldn't be seen together for a while.

"Mrs. Callahan, my stomach hurts." Gabe stood with a hunch, one hand on his abdomen. "I think I need to go home."

She pursed her lips and raised an eyebrow. "Lying is a sin, Gabriel, and idle hands are the devil's workshop. I don't care to contribute to your idleness."

"It really hurts, though. Look." He pulled up his shirt to reveal the bruises and welts.

A flicker of alarm crossed Mrs. Callahan's face, but she appeared to shake it off right away. "That looks like discipline to me, Gabriel. Righteously delivered."

"Yes, Ma'am. There's pain deep down, though, not like usual. I've been punished a lot, and it never hurt like this before. I'm afraid it's an organ or something."

Another flicker. He knew he was getting through to her soft side. "What makes you think that? I don't believe you're trained as a doctor."

"No, Ma'am. But . . ." He lowered his voice and tried to look scared. "There's blood in my ur- . . . uh, when I relieve myself. That's not good, is it?"

Her face went pale. "Very well. Go see Doc Jones and make sure he lets me know if you can't work tomorrow."

"I will, Ma'am, and thank you." He turned around, and his mouth twisted into a wry smile as he fake-limped out of the barn. Once out of Mrs. Callahan's sight, he relaxed and walked toward the neighborhood at a brisk pace, as if he'd been sent on an errand. If you looked like you were doing something important, the Butler's Shaft peeps assumed someone more important than them sent you to do it and left you alone.

He walked into the community building and checked with the kitchen to see how soon they'd need more milk. That allowed him easy access to the side door—the one closest to Barnabas's house and out-back, where he could get Internet access.

He'd go see Doc Jones afterward, just in case Mrs. Callahan got nosy.

An hour into his shift, Zeke startled when Gabe emerged from the edge of the woods and waved him over. He glanced around to make sure no eyes were on them, then ordered the sheep and dogs to stay in the field. He pointed at the willful and cantankerous ewe. "Eleanor, you stay put, too, you troublemaker." Satisfied the animals would behave themselves, Zeke trotted across the field and the two boys ducked into the trees.

"What are you doing here?" Zeke asked.

"What did you think about the video Mrs. Clark showed us, of the dragonfly girl?"

Zeke hung his head. "I didn't expect them to come for us so soon, but I guess it's good that we're ready to defend ourselves."

Gabe shook his head. "Seriously, dude? You bought that? The way it was edited, showing the reporter while the girl was talking, and the way her audio sounded all glitchy and disconnected—I suspected they'd tampered with it, and I was right." He pulled out his tablet. "I slipped over to outback and downloaded this. Take a look."

The reporter came on. "Hate groups have been bolder of late, in response to the current political climate as well as because of Zayden's para-supremacist agenda. Chloe, what would you say to people who believe there's something wrong with parahumans, or that parahumans feel superior to those of us without powers?"

"I guess I'd say . . .we're just like everybody else. All the parahumans I know—well, except for Zayden and Izzy and Lucia—they want to help people. My friends at the Academy proved that when they put themselves at risk to stop Zayden. Just Cause and the Champions prove that every day. People think it's some glamorous life, like actors and rock stars and stuff, but really, it's a lot of hard work, and it's scary, and people you care about get hurt and killed. Then there's the media attention . . . Sorry, but it's not fun at all. I hated it after my wings first came out, and I hate it now. I'm only doing this interview because I got sick of hiding inside my house. Heroes are way more like police or firefighters than celebrities. We all need to pull together for everyone's sake, not fight against each other."

Zeke squinted at the small screen, confused. "Wait, that's not what we saw in class."

Gabe sighed. "Of course, it's not. Barnabas or somebody edited the interview, so it'd say what they wanted it to."

"But why would they want her to say the fr-, uh, the parahumans was coming for us?"

"Because, dude." Gabe put a hand on his shoulder. "They want you guys to *think* outside forces are against you. They want to make you fear them, and hate them, and want to kill them. They're manipulating the crap out everybody here. It's all lies, Zeke."

Zeke reeled. He didn't want to believe everything he'd been taught was a lie, but this interview amounted to pretty strong evidence. "Let me watch that again."

He watched it three more times and began to see how someone had picked out certain phrases and strung them together to change their meaning. After that, Gabe showed him other news clips and articles he'd collected. The more he read and watched, the more his shock wore off and anger took its place.

If they've lied about all this, how can I believe anything they've ever said? Images ran through his mind of grasshoppers, spiders, toads, and rats flooding the compound. He wanted to make it happen, wanted to scare them, but he knew he'd never have the courage to go through with it. Not really.

Gabe headed back toward the barracks while Zeke finished his shift so they wouldn't be seen together. He felt bad for the big lug—his whole worldview was crumbling. That was tough, but since it had been Gabe's goal for months, he felt pretty proud of himself for getting the evidence.

"What do you have to smile about, faggot?"

Gabe froze at Justice White's mocking voice. The thug and two buddies had just stepped out of the barracks and blocked Gabe from entering. His heart raced. If he got another beating, he really *would* pee blood.

A proud Justice held a Christian soldier uniform on a hanger. A lump formed in Gabe's gut as he realized the bully must have just been promoted from soldier-in-training to the real thing. That meant he could get away with a lot more abuse than he used to, which meant Gabe was in deep shit.

"Hold this. I don't want him to breathe his gay cooties on it." Justice thrust the uniform at one of his friends and strode toward Gabe.

Gabe wondered if he could run fast enough to get away from them. Justice towered over him almost as much as Zeke. "C-congratulations on your promotion."

"Don't you speak to me like we're friends." Justice jabbed Gabe's chest. "I'm your superior now, *Gay*-briel. You call me *Sir*. How do you like that?"

"If anyone on the compound belongs with the soldiers, it's you. S-sir." Gabe cursed his voice for shaking.

"You trying to be some kind of smart mouth, fag?"

"No, Sir. Just trying to go to my room."

Justice punched him in the gut and Gabe cried out in real pain when Justice's fist connected with his ribs. "Go on to your room, faggot. The decent folk don't want to look at you."

Clutching his side, Gabe limped to the barracks as Justice and his buddies laughed and jeered. It wasn't long before he heard screams.

Zeke rounded the barn on his way home and saw Gabe limping toward him, panic in his eyes.

"Dude, what did you do?"

"Wh-what do you mean?"

Gabe pointed back toward the neighborhood. "They're everywhere. Freaking everywhere!"

The blood drained from Zeke's face and he sprinted toward the neighborhood. What he saw filled him with an odd mix of awe, malicious power, and dread.

All around the houses, women shooed toads and rats away with brooms. Jemima Jones pressed her back up against a storage shed and sprayed the ground with bug killer. Men stomped around in their boots, killing the small vermin underfoot and frightening away the larger creatures. Zeke froze. Rats, toads, spiders, and grasshoppers boiled over the dirt roads and the small patches of grass. The walls writhed with them.

Gabe came up beside him. "Seriously, how did you manage this? Even out in the woods, I can't believe this many things heard you."

Zeke shook his head. "I don't know. I never even said it out loud."

"Well, make it stop before someone figures it out. Especially the spiders. Gross!"

Zeke thought it would be a bad idea to send them all away at once, in case anyone had noticed him arrive. He tried to focus through panic and thought, *Spiders, go away.* Nothing happened. He wandered through the neighborhood and muttered, "Go away, spiders," whenever no people would overhear. The creepy crawlies began moving away and he started to dismiss the other creatures. Things started to calm down.

Dead vermin carpeted the neighborhood. The bugs didn't bother him too bad, but the blood and viscera of the larger creatures turned his stomach and made him sad. He was responsible for every single death. *Freak.*

He caught Gabe's eye from a few houses away and gave a pointed look at the school, which should be empty this time of day. Gabe meandered that way, and after a glance around to make sure he wasn't being watched, Zeke followed. When he went through the open door, he found Gabe standing on a desk and staring in fear at the floor where a handful of spiders roamed.

"All of you go back to where you came from," Zeke ordered. Spiders didn't bother him much, but he did find it disconcerting to see how many slipped away through invisible gaps between floorboards. He looked up at Gabe. "Okay, little girl. You can come down now."

Gabe put his hands on his hips. "Seriously? How do I even begin to tell you what's wrong with saying that?" He climbed down onto the chair, scoped out the floor one more time, then sat. He kept his feet on the seat, though. "Now tell me how that all happened if you didn't even say anything."

Zeke told him about picturing those exact things in anger. "You was there, though. You know I didn't say it."

"So, that means you directed them . . . telepathically or something."

"What does that mean?"

Gabe sighed and dropped into a seat. "It means you told them with your brain."

Zeke scrunched up his face, trying to puzzle that out. "When a frog couldn't hear me before 'cause it was in the water, it didn't respond. And when I tried to *think* at the spiders, they didn't leave. How come?"

"Shit, I don't know!" Gabe shrugged. "I'm not an expert in parahuman mental abilities, but if I had to guess . . . maybe it's because you were mad? Maybe you *thought* it intensely enough."

"Okay, that's weird."

"*That's* weird? I'm pretty sure everything about this situation is weird."

Zeke nodded. "Yeah, you said a mouthful, right there."

Gabe gave the floor a close examination and then stood. "I'll head out the back door and see if I can help with the cleanup out there. You come out the front in a couple minutes, okay, Plague Master Z?"

Zeke nodded and stood there thinking as Gabe left. *Plague Master.* Is that what he was? It sounded more like a supervillain's name than a hero's, that's for sure.

Closer to Satan than Jesus, too. *Does that mean it's a curse? That I'm an evil freak?* But he didn't feel evil. Weak, yes. Inadequate, certainly. Not evil, though. That made him wonder if evil people realized they were evil, and that was a deeper thought than he knew how to process. Even so, he felt pretty sure evil people didn't feel remorse for hurting rats and toads.

Then it dawned on him what the plagues were: punishment, sent by God. Was his ability a sign that God didn't like what Bruderschaft was doing?

Zeke left the school and went home through the masses of grasshoppers leaping every which way and tried not to step on anything living. A toad croaked at him from underneath the porch swing and he told it, with his mind, to go home.

It hopped away.

CHAPTER FIVE

Wednesday, July 26, 2017
Coeur d'Alene, Idaho

Chloe's eyes flew open, her heart pounding. The morning sunlight streaming through her bedroom window revealed nothing about the boom that had awakened her, but the repetitive chirp of car alarms confirmed something was wrong.

She half-ran, half-flew down the stairs as her white-faced parents stumbled in from the patio. "What was that bang?" Phil asked.

They all stared at each other for a moment. Chloe realized they didn't know any more than she did and raced to the great room window.

The street looked the same as always except for neighbors staring out of their open doors. A puff of smoke caught her eye and she realized what had changed. Or rather, what was missing. "Um, I think our mailbox exploded."

Her parents crowded in to look out the window.

"Holy hell, I think you're right," Heather said. Phil called 9-1-1.

Stomach churning, Chloe turned to her mom. "I feel like I should go out and look, but that's probably kinda stupid, huh?"

"Yeah, you're not going out there." Heather hugged her. "Let someone else be the hero today, Fly Girl."

"You see what your faggoty friend caused yesterday?"

Zeke jumped and spun around. Tom Shepherd leaned against the door jamb, chewing his ubiquitous toothpick. "I didn't know you was here, Sir. Why aren't you on duty already?"

"I asked you a question, boy."

Zeke pulled a camo-print t-shirt down over his head and reached for the gray sweatshirt with the red iron cross emblem on the chest. "What about Gabe?"

"The vermin yesterday. The plagues. You don't think that was no accident, now, do you? It sure as shit wasn't natural." He shifted the toothpick from right to left. "Barnabas figures God's sending plagues to punish us for letting the faggot kid on the compound. Preacher, he thinks it's what you and Beck was doing in the field the other day."

Zeke sighed. "Pa, I told you, we wasn't doing nothing. If Mercy says anything other than us just looking at the ground, she's a liar and going to Hell for bearing false witness. I swear it, we was just looking at some ants."

Tom raised an eyebrow. "Ants, you say. Like the ones that invaded this very house. Like you're being singled out for what you done."

"You serious? You think I'd do . . . gay stuff with Gabe?" Zeke clenched his fists, anger rising.

"Hell, maybe you would, Ezekiel. You're always out in the fields with those damn animals. Maybe you got some kind of messed up notion in your head about how stuff is supposed to be." Tom rolled the toothpick back across his mouth. "Like maybe this place ain't good enough for you. Maybe *I* ain't good enough for you. Maybe womenfolk ain't good enough for you, neither."

"You know I like Naomi Jones, Pa. I want to marry her. Would I want that if I was some f-faggot?" He felt guilty, once again, for talking that way about his friend. He also realized images of bugs and small animals once again flashed through his head, more and more of them as he got madder. He tried to push the images away but couldn't. The last thing he needed another accidental swarm. *Freak.* "Can you move out of the way, please, Sir? I don't want to be late for work."

His father stared, eyes narrowed to slits. "You said you was looking at ants, and then we had ants here in the house. Then your sheep got out too, didn't they? Ran all over creation." He pulled the toothpick from his lips and regarded it as if contemplating what secrets it might hold. "Makes a fellow think."

Zeke hung his head, not daring to argue with his father. Straining to keep his anger from summoning every bug in the county made his head throb.

"Thing is," Tom said, "I can't let accusations against my kid stand. I got a position here, understand? I can't let nothing threaten that. I'll swear to God and everyone else you're using Jemima and Esther to satisfy your urges already. You hear what I'm saying, boy? I'll lie—I'll *sin*—to protect my standing here, and that'll save you some punishment. But I might just see fit to make amends to the Almighty by punishing you myself. You keep yourself out of trouble, you hear? You stay away from that Beck kid or I swear I'll beat you bloody."

Zeke reeled, feeling dirty and guilty. His father intended to lie, to tarnish his own soul because of him. "I hear you, Sir."

Wednesday, July 26, 2017
Boise, Idaho

"Jeffrey, did you hear a word I said?"

Jeffrey looked up to see Tamara beside his desk. He shook his head. "Sorry, that freaking band is so loud."

She raised an eyebrow. "What?"

"Right? I can't hear myself think!"

"No, I heard you just fine. I meant, what are you talking about?"

"The marching band." He waved a hand toward the window. "Any idea how long they're supposed to be practicing out there?"

"They're *not* out there."

He looked at his supervisor and friend, unsure whether she was messing with him. No way did she not hear that cacophony. "Tamara, come on."

"Seriously! Unless I'm losing my mind—which, I'll grant, is possible—you're having a vision." She cocked her head. "Or an . . . audio-sion? Whatever you call an auditory premonition."

"I'm guessing it's called an 'auditory premonition,' but my forecasting isn't like that." He pushed off from the desk and rolled his chair toward the window. "Are you seriously trying to tell me you don't hear that—" He pivoted away and looked out the window. "Wait, what?"

Tamara leaned over him. "Oh, the Seven Cars in the Otherwise-Empty Parking Lot Band! Yeah, they're legendary. What they do with Sousa . . ."

The senator's ringtone came from Tamara's phone and she answered. "Senator, what can I do for you?"

The band music cut out like someone threw a switch. Images flashed through Jeffrey's mind as his forecasting switched from auditory to visual. *Parade. Marching band. Lake. Raven. A distant scream.*

"Coeur d'Alene's Diversity Day parade is coming up. The one they always invite me to." Even though Tamara wasn't using the speakerphone function, Jeffrey could hear the Senator plain as day.

"Yes, Ma'am. Declining the invitation is on my list for today."

"Don't decline," the senator said. "The dragonfly girl will be on a float. With how hot she is right now, I can't pass up the photo op. Tell them I'd be delighted to attend."

Jeffrey spun around and gave her a frantic head shake. He wanted to scream no, but he didn't dare. Not while he remained on thin ice with the senator. Tamara turned away. "We've been trying to find a good time to talk to that reporter—what's his name, with the bushy mustache? The one who was so big with parahuman rights back in the day and came out of retirement after the last election."

"Ah, yes. Mr. Lee."

"I'll see if he can come up for the parade. We can turn the photo op into a media event."

"Excellent idea, Tamara. Get on those arrangements." The Senator disconnected.

Looking proud of herself, she hung up and noticed the concern on Jeffrey's face. "What? Does this have something to do with your imaginary marching band?"

Jeffrey raised his eyebrows. "Marching band? Parade? It fits."

She sighed. "Shit. What's going to happen?"

He shook his head. "You know it doesn't work like that. I won't know until we get closer to the event." He returned to his chair. "Someone's in danger. I think . . . I think someone's going to die. Should we tell her?"

Tamara laughed. "Yeah, right. After the last time nothing happened? That'd go over well." She paused, hand on her hip. "If you forecast anything else, anything specific, let me know."

He shook his head, lips pressed tight together so he wouldn't explode. "Why is she such a miserable hard ass?" he asked under his breath.

Tamara gave him her best why-are-you-so-obtuse look. "Because she has to be. You want change? That's what it takes."

Wednesday, July 26, 2017
Bruderschaft Compound, North Idaho

Eleanor stayed close to Zeke's side, and he found her presence comforting. He patted her on the head and laughed as some lambs cavorted through the stream. He needed the distraction the animals provided.

"April and May, spin around in circles," he told the rambunctious lambs. They leaped and spun, and their excited bleats sounded almost like laughter. Since they seemed to be enjoying themselves, he decided to make it a little party. He pointed at a ewe. "Belinda, bleat in rhythm, like this: Bah, bah, bah. Huckleberry . . ." He looked another lamb in the eyes. "Hop up and down to the rhythm." He laughed as more lambs joined in the spinning and hopping without being commanded. He leaned back against a tree and laughed as he conducted the antics. By the time Gabe walked up the hill toward him, he had a chorus of sparrows sitting on the lambs' heads, adding their cheerful tweets to Belinda's song. His amusement died when he saw fresh bruises around Gabe's eyes.

"You don't look so good." He told the sheep to go back to grazing and sent the sparrows flying away. "That have anything to do with the council thinking you're behind the plagues?"

Gabe shrugged and stared at his feet.

"Sorry, man," Zeke said. "I should've realized they'd think that. 'Course, they think it's because of me, too. Because of what Mercy told them."

"So, what are they gonna do?" Gabe sat, moving with caution, like an old man.

"I don't know. They'll probably meet soon to talk about it. My pa says he'll keep them from accusing me. To protect his position, though, not 'cause he gives a damn what happens to me."

Gabe shook his head. "Figures. What about me?"

Zeke plucked a few blades of grass from the ground. He couldn't meet Gabe's eye. "Could be a lot of things. Could be they'll try some more of that conversion therapy stuff on you."

Gabe's chin quivered at the thought and he looked away. "I'll kill myself before I go through that bullshit again."

Zeke's stopped himself from blurting out that suicide was a sin of weakness. "There could be public beatings. Or they could banish you."

"Damn, that sure wouldn't suck! Except, of course, I have nowhere to go. It's Butler's Shaft or the streets."

Zeke swallowed hard. "A few times, when someone's done something really bad—and I mean really, really bad . . . It-it doesn't happen very often . . ."

"Cut to the chase, dude."

"It's possible they'll . . . execute you."

Gabe's eyes went wide. "Are you serious? What, like a firing squad, or hanging?"

Zeke looked away, shaking his head.

"Worse? What, crucifixion?"

"They'll beat you till you can't stand, and then . . ." Zeke struggled to get the words out and couldn't manage more than a whisper. "They'll stone you to death."

Gabe froze. "Holy shit. Have you seen it happen?"

Zeke closed his eyes, trying to drive away the mental images. "Just once."

Wednesday, July 26, 2017
Coeur d'Alene, Idaho

"The good news is that it was a pretty shoddy attempt," Detective Abara told the Wylds. They sat around the kitchen table, Heather pouring Irish cream and vodka into her steaming coffee, despite the day's rising heat. "The organized hate groups have explosives experts, and those guys know what they're doing. This device was crude and sloppy—which is fortunate. That's why it went off early rather than when you opened the mailbox. Forensics is investigating the residue, but I think they'll find it was someone's leftover 4th-of-July fireworks."

"It still could have hurt someone," Chloe said. "Or . . . or worse."

Abara looked troubled. "Sure could've. We've got uniformed officers canvassing the neighborhood and checking for security cam footage. You may want to invest in some home security yourself."

Phil nodded. "I'm already working on it."

"Any lead yet on who's behind the leaflet?" Heather asked.

Abara shook his head. "We're pretty sure it was just one guy. We've got security video of the suspect, but he wore a hat and sunglasses, generic clothing, and an oversized coat that makes it difficult to see his build. We're still looking for witnesses, though." He pulled out a handkerchief and dabbed at his forehead. "I miss the days when you had to go to Kinko's to get something photocopied. Now that everyone can do it at home, it makes things like this impossible to trace. We'll keep looking, though. Something will turn up."

He stood, ducked around the light fixture, and headed to the door. Chloe and her parents followed.

"I'll do what I can to keep this out of the news. The last thing we need are copycats, and that's usually what publicity gets us. Meanwhile . . ."

Chloe sighed. "Stay inside and keep my head down. Yeah."

Gabe wasn't at dinner. His parents sat hunched over their trays. John Beck gave off a foreboding vibe that kept everyone away. His wife, drunk and dazed, picked at her food without speaking. Zeke noticed bandages over the knuckles of John's right hand and had the sinking feeling he'd hurt himself beating to his son yet again.

The council elders—including Zeke's pa—ate in silence and left early. Zeke knew they'd head out-back, which meant something was up. Zeke feared it had to do with him and Gabe.

He hurried through dinner, slipped out of the community room, and headed straight to the barracks. He tapped on Gabe's window. "Gabe? You in there?"

The curtain moved aside just enough for an eye to peek through, then closed. Zeke tapped again. Gabe's hand reached up under the curtain and slid the window open a crack. "Go away." His voice gurgled like he had a mouth full of mud.

"Gabe, come out here. I have an idea."

Silence stretched out and Zeke was about to give up when Gabe pushed aside the curtain. His left eye was swelled shut and sickly colors marred the flesh where bruises just started to form. His lips bled from numerous splits. Zeke gasped.

"Go 'way, Zeke. I don' wanna do anythin' but lay here an' die. Or wait till they kill me."

Something gnawed at his stomach as he thought about Gabe being gone. Being dead.

"Dude, the council's having a special meeting right now, and I'm pretty sure it's about us. We need to sneak into out-back and see what's going on."

Gabe's one good eye widened and he climbed out the window. "Was my dad still at dinner?"

"Yeah, but hold on." Zeke looked around the corner of the building and saw John Beck wasn't among the men who'd emerged and headed home. As always, they left the women behind to wash the dishes. "He must still be in there."

Gabe motioned the other direction with his head. "Let's go th' long way around, so we don' risk runnin' inno him."

They slipped around the other side of the building, circled the outside of the neighborhood and around to Barnabas' back field.

"You know how to get in, right?" Zeke whispered.

Gabe nodded. "I c'n pick th' lock. Migh' be loud, though. We need a dis'rac'tion."

Zeke had to ask him to repeat it so he could understand the garbled speech. "Distraction. Got it." He jogged over to the nearby tree line, where he'd spotted some crows perched high in the pine trees. "Hey, crows. Follow me over to the building and then—without hurting yourselves—bang your wings against the windows and make as much noise as you can." He turned and hurried back to Gabe., The birds followed, circling until Zeke pointed to the windows. They dive-bombed the building, beating their wings and even their bodies against the windows and cawing like mad.

Gabe went to work on the lock with a bent piece of metal and a wire he'd pulled from his jacket pocket. His jiggering rattled the lock enough to make Zeke grateful for the avian noise camouflage. The elders yelled, trying to shoo away the birds.

"Got it," Gabe whispered. He unlatched the door.

"Go away, crows," Zeke whisper-shouted. "And, uh, thanks." The crows flew off, still cawing, as the boys slipped through the door and eased it shut behind them.

They found themselves in a small foyer with a coarse rug for catching the mud on men's boots, a rough-hewn bench, and coat hooks lined up on one wall. Voices behind the nearest door cursed the birds' strange behavior. Gabe motioned him to another door and they slipped into a large but sparse office. A bulky tan computer squatted atop a metal desk, and topographical maps adorned two walls. A gun rack full of black assault rifles took up most of the third. Gabe pointed to a vent down near the floor, near the rack, and they knelt in front of it. Gabe pulled a screwdriver from his pocket and pried off the vent cover. The voices in the next room came through loud and clear.

Preacher's voice cut through muddled conversation. "His folks already tried therapy. It didn't work."

"Maybe they wasn't tough enough on him." That was Barnabas.

"I don't think we can afford to wait and see if it works this time," Tom Shepherd said. "We already got Biblical plague shit going on, in case you ain't noticed." Zeke chewed at a fingernail as he pictured his father pacing back and forth.

Preacher banged a fist. "Thomas, I'm sick of telling you to stop using profane language alongside sacred words. Between that and your drinking, I'm starting to wonder whether you belong on this council."

"Sorry, Preacher." Tom sounded more angry than apologetic.

"I agree with Tom's sentiment, though," said one of the other men. "No use trying what's already failed. We need a solution right now."

"Beatings, then?" Barnabas asked.

"His pa already tried that approach plenty." That was Mr. Callahan, whose wife was Gabe's boss at the barn.

"I say we beat him as a warning to the other kids, then send him packing," Mr. White said.

A few of the others voiced support for his idea.

Preacher cut in. "I'm afraid God won't find that a severe enough punishment, gentlemen. He has unleashed plagues on us as a warning, and you witnessed it just now

—we mentioned conversion therapy and He sent the black birds to warn us against that path. Do you deny it was a sign from the Lord Himself?"

Zeke winced.

"So, what, you want to execute him?" Callahan asked. "We ain't never executed a kid."

"We ain't never had a faggot infecting other kids with his sin, neither," Barnabas told them.

"Watch what you say," Tom warned, voice almost a growl. "My boy ain't no faggot or no sinner. He's already bedding the pass-around girls on the regular and got his eye on Jones's youngest as a bride."

Gabe turned to him, good eye wide and questioning. Zeke scowled and shook his head, wanting to make sure Gabe knew it wasn't true about the pass-around girls.

"Hoping she'll fuck like her big sis, eh?" another man said. "Wouldn't mind having a go at the younger one myself, just to see. She got them nice Jones titties already. You notice that?"

Several of them laughed. Zeke's face got hot and red hearing him talk about Naomi that way and he thought he might punch the man if they were face to face.

"Language." Preacher's voice dripped with disdain. "The Lord is always listening, gentlemen. If you're done being crass, I call for a vote."

"Alrighty, then." Barnabas cleared his voice and slipped into an official tone. "All in favor of conversion therapy say *aye*."

Silence.

"All in favor of a public beating and banishment, say *aye*."

Two voices said "aye," including Zeke's father. Surprise and gratitude welled up in his heart. He'd been sure his father would vote for the most extreme punishment and wondered if he made this decision with Zeke's feelings in mind. He doubted it but felt gratitude anyway.

"All in favor of execution say *aye*."

The rest said a resounding "aye."

Zeke's stomach lurched and the color drained from Gabe's face, making the bruises stand out more than ever, even in the dim light.

"That's settled then. We got fields to get fertilized over the next couple of days, so we'll do it after dinner on Saturday. Any objections?" No one voiced any, and Barnabas declared the meeting adjourned. Zeke realized too late they were trapped in the office with nowhere to go if Barnabas or one of the others came in. He reached for Gabe to pull him behind the desk, but the elders all left together and locked the door behind them.

Gabe fell back onto his butt and stared at the wall. "Holy shit. They're gonna kill me."

Zeke leaped to his feet, fists clenched. "No, they ain't! We're gonna get you off the compound before then, I promise. You can find somewhere safe out there. I know you can."

Gabe looked up at him, a tear rolling down his right cheek. "Come wit' me, Zeke. Get away from here while you can."

Icy splinters dug into Zeke's stomach. "Leave? Where would I go?"

Gabe shrugged. "I dunno. Maybe there's a halfway house f'r reformed racists or somethin'. We can go to th' police. Or Just Cause."

"No way! You can't trust cops or fr—" He broke off when Gabe looked at him like he was an idiot. "Is that another lie?"

"Yeah, mostly."

He sat down in the task chair. "Gabe, man, I don't know if I can make it out there. The world . . . I don't know anything about it, and I can't trust what I been taught here."

"I know, but you're a decent person. An' if you stay here, they'll beat it out of you evench'lly."

Zeke looked down at his boots and kicked at a loose floorboard. "You're probably right. I don't know if I can do it though."

Gabe stood up and went to the desk. "Lessee if we c'n find contact information f'r Just Cause. I c'n put it in my tablet and get a hold of them as soon as we ditch this place." He did some stuff on the computer Zeke couldn't follow and pictures flashed up, only to disappear and be replaced by something else after a click on the deelybob under Gabe's hand. "I'm not seein' anythin'. Hey, there's that girl, though! WyldWing. Wha's her real name?" He clicked through a few more screens and pulled up a news article. "Chloe Wyld. Coeur d'Alene's not that big. We c'n find her."

Zeke gaped. "Coeur d'Alene has like fifty-thousand people! It's huge!"

"Ah, dude. That's jus' sad." Gabe wrote her name on a piece of paper from the desk and shoved it into his pocket. "If nothin' else, we c'n go to her." After closing windows in preparation to leave, something on the desktop caught his eye. He pointed to a folder icon. "Any idea what *Operation 88* is?"

Zeke shook his head. "I mean, 88 stands for H.H. Heil, Hitler. But I never heard of no *Operation 88*."

"Sounds important." Gabe clicked on the icon and found a list of documents, numerous photos, and a few maps. He opened a document titled *Hit List*. "Holy fuckin' Christ!"

"Shhh! Someone'll hear. Plus, serious blasphemy."

"You wanna talk bla'phemy? Fine, what about *thou shalt not kill*? Or don't they teach that one here?"

"Um, I know the Ten Commandments, Gabe. I ain't a moron."

"Okay, then, look at his. These are plans for assassinatin' all these people. Pretty sure that means killin' 'em."

Zeke started for the door. "Let's just get out of here. I'm nervous as all get out."

"Hold on." Gabe pulled up a page that said *Drive* and dragged the *Operation 88* folder over to it. He stared at the screen while Zeke fidgeted behind him, every second dragging on forever. At last, a message popped up saying it was done. Gabe stood up. "Okay, now we c'n go."

CHAPTER SIX

Thursday, July 27, 2017
Bruderschaft Compound, North Idaho

Gabe wasn't at breakfast. Worried, Zeke swung by the milk barn to check on him. Instead of Gabe, he found Naomi. She was red-faced and rushing around, tending to the cattle all by herself. He stopped short, wondering why she was there. She'd moved to housekeeping months ago.

She noticed him and froze, blushing. "Oh, Ezekiel. Hi. If you're looking for Gabriel, he's sick again."

"Is that why you're here? I didn't expect to see you, but I'm glad I did."

"Not just that. Mrs. Edwards had her baby last night, so they're down two here."

"Oh yeah, I heard about the baby at breakfast." Zeke stood there, hands in his pockets, feeling like a wet lump of nothing good. "I best get out of your way, then."

She put down a bucket and hurried over to him. "It was good of you to stop by, Zeke. I miss seeing you in school."

Zeke grinned, feeling dopey. "I miss seeing you, too. Maybe . . . Do you think your pa would let me come visit sometime?"

She blushed. "Like, to court me?"

"Oh, uh, I mean, if you don't want me to . . ."

She touched his hand. He stared at it, eyes wide. "I'd like that." They grinned at each other, and she took his hand in hers. The warmth of it made him dizzy. Then a concerned expression stole her smile. "About the trouble with you and Gabriel. I've heard the rumors, but I don't believe them. What really happened?"

He sighed. "We was being dumb. Messing with an anthill, watching them all scatter. Please believe me!"

She laughed. "Of course, I believe you. That sounds like much more of a Zeke thing than what people have been saying." She glanced around, looking anxious, then stood on tippy toes and leaned toward him. Zeke gaped, not knowing what to do. Naomi put a hand on the back of his neck, pulled his face down, and gave him a soft kiss on the cheek.

His face burned and he smiled so hard he thought he might split his ears. She beamed back and put a finger to her lips to let him know this was their secret. Then she grabbed the bucket and went back to work.

Zeke, still grinning like a fool, slipped out of the barn and went on to the sheepfold, feeling pretty good about the day. Pleasant fantasies of Naomi filled his mind, keeping his worries about Gabe at bay for a few minutes, at least. He took the flock farther away from the compound than normal, not because the closer fields were picked clean, but because he wanted to be as far as possible from the men who wanted to kill his friend. He needed space to think about how to get Gabe off the compound. *Could I really go with him?*

Zeke still couldn't wrap his head around the idea of leaving Bruderschaft. Sure, he questioned a lot of what he'd been taught. He was dying to know what Gabe had learned from the out-back computer. But he'd never ventured very far out into the world. He'd been to Clagstone, the nearest town, often enough, but Coeur d'Alene was a different matter. He'd only been there once, with his pa and Barnabas because they needed tractor parts in a hurry, and it had overwhelmed him. Gabe said it was a small town, but it sure looked big to Zeke.

A flock of sparrows landed in the tree he lounged against and he took advantage of the distraction. Before long, he had the birds flying in a figure-eight formation above the flock. That got boring pretty fast, though. "All of you, land right in that tall patch of grass right there." He gave them some more instructions and then lay down on his belly and aimed with an imaginary rifle. "Three, two, one, *boom!*" The birds erupted out of the grass right on cue, scattering like exploding shrapnel. Zeke burst out laughing and rolled over on his back, thinking no way could he make it out in the world. This was home. This was the life he knew, and where he had a place.

"What in tarnation was that?" Mercy White stared at him from a stand of trees. She'd been watching him.

She saw him with the birds. She saw it all. He couldn't find any words of defense beyond, "Mercy, please . . ."

She turned and ran.

Thursday, July 27, 2017
Coeur d'Alene, Idaho

list hate groups north idaho.

Chloe hit ENTER and the first result was an interactive map from the Southern Poverty Law Center. She clicked on it, and up popped her home state with ten dots on it—two down near Boise, where the bulk of the state's population lived, and eight up north. She scanned their affiliations to see if she could eliminate potential mail bomb suspects based on who they hated. She found three *General hates*, two *racist skinheads*, and one each *neo-Nazi*, *Holocaust denial*, and *Christian identity*.

She shook her head, feeling sick. She decided it was safe to eliminate the Holocaust deniers since parahumans weren't part of Hitler's agenda. The rest, though, had to remain viable suspects. Even the Christian identity folks probably thought her an abomination.

Seven organized groups in my area most likely want me dead. She sat still for a minute, letting it sink in. *Seven groups. And that doesn't include all the random, unorganized racists.* No matter how much good she did in her lifetime, that would never change. The knowledge felt heavy.

She searched next for the general hate group located in Coeur d'Alene and found a website describing it as a church. Chloe found its rhetoric disturbing, but the focus appeared to be hatred of homosexuality. *They're messed up, but low on the list,* she decided.

The next closest group, 88 Statesmen, had a red and black site with screaming white letters. It bashed all non-white races, homosexuals, and—bingo!—parahumans. She pasted their web address in a document and designated them as number one.

The next two she checked on appeared to be defunct. *Okay, a little good news, anyway.*

Moving a little farther from home, she found a dated and amateurish site for a group called Bruderschaft. They had a chat room that seemed primarily for recruiting. Few comments had been posted in the past few months, and while they were full of awfulness, they didn't point toward anti-parahumanism as a major focus. She listed them as number two.

After investigating the next two, she eliminated one and added the other in third place. The final group, called Aryan Resistance Movement, had a chat room. Chloe's heart leaped into her throat when she saw her name amid the litany of hatred.

TheGnasher88: *Did you see that Wyld whore on the tv? Someone needs to let that little bitch know we don't want her and her kind around hear!*

Her jaw dropped. The leaflet used some of the same language, if her memory served, but Detective Abara had taken theirs so she couldn't compare them. She dialed his number. He answered right away.

"Hi, Detective. It's Chloe Wyld. Sorry to bother you, but I might have found a lead."

"It's no bother, I told you to call me any time. What've you got?"

"I looked up local hate groups, and on one of their websites, I found a comment that mentions me specifically and has wording similar to the leaflet." She read it to him and mentioned the misspelling of *here.*

"Good catch," he said. "Send me the URL and some screen-shots and I'll get it to our tech guys. It might be possible to figure out who made the comment."

She grinned and thanked him, then sent everything to the email address on his card right after they hung up. Then she poked around and tried to see if she could find TheGnasher88 anywhere else online, but nothing came up.

Bored with her research already, she started to close the laptop, but then it occurred to her she didn't know how the internet had reacted to her interview. Knowing it was probably a stupid choice on her part, she Googled herself.

In addition to all the news stories based on the interview, she found a few critical comment threads. It was pretty much the standard anti-parahuman stuff, though, and nothing bothersome. BuzzFeed had dubbed her the Dragonfly Detective and she thought that was kind of cool.

No one mentioned the mailbox bomb, so it seemed Detective Abara had kept it quiet. Best of all, she didn't find any memes or GIFs making fun of her, and nothing new had been posted in the past day. Before long, she'd be old news.

Charlie, on the other hand, had become an instant heartthrob. She didn't want that to bug her, but it did. TMZ had found a picture of them together on someone's social media, so now it was everywhere. It showed them flying above the quad on the Hero Academy campus. She was looking at the ground, but he was focused on her. The grin on his face made all his feelings clear. Chloe found a few pics where girls had Photoshopped their faces over hers.

Looking at the pics made her miss him, so she called him.

He answered. "Hey, Wyld! What's up?"

"Googling us and seeing what's out there."

He clucked his tongue. "You know better than that. Why would you want to see horrible people being horrible?"

She chuckled. "Actually, there's nothing really bad. Except for the Photoshop jobs of girls replacing my face."

"Why would they do that?"

"So they can pretend you're looking at them instead of me." She tried to make it sound like a joke, but her tone of voice betrayed her insecurity.

"Well, that's just dumb. No way can anyone replace you."

She blushed and grinned, feeling better. "You're so sweet." They chatted for a few minutes about the interviews they'd done, then Charlie brought up his upcoming visit.

"Oh, I almost forgot!" Chloe said. "The city wants me to be on a float for the Diversity Day Parade. It's while you and Lindsay will be here. Will you do it with me?"

"Yeah, I guess. What's Diversity Day?"

"Oh, the big hate group that used to be here marched through downtown every year, and once they got shut down, the city started doing this parade instead. It's a pretty big deal. Tons of floats and marching bands and stuff."

"Is Lindsay doing it, too?" Charlie asked.

"I haven't asked yet. I'm sure she'll say yes. Roommate solidarity and all that." She messaged Lindsay to ask.

That sounds awesome! Lindsay replied right away. *Should I bring my school uniform?*

Probably. I hadn't thought about that. Chloe told Charlie to bring his training uniform as well as his brand-new costume. All Academy students had uniforms customized for their abilities, but they didn't get *official* costumes until after their sophomore year. The Just Cause costumers came in to get everyone's measurements and specifications before school ended, then worked on them over the summer. Subsequent outfits would be made with 3D body scanners and nanotech fabric printers, but every student's first costume was hand-crafted. It made them unique and special. Most Academy graduates saved their original costumes as trophies or wore them on special occasions.

Chloe's mom had gotten permission from the school to make her a hero costume for the 9/11 awards ceremony after she stopped Zayden's plot. She hadn't worn it since. She was self-conscious about being the only freshman with something other than the standard Academy colors—especially since it was bold lime green and purple. Not at all subtle. She wasn't sure yet which one she wanted to wear for the parade.

Her dad knocked on the door and called her name. She opened it while still talking to Charlie. "Want to go train?" he asked.

She nodded with enthusiasm and closed the door. "I gotta go," she told Charlie. "Time for some training."

"Ah, that's my little over-achiever," Charlie teased.

"Maybe if you trained more, you'd be able to keep up, O'Neal," she teased back.

He laughed. "Yeah, right. I'll never be as fast as you, Wyld."

"I suppose you can't help that you mutated into an inferior insect."

"Watch out, you're starting to bug me."

She groaned. "You did not just say that!"

"Yeah, I really wish I hadn't. Still love me?"

"Hmm, let me check." She paused. "Looks like I do. It's your lucky day."

"Hell yeah, it is."

Thursday, July 27, 2017
Bruderschaft Compound, North Idaho

Sweat ran down Zeke's face as he slipped into the barracks and rapped on Gabe's door. "Gabe, it's me."

Gabe opened it with a wary expression and slouchy look Zeke often noticed at a distance, but not when the two of them hung out. Gabe's eyes darted both ways down the hall. "I don't think you should come in."

"Not wanting to. Come with me."

They headed outside, checking to make sure nobody saw them, and Zeke led the way north. He didn't speak until the trees had them well hidden.

"Mercy caught me."

Gabe stared at him. "Caught you? Doing what?"

Zeke thrust his hands in his pants pockets. "Making the animals do tricks."

The color drained from Gabe's face. "Tell me you're talking about sit and fetch kinds of tricks."

Zeke shook his head and kicked at a rock. "More like flying-in-formation kinds of tricks. And when I got back to the neighborhood, I saw my pa and Edwards heading toward out-back."

"Shit." Gabe stared at the ground for several seconds. "We better go see what today's topic is."

Zeke nodded. Keeping within the tree line, they headed for the private building. As they got close, they saw an open window, which made Zeke grateful for the heat. They wouldn't have to risk breaking in again, and he wouldn't have to create a diversion. Any strange animal behavior now would make the elders suspicious.

In hurried whispers, the boys discussed the best way to get to the window unseen, then set off. First, they crawled along the forest-side of the fence to the rear of the building. Then, after a quick glance around, they hopped the fence and crouch-ran across the small open area to the concealment of the outbuilding.

Zeke crawled into place under the window and hunched on the hard-packed ground. Gabe sat beside him, looking pale and small.

"Thank you, Mercy," Barnabas said from inside. "You done well, bringing this to us. You'll be rewarded. Run along, now."

The boys shot each other a panicked glance and Gabe turned to crawl around the corner, but then the door opened and they froze. Zeke gave a silent prayer for her to head off toward the compound and never look their direction, but his thudding heart seemed to think they were already caught.

Mercy, wearing a bonnet like a proper girl, emerged, turned her back to them, and disappeared around Barnabas' house.

Thank you, God, for blocking her side vision with that silly ruffle!

"Still trying to say there's nothing up with your boy?" Barnabas asked inside.

Tom didn't respond.

"How's it possible?" Mr. Edwards asked. "We all been tested for the Mush-a-what-ee gene."

"Musashi," Barnabas corrected. "Preacher, could there be any truth behind the rumors that God grants powers to some folks who ain't got the gene?"

"I don't believe it, but I'll pray on it and see what I can learn. If the Almighty wants to grant powers, it's certainly within His ability to do so."

"Maybe my son is chosen by God, then. Maybe he's a freak, but he's still one of us," Tom said. *Freak*. Zeke thought his pa would love the boost in status that would come with having a powerful son.

Someone spat on the floor. "No way I'll ever buy that load of manure. We need to execute him, too."

"First thing we gotta do is get him tested again. Maybe the first test got it wrong, or maybe he somehow mutated later," Barnabas said. "Edwards, go into town and pick up one of them testing kits. If he still ain't got the gene, well then, we got some evidence he just might have God-given powers."

"If he does," Preacher said, "we may be able to put them to good use."

Zeke's stomach lurched. He didn't know much, but he knew he didn't want to be used as a weapon. *God damn you, Mercy! Why was you out there, anyway?* She should've been in school, not out hiding in a stand of trees. Then it dawned on him—someone must've told her to spy on him. Considering it was Barnabas's wife who'd need to excuse her from class, Zeke figured the order had come straight from him. No one would risk something like that without Barnabas's okay. If Barnabas stood against him, Zeke didn't stand a chance. And if Barnabas wanted to use him to hurt people, he didn't stand a chance of resisting.

Zeke realized he didn't have any options left. He had to leave the compound.

He and Gabe slipped around the corner while the councilmen left, then headed back out to the woods. Paranoia dug its hooks into Zeke, and he kept watching over his shoulder for any sign they'd been followed.

"We should use the birds to keep watch," Gabe suggested.

"But how? It's not like I can understand them or anything."

Gabe rolled his eyes. "Tell them if they see humans, they should swoop around them and make a bunch of noise."

"Oh. Yeah. That's a good idea." Zeke rubbed the back of his neck. "You know, you don't have to make me feel stupid. I know most of the kids here are smarter than me, and the kids out in the world are probably smarter than most of them, but you're supposed to be my friend."

Gabe looked sheepish. "Sorry, dude. You're totally right."

Zeke nodded and called for any nearby birds to come to him. Thirty seconds later, at least two dozen perched on nearby branches, and a dozen more stood on the ground a few feet away. The way creatures stared at him when waiting for commands was downright creepy. He gave them instructions and sent them on their way.

"What are we gonna do? Gabe, this whole thing is freaking me out, bad."

"We've got to leave. Both of us. We don't have any other choice."

Zeke sighed and leaned back against a tree. "Yeah. I sure as heck don't want to be used as some kind of weapon."

"All right, then. My execution is scheduled for forty-eight hours from now, and by then, they'll have your test results. The sooner we're out of here, the better."

They froze, hearing something crash through the underbrush. The boys locked eyes and a bead of sweat trickled down the back of Zeke's neck—had the birds failed to warn them?

Then a bull moose emerged from the trees and stopped to look down at them with eyes that had to be ten feet off the ground.

"Oh, shit, he's huge," Gabe whispered. "Make him go away."

Zeke's nerves clanged too hard for him to focus, so he gave the instructions out loud. "Go away, Moose."

The enormous animal shook his head, laid his ears back, and clicked his teeth. Zeke recognized the actions as warning signs.

"I'm sorry, Mr. Moose, sir! Just . . . do whatever you want."

Nothing moved for several long moments, then the moose continued on his path across the clearing. The moment his back leg moved into the trees, he became invisible.

"God damn, these woods are scary," Gabe said with a trembling voice. "I hate how dense they are."

"At least you know we can just walk off and disappear."

Gabe shook his head. "Hell, no. With huge frigging moose, plus cougars, wolves, and bears? Even if they didn't eat us for dinner, we could wander out here for weeks."

Zeke snorted. "Maybe you would. Give me a compass and a map and I can get us anywhere. Who's the smart one now?"

"Okay, I'll give you that. But even so, it's a long walk, it's the middle of summer, and I don't know if I'm up to it. You know, at the moment." Gabe gestured to his wreck of a face.

Zeke winced. He'd forgotten how carefully Gabe had been moving. "So, what's your plan?"

"I've thought it over a million times. The only way is to steal a truck and head for the nearest town."

"We can't go to Clagstone. Too many people there would recognize the truck, and probably me, too." Zeke thought for a minute. "If we head southwest instead of east, we should hit Blanchard before too long."

Gabe looked up Blanchard on the maps saved to his tablet and nodded. "Then it's just a straight shot down 41 to Coeur d'Alene."

"Then what? We find the fr-, uh, the parahuman girl?"

Gabe shrugged. "Yep, or the police."

The blood drained from Zeke's face. "Are you sure about the police?"

"After what I found on the computer?" Gabe pulled up the *Operation 88* file. "Hells, yeah. There's some serious shit in the works. Look at this."

Zeke lay awake, trying to make sense of this being his last night in this bed, in this house, on this land. *How did it all go so wrong so fast?*

But then, he had to admit everything Gabe had told him was true. Bruderschaft wasn't a paradise, sheltering its members from the evils of the outside world. *They* were the evils of the world, and Zeke had been living among them his whole life. The things Gabe showed him from that computer in the office . . . He couldn't stand to think about it. He already had too much to deal with—leaving behind everyone he'd known since birth, leaving behind his way of life, leaving behind his future with Naomi.

He didn't feel as bad about leaving his pa, though. A weight lifted at the thought of not getting hit anymore. For the first time in his life, Zeke was relieved his mother had died. Leaving here wouldn't mean leaving her.

He didn't remember her very well. She'd been gone since he was not quite five, but he still remembered what it felt like when she'd held him. Nobody had held him that way ever since.

If Gabe was right about everything else, would that mean God didn't punish people like Preacher said? Gabe said God was kind and loving to all people, not the jealous and hateful God of Preacher's fiery sermons. Was his mother's death, just maybe, not a punishment for Zeke's weakness as a man? He wanted to believe that, but he didn't know if he ever could.

He got down on his knees and clasped his hands. "Lord, I don't know what to believe anymore. Everything used to be so simple and now it's all a big mess and . . . and Preacher always said you hate cowards. I hope that's not true, Lord, 'cause I'm real scared right now. I ask you to help me see what's right and what's true. I just want to be a good man, and I need your help to know what that is. Amen."

CHAPTER SEVEN

Friday, July 28, 2017
Bruderschaft Compound, North Idaho

Zeke woke up to his alarm at four a.m. rather than the usual five. His pa should already be on patrol duty, but Zeke peeked into his room, just to be sure. The rumpled bed was empty and so was the bathroom. He breathed a sigh of relief. He'd packed his duffel bag the previous evening and hid it between his bed and the wall. He retrieved it and slipped outside, keeping to the shadows and grateful for three years of combat and infiltration training. Stealth he understood.

The milk barn already bustled with workers. He gave it a wide berth and headed straight for the wooded area beyond. He had a compass and the map he'd traced off of Gabe's tablet, but it was still too dark to read either one. Mostly by instinct, he trekked through the woods toward the strategic spot he and Gabe picked last night. He left his bag there, behind a distinctive lightning-struck tree he'd be able to find later. Patrols didn't range out this far, so it should be secure.

Now for the dangerous part. He crept through the darkness toward the nearest Bruderschaft truck. Barnabas insisted upon keeping several hidden around the compound in case the government or Just Cause attacked. It would give the soldiers immediate mobility to counterattack and allow women and children to flee.

I should be there by now, Zeke thought after a while. *Where's the damn truck?* He started to panic and told himself to calm the hell down, but it didn't work. *Think, freak!* He wondered if any animals could lead him to it.

He jumped as a loud caw came from a few yards away. Another crow joined the first, and a squirrel chittered. Moving toward the sound, he saw two crows hopping up and down on a branch. Something didn't look right, though, and he realized it wasn't a real branch—it was part of a real-tree camo pattern. The truck stood right in front of him, covered in a camouflage sheet and with boughs piled on the roof and bed. Without the animals' help, he'd have walked right past it in the dark and never seen it. He sent a message of thanks, and they quieted down.

Zeke moved slow, the way he'd been taught, placing each foot with care so no noises gave him away. He peeked around the rear of the truck and confirmed he was alone. He ducked underneath the camo sheet and opened the driver's side door. Reaching underneath the steering wheel, he popped the cover off the fuse panel, pulled out the fuel pump relay fuse, and pocketed it. Simple enough to fix, but tough to figure out. Anyone who tried to start it would assume it needed gas.

Neither boy knew how to hot-wire a vehicle, though, so as long as Gabe got the keys, they'd be set.

He heard someone crashing through the underbrush, but the footsteps sounded too heavy to be Gabe, and they approached from the wrong direction. Zeke dropped to his belly and slithered underneath the truck.

Light had just begun to infiltrate the dense forest, enough for Zeke to see a familiar pair of work boots stop right beside the truck. His heart thudded so loud he couldn't hear himself think. Once his pa stopped moving, Zeke feared his panicky breathing would give him away.

Be noisy, be noisy, he sent out with his mind, concentrating as hard as he could and funneling all his anxiety into it. In an instant, the woods went from near-silent to a cacophony of animal sounds—crows, sparrows, owls, squirrels, and coyotes.

"Wha' the fuggin' hell?" Tom slurred his shouted words, and Zeke realized in shock that his pa was drunk. *Patrolling drunk? And he's worried about me embarrassing him?* If the compound were compromised somehow because Tom was drunk, the punishment would be swift and immediate, no matter his status. Zeke couldn't imagine a worse infraction. *Where's that tattle-tale Mercy when you need her?*

Tom stumbled on along his patrol route, shouting something incoherent at the animals. Zeke crawled forward so he could see his father's back moving off through the trees. Once the man was gone, he told the owls and coyotes to quiet down, then went through the rest at a slow pace so the noise tapered off. Once satisfied he was alone, he crawled out from beneath the truck. He checked the compass and headed on a straight trajectory toward the sheepfold.

He reached the tree line and scanned the field between it and the fold. Nothing. With a grin, he emerged and headed for the gate. Just as he reached it, Naomi stepped out from behind the corner of a shed and startled him.

"Whoa! Hey, Naomi." He hoped she didn't notice the tremble in his voice. "What are you doing out here?"

"I was planning to ask you the same question."

He tried to give a casual shrug, but he'd never considered what made a shrug casual before and was pretty sure it didn't come off that way. "I'm getting to work, is all." He met her eye, expecting anger, but it was even worse—she was hurt.

She crossed her arms. "Sure, *now* you're getting to work. But what was you doing more than an hour ago, heading into the woods with a big duffel?"

"I, um, went for a hike."

"Did you lose your bag along the way? Or did you stash it in the woods somewhere?"

Beads of sweat broke out on Zeke's forehead. "Why . . . uh, why would I do that?"

"I heard what the council's planning for Gabe, and I know you're in trouble, too. Mercy says you're a freak, controlling animals somehow?" Naomi's voice shook now, too. "So what I'm thinking is, you're either helping Gabe escape, or you're both leaving. You owe me the truth, Ezekiel. Which is it?"

He hesitated, thinking he should lie to her. He knew he wasn't any good at it, though, plus Naomi was way smarter than him. She'd know. Still, if she told anyone . . .

But then he remembered her kiss on his cheek. She'd taken a risk he would tell someone and get her in trouble. She'd trusted him, even after Mercy lied about him fooling around in the field with Gabe. She deserved the same respect.

He looked around to make sure no one was in earshot. "We're both going. Today. Promise me you won't tell no one."

She blinked a bunch and her chin quivered, but she drew a finger in an X over her heart. "I won't say nothing, hope to die. I suppose I wouldn't be able to marry you, anyway, if you're some kind of . . . parahuman. Are you?"

He rubbed the back of his neck. "I don't know what I am. I got tested for the gene just like everyone else, but Gabe says sometimes God gives people powers. I never heard of that, but Preacher and Barnabas was talking about it, so maybe it's true. But yeah, I can control bugs and birds and all kinds of things. Guess that's why I always been so good with the sheep."

"You're sure the only one who can keep Eleanor and her brood in line." They chuckled together, then

Naomi stood there quiet for a long time. When she did speak, it was a whisper. "When are you going?"

"Partway through my shift. It'll give us the longest head start before someone comes looking."

She nodded, eyes on the ground. "Good luck to you, Ezekiel. I think I would've liked being married to you." She wiped a tear, then turned and ran toward the milk barn.

Gabe's hands shook and his heart pounded. He had to work fast, but if he made a mistake, it would be his last.

He checked the instructions on the website once more, twisted the last two wires together, and put a cap over them. Careful to keep the pin depressed, he set the apparatus down and let out the breath he'd been holding. Tools cluttered the shelf but decided he couldn't take the time to put them away, plus he really wanted to put distance between himself and the armed device. He slipped out of the explosives depot.

You're welcome, he thought, picturing the cops who wouldn't get blown up by that shit. So long as he hadn't botched it, the soldiers who went to retrieve the explosives would set off the bomb as soon as they picked it up off the floor and that pin popped out. Who would expect it to be armed and ready? He hoped his research proved right and one explosion would trigger a bunch of others. He hoped the building contained enough explosives to wipe Butler's Shaft and its miserable little compound right off the map.

He only regretted that he wouldn't be able to see it happen in person.

He peeked around the corner of the shed to make sure no one was watching, then slipped off through the shadows to complete his part of the escape plan. Time to get the fuck out of Dodge.

As Zeke waited for the school bell, he wandered amongst the flock and touched each animal on the head or the back, saying good-bye one-by-one. Eleanor seemed to understand and leaned against his leg. "You cantankerous old girl, I'm gonna miss you."

He couldn't remember ever being so anxious, not even when he was little and knew his papa was coming with a switch. At last, the bell tolled. The last one he'd ever hear, he told himself. He repeated the instructions to the sheep. "Stay here until the next bell rings and then go on a rampage through the neighborhood." He'd given the same commands to the dogs and all the vermin in the vicinity. He whistled for Jimmy and Bob to come to him and gave them both a good head scratch. With a deep sigh, he looked over his flock. "I'll miss you all, you ewes." He chuckled at the silly joke, thrust his hands in his pockets, and walked into the woods.

Zeke kept to the trees as much as possible and avoided the areas he knew had video surveillance. Gabe was supposed to take out a couple of cameras, but they hadn't spoken all day and Zeke had to trust his friend would come through.

He retrieved his hidden duffel and headed for the sabotaged truck. The likelihood of someone already finding out it wasn't running was slim. Even if they did, it would take hours for the mechanics to get out there and check on it. Most of the council members could do simple repairs, but they were too busy and most of them thought they were too good for it, anyway. They'd just take another truck and put in a work order. That was how things went.

Zeke's heart leaped into his throat when he stepped from behind a stand of trees and there stood his father, staring at the engine under the raised hood. The camo sheet puddled between the hood and the windshield.

Zeke froze for a moment, sure he'd be seen if he tried to slip back into the woods, but just as sure he'd be seen if he didn't. He glanced to the side and found a clear spot to place a foot. As he moved behind cover, though, the toe of one boot scuffed against the bark.

"Hello? Someone there?" Tom Shepherd called. Zeke froze, certain his pa would come around the tree at any second. After what seemed like way too long to hold his breath, he let it out, slow and measured. He started to relax, then realized Gabe would be coming from the other direction at any moment, and that guy did not know how to sneak through the woods. *I gotta come up with something, fast,* he thought. Zeke knew he wasn't good at thinking on his feet, so that made him all the more anxious. After a few seconds of frantic thought, he tucked his duffel behind a bush and stepped out of the hiding place.

"Hey, Pa. There you are, finally."

Tom spun around like he'd been caught red-handed. "What the hell you doin' out here, boy? Ain't you supposed to be working?"

Zeke swallowed hard and said a silent prayer that he'd guessed right, and his pa hadn't been sent here on official business. "Barnabas didn't know where you was. I guess he needs you real bad, 'cause he came out to the field himself and told me to find you."

Tom scowled. "Well, that don't make no sense. Andy just seen me out here when he was patrolling. I told him to put in a work order on the truck in case I couldn't figure out what was wrong with it."

Zeke shrugged, feeling a little more confident he could make it look casual. "Yeah, but he'd only just be getting back now, wouldn't he? I been out here a while, and Barnabas was looking for a while before then." Tom didn't respond right away, and Zeke felt exposed.

I can't do it, I ain't strong enough! He opened his mouth, ready to confess everything, then imagined

Gabe on the ground with all the Bruderschaft men pelting him with rocks. "You trying to go somewhere? What's wrong with the truck?"

Guilt flashed across Tom's face again. "Uh, I just tried to start it up, like we gotta do every so often. You know, to make sure it's running good. Shouldn't be out of gas, but I'm thinking maybe the fuel pump's busted. I'll make sure Andy turned in the order." He slammed the hood. "After I figure out what Barnabas wants, anyway. Did he say anything about that?"

Zeke shook his head and tried to look dumb rather than guilty.

"Well, thanks for coming to get me, I guess." Tom grabbed the keys from the ignition and tucked them into his pocket. As he walked past his son, he clapped a hand on his shoulder. Zeke couldn't suppress a startle response at the touch, but Tom didn't seem to register it. Tom trudged off into the woods. Zeke expected him to turn around and say something about getting back to the sheep, but he didn't. *What the heck you up to, Pa?* Zeke wondered.

Zeke finished uncovering the truck, tossed his bag in back, replaced the fuse, and waited. He heard Gabe approaching well before he saw him.

His friend stepped into the small clearing with a big grin on his bruised face. "Did I sneak up on you?"

Zeke laughed. "I heard you half a mile away, Bigfoot."

"Really? I thought I did pretty well."

"Guess again. Lucky I got rid of my pa when I did."

Gabe's jaw dropped. "He was here? Why?"

"Don't know. He had the hood up and was trying to figure out what was wrong, and he acted real guilty." Zeke went around to the passenger seat while Gabe climbed behind the wheel. "Tell me you got the spare keys."

Each barracks had a labeled pegboard of keys to all the escape vehicles, so they could be grabbed in an emergency. "Of course, I got the keys! I even moved a bunch of them around to the wrong pegs, so it wasn't obvious which ones were missing."

They chuckled. "Ah, man! That'll take them forever to straighten out."

"Yeah, I almost wish I could see it."

The truck started right up, and Zeke relaxed a little. "What about the money?"

Gabe smiled. "Took a little from the office, then decided to check my parents' room, just to make sure. Found a few twenties in my dad's sock drawer and a couple hundred stashed in a purse in the back of my mom's closet."

"Why would she have so much?" Zeke asked.

Gabe shrugged. "She's a flake. I kinda figured she'd have a bug-out plan." He swallowed. "You'd think she'd've taken me out of here when the beatings got bad, but I guess she didn't give a shit. Even so, I only took half, so she could still get out if she wanted. Cleaned out my dad, though, so we've got about three hundred bucks."

The cab heated up fast after they hit the dirt road and had to roll up the windows, but it was that or choke on dust the whole way. Air conditioning was a luxury option Bruderschaft personnel had deemed unnecessary.

"What's in that envelope there?" Gabe asked.

For the first time, Zeke noticed a white envelope tucked into a little compartment in the dash, right in front of the stick shift. He grabbed it and pulled out a strip of paper with lots of stuff printed in little boxes. "What in the world?"

Gabe glanced over. "Holy shit! It's a boarding pass. For an airplane," he added when Zeke look confused. "Does it have a name on it?"

Zeke searched, struggling to make sense of all the numbers and abbreviations in the grids, then came across the name field. "Thomas Shepherd." He stared in shock. "Why in hell would my pa be flying somewhere, especially without telling me, or Barnabas?"

"Where's it for?"

Zeke searched some more. "Departing from Spokane, arriving in . . . Springfield, Missouri. That's where my ma was from. It don't make no sense."

A lamb darted out into the dirt road and Zeke yelled for Gabe to stop. He dropped the boarding pass and it fluttered forgotten to the floorboards as the truck skidded, sending up dust plumes all around them. Hearts racing, the boys waited for the air to clear. The lamb appeared unharmed a few feet down the road. Beyond it, they saw the silhouette of a girl in a dress and bonnet, but the sun shining through the dusty air obscured her identity.

Oh God, please don't let it be Mercy!

As the dust settled, though, he recognized Naomi and let out a shaking breath. She glanced over toward the trees as she hurried to the passenger-side window. Zeke rolled it down.

"The compound's overrun with animals." She rested her hands on the rim of the open window. "You do that?" Zeke nodded, and she glanced back toward the trees again. "I'm not alone out here. You need to go, and fast."

"We're trying to." Zeke's heart ached, thinking he'd never see her again. He put his hand on hers. "Come with us, Naomi."

She gaped at him. "Zeke, I . . . Do you mean it?"

"We've always wanted to be together. Now we can be, out in the world where there aren't so many rules."

"I wish I could, but . . ." She shook her head, a tear slipping down one cheek.

He wiped the tear away with his free hand and leaned forward to kiss the spot. "It's okay. I get it."

They sat in tense silence for several seconds before Gabe put an end to it.

"Hey, if anyone notices the truck is missing, say it's being used to herd the sheep."

Naomi gave him a shaky smile. "That's a good idea. I always liked you, Gabriel. I never talked to you much because my papa would whup me, but I wanted you to know that." She backed up two steps, blew a solemn kiss to Zeke, then turned away and shooed the lamb back toward the woods. "Hey, Mercy!" she called. "Head back toward the fold with those two—I got April."

It was May, Zeke could tell even from that distance, but at least she was close. He watched Naomi disappear into the woods and tried not to cry.

Gabe took his foot off the brake and let the truck roll forward down the gradual slope for a while to make sure they were past the area where someone might hear them. "How the hell did that lamb get all the way out here?" He tried to look calm, but a nervous edge to his voice gave him away.

"Damned if I know. I told them to head toward the neighborhood, but sheep ain't that smart, and they spook easy. Especially the little ones." Zeke wiped sweat from his brow. "Sure glad we didn't hit her. She's Sadie's lamb, and the poor girl lost her last three. Grieved harder every time."

"Dude. Sheep grieve?"

Zeke's eyes went wide. "Oh, yeah. They grieve hard, and it's something awful to hear them cry." He wondered if they'd grieve for him.

They drove on, and before long, arrived at the gate marking the edge of Bruderschaft property. "You took out this camera, right?" Zeke asked. Gabe nodded. Zeke hopped out of the truck, entered the code into the keypad, and held his breath until the gate slid off to the left side of the road. He climbed back in the truck, and Gabe gunned it with a loud whoop. Zeke got a lump in his throat. *It's official. I don't have a home. Or a family. Or anyone in the whole world except Gabe.*

"That was the most ridiculous thing I ever seen! Where in blazes is Ezekiel Shepherd?" Barnabas's voice boomed through the community room. "Why ain't he here helping with the sheep, for God's sake?" Tom Shepherd wondered the same thing but said nothing about his encounter with Zeke earlier in the day. The last thing he needed was for Barnabas to start asking *him* questions.

Every Bruderschaft member sat on the wooden benches facing their leader. Many wore bandages spattered with blood from shooting the swarms of coyotes, raccoons, and possums. An over-eager SIT shot a skunk under one of the barracks, so it stank to high heaven. Doc Jones and his nurses tended to the worst injuries while other folks patched themselves up or got help from their families. Cleaning up the compound would take days, maybe weeks.

Naomi Jones raised a hand and Barnabas nodded at her. "I saw Zeke and Gabe heading north, after some lambs. I ain't seen neither of them since."

Barnabas turned to Mrs. Edwards. "Could there still be sheep out there, or are they all accounted for?"

She shook her head as she bounced her new baby boy on her shoulder, trying to keep him from fussing. "We got six or seven still missing."

Barnabas' scowl said he didn't care for that answer. "Well, which is it—six or seven?"

"I don't know. I'm sorry." She looked down at the floor. "It was hard to get a good count with them being all riled up. I'll check again soon as we're done here."

"Yeah, you better." His eyes bored holes into her. He directed three men to go look for the missing boys up north and told the rest to start the clean-up. As Tom started to follow the others out, Barnabas intercepted him. "The sheep are your boy's responsibility, and if it's true he can control animals, this never should've happened. If I find out he did it on purpose . . . It won't help his case none, that's for sure."

Tom slunk home to ponder his next move in private. After his conversation with Zeke, he'd been heading in to ask Barnabas what he needed when all hell broke loose. He never had the chance to ask the leader about being summoned, and Barnabas hadn't seemed to need him, anyway. Tom knew the Jones girl couldn't have seen Zeke heading north, now, could she? Not when Tom had seen his son to the southwest just minutes before. He hadn't wondered at the time why Zeke didn't follow him back, but now he wondered plenty. The truck being dead was weird on its own. Then there was Zeke finding him there. Then Zeke's flock and all the other animals went crazy, and now both his son and the faggot boy were missing. Funny how the only one offering information about where he might be was the girl he was sweet on. Too many coincidences for comfort and Tom felt like he was being played a fool.

He went into Zeke's bedroom and opened the closet. The duffel bag that lived on the top shelf was gone and so were half his son's clothes and his extra pair of boots. He slammed the bedroom door on his way out and grabbed a cold beer from the fridge.

Dammit, boy, he thought, *I didn't think you had it in you. Why'd you have to run now?* If Zeke had just waited a few hours, or if Tom hadn't been too scared to let him in on the plan, they'd be heading to the Spokane Airport right now, the two of them and—if Zeke had insisted—even the damned gay kid. Now, would he ever see his son again? Would he ever be able to tell him the truth about his mother?

Tom grabbed the whole twelve-pack—his only solace—and slumped onto the couch.

Friday, July 28, 2017
Coeur d'Alene, Idaho

Zeke and Gabe abandoned the Bruderschaft pickup in a busy parking lot on the northern edge of town. They wandered down a street crowded with fast food places, strip malls, and rush-hour traffic.

"Damn, it feels good to be back in civilization," Gabe said.

Zeke looked around, wide-eyed. "I think I could do with a little less of it."

"So, who first? Cops or dragonfly girl?" Gabe's face still looked rough, but he talked better now that his lips weren't so swollen.

"I don't think I can deal with the cops right now." Zeke sighed. "Plus, how do we know they're not gonna take us straight back there?"

Gabe frowned. "You might be onto something. We're minors. Technically, runaways. Plus, we stole a truck. Maybe WyldWing should be our first stop. Her mom's a lawyer, and it wouldn't suck to have her on our side."

Zeke nodded, relieved. "Maybe they'll give us something to eat, too. Lunch was a long time ago." Zeke wondered if he'd ever again eat a sandwich under a shade tree while tending sheep. He hoped Sadie's lamb had gotten back to her okay.

"I'm too keyed up to eat. It's good to be out of that truck and not looking over my shoulder all the time." Gabe stopped, grabbed Zeke's arm, and gasped. "Starbucks! Okay, I'm not too keyed up for a Frappuccino." He pulled his friend inside the coffee shop. "Mmm, that smell!"

"Smells like coffee."

"Gee, really? It's a coffee shop, dude. And not just *a* coffee shop, but *the* coffee shop." Gabe eyed the menu above the counter. "Some hipster snobs say they over-roast the beans, but I don't give a shit what they do to them as long as their coffee tastes better than everyone else's. And it does."

Zeke raised an eyebrow. He'd never seen Gabe this excited about anything. He may never have seen anyone this excited about anything. "Um, it's just coffee. You usually make a face when you drink it."

"Yeah, this isn't that compound swill. Wait until you taste it, my friend." He stepped up to the counter and ordered a triple mocha Frappuccino. Zeke stared open-mouthed at the cashier behind the counter. She was so beautiful! He thought she might be wearing makeup because her skin looked softer and clearer than any girl he'd ever known. He'd never seen eyelashes like that in his life. He wondered how Naomi would look with makeup and felt a pang of regret with a side of guilt, then cast his eyes away from the cashier.

They sat down and Gabe took a long drink of his fancy-looking coffee that didn't look like coffee at all, in Zeke's opinion. Then Gabe offered the cup to him and he shook his head. "I don't like coffee. You know that."

"You've never tasted anything like this. I guarantee it." He put the tall cup in front of Zeke and stared at him, expectant.

Zeke picked up the cup and took a sip. It was sweet and creamy and chocolaty, like cake turned into a frozen drink. His eyes flew open wide. "Whoa! This is coffee?"

Gabe chuckled, taking the cup back. "This is coffee done right." He pulled out his tablet and looked for Chloe's address. "Figures it's not listed," he muttered as Zeke took possession of the drink again. Gabe scowled at the screen for a few minutes before his face lit up. "Yes! Check it out. There's a sign for the park across the street in one of the news stories, and another one shows the front of the house. Now we can find it. No problem." He looked up and saw Zeke taking a long pull on the straw. "Dude, don't drink it all. That stuff's expensive."

Chloe had just polished off her third bowl of pad thai when the doorbell rang. Her parents had gone to the back yard with glasses of wine, so she peered through the peephole. Two boys she didn't know, about her age, stood on the patio. The one in front had a battered face, and the big guy behind him fidgeted and looked out of place. It put her on edge right away. She cracked the door, leaving the chain fastened.

"Hello?"

The bruised one flashed a big smile that had to have hurt. "Hey, are you Chloe Wyld? The hero?"

"Who are you?"

"Um, to be honest, we're . . . runaways? Or refugees, maybe. We need some help, and we have information the police and Just Cause and probably the FBI and ATF should have, too." He swallowed hard, just as nervous as his companion.

"Wait here a sec." She closed the door and hurried to the back yard to retrieve her parents.

"I'll handle this, Chlo," Heather said as they headed through the house. She opened the door, chain still in place. "You boys have evidence of a crime?"

"Uh, yes, Ma'am. Plans for lots of them, actually," said the smaller boy.

"Why did you come here, instead of going to the police?"

"Um, my friend here, Zeke? He was raised not to trust law enforcement. His dad—and mine, too—are part of Butler's . . . uh, Bruderschaft. I don't know if you've heard of it."

Heather's gaze narrowed in suspicion. "Oh, yes. I've heard of it. Do you know anything about leaflets being circulated about my daughter or the bomb in our mailbox?"

The big one's eyes widened. The talker looked rattled. "Uh, no. I don't . . . I don't think that was them, but we were never exactly in the loop."

"Who did that to your face?" Phil asked over his wife's shoulder.

The smaller boy's eyes dimmed, and he looked away. "Oh, uh. My dad."

"Is that why you ran away?" Heather asked.

He shook his head and looked sick. "No, Ma'am. We left because . . . because they were gonna execute me tomorrow, 'cause I'm gay. And they were trying to figure out what to do about Zeke, 'cause he's a parahuman."

Heather looked at her husband and daughter, who nodded back at her. She undid the chain and opened the door. "Come in. Sounds like you've got quite a story to tell."

An hour later, they all sat around the coffee table, which was littered with Bruderschaft documents Heather had printed out so they could all look them over. Phil had made the boys sandwiches and milkshakes and treated the cuts and scrapes on Gabe's face.

Heather ran a hand through her hair. "You've done a good thing, gathering this information. Phil has a good friend on the Hate Crimes Task Force. I'd like us to speak with him here, tonight, rather than just showing up at the police station. Are you comfortable with that?"

Gabe nodded with enthusiasm.

Zeke sighed and stared at his boots. "I don't know. I guess we gotta tell someone at some point, but the police . . . It's hard to know what's right when you find out everything you've been taught is wrong."

"I can't imagine how hard this is for you." Phil gathered their empty plates. "I'll call Sam. I promise you boys can trust him."

"You said your fathers are both Bruderschaft—what about your mothers?" Heather asked.

Gabe sighed. "My mom's on the compound, too. My dad dragged us there a few months ago. I've got an aunt in Wisconsin, but I haven't heard from her in a long time."

"My mama's dead," Zeke said. "She got real sick when I was little."

"I'm going to assume, since you're here, that you don't have anyone in the area you can stay with."

The boys shook their heads. "I figured we'd find a shelter or something," Gabe said.

"If the organization is looking for you, is there any reason they'd suspect you'd come here?"

They shook their heads again. "Mostly, we just came here 'cause we thought you'd be able to get Zeke in touch with Just Cause or the PRA or something, since he's powered," Gabe said.

"It's possible, but we'll have to get the police involved before we do anything like that." Heather took a deep breath. "It would be safer for you to stay here than going to a shelter, where they might look for you. Also, there are laws about harboring runaways, so shelters probably wouldn't even take you. However, evidence of abuse is a legal defense." She gestured to Gabe's face. "But Zeke, I have to report your whereabouts to the police, so Phil and I don't risk facing charges."

"Will they send us back?" Zeke asked.

"Nothing in the law says the police have to return you to your parents. Under the circumstances, I'm sure they'll make no effort to get you back to the compound. If they try, I'll represent you and fight them with everything I can."

"We . . . don't have much money—" Gabe began.

Heather cut him off with a wave of her hand. "Some things I do for free."

"Thank you, Ma'am." Emotion strained Zeke's voice. "I don't understand why you're being so nice to us, but I sure do appreciate it."

Heather had Chloe show the boys to the guest room. "You need anything, I'm right next door," Chloe said. The boys stared at the wings sprouting from her back and thanked her. A few minutes later, the doorbell rang and Phil called for them. As they came down the stairs into the great room, where the dark-skinned Detective Abara towered over Phil, Zeke froze and gaped.

"Zeke, dude, it's okay," Gabe said. "You and Chloe and I fall under two of the *Four F*s and Mrs. Wyld is the third. He's the fourth, so now we've got all of them covered. Nothing to worry about."

Zeke shook his head as if to clear it. "Yeah, yeah, you're right." He drew a shuddering breath and continued down to the ground level.

Gabe shook hands with the detective while Phil made introductions. Then Abara held out a massive hand to Zeke. "Ezekiel, is it?"

"Uh, yes. Sir. Yes Sir." Zeke wiped his hand on his pants, hesitated, then took the proffered hand.

"Detective, have you found out anything about that chat room post?" Chloe asked as they all took seats around the coffee table.

Abara shook his head. "Sorry, Chloe. The tech guys said the IP was hidden. We'll keep looking, though." He turned to the boys. "I hear you've brought some evidence from the compound. What's Bruderschaft up to now?"

Gabe smirked. "I prefer to call it Butler's Shaft."

Abara burst into a deep, hearty laugh. "I'm gonna steal that one, I'll tell you right now. Man, did we celebrate when that old son of a bitch died."

Zeke gasped and seemed to shrink as all eyes turned to him. "Sorry. He's like a saint on the compound. This is weird."

"It must be quite the culture shock." Abara gave him a sympathetic look. "What's that you said on the stairs there, Gabe? About the *Four Fs*?"

Gabe squirmed. "Oh, it's, uh . . .the groups Butler's Shaft hates. Freaks . . ." He gestured to Chloe and Zeke. ". . . Faggots—that's me. Foreigners—" he nodded toward the detective, "—which means anyone with dark skin, and feminists." He nodded toward Heather. "So just about everyone here."

"Better include me," Phil said.

"Are you a parahuman, too?" Zeke asked.

"No, but I am a feminist."

Zeke gave him a skeptical look. "Men can be feminists?"

"You think she would've married me if I weren't?" Phil chuckled. "Look, all it means to be a feminist is that you think everyone is equal. I married a powerful woman. I'm raising a powerful woman, and I coach powerful women. So yeah, count me in, and I'm proud to be part of any group Bruderschaft doesn't like."

"Forgive my friend. He's got a lot of reality to adjust to out here," Gabe said.

"It'll take some time. I'm certain." Abara motioned toward the papers on the coffee table. "May I?"

Heather slid them toward him. "Be my guest. Oh, and can I consider law enforcement officially notified that we're providing shelter to two at-risk runaways?"

He waved a hand. "I'll get it reported, no worries, Counselor."

"And we won't have to go back?" Zeke asked.

"Back to Brud—, er, Butler's Shaft? Hell, no." Abara looked them each in the eye for several seconds. "If what Phil told me about this so-called *Operation 88* is true, the next time you see that compound, it'll be on the news and under siege."

CHAPTER EIGHT

Saturday, July 29, 2017
Coeur d'Alene, Idaho

The next morning, Detective Abara picked up Heather and the boys and drove them to the police station himself. He parked right at the back door and slipped them inside, just in case Bruderschaft had eyes out. Inside the sterile, cinder block hallway, he led them past two closed doors and into a conference room. Three people sat there on one side of a conference table, drinking coffee. An open Krispy Kreme box sat on the table. Gabe helped himself to a doughnut as the three of them sat on the empty side of the table and Abara took his place at the head.

"Heather, good to see you," said a woman in a crisp white button-down. Her severe features clashed with a kind smile and friendly voice.

"Hey, Molly. Good work on the stand last week. Sure glad you were on my side."

Alarm bells clanged in Zeke's head. He was in a police station, in a room with four cops. He'd been taught since he could talk that this was a nightmare scenario. Guys like him never walked free out of places like this and rarely left them alive, according to the lessons taught at Bruderschaft. He clenched his clammy fists.

"Gabriel Beck, Ezekiel Shepherd, Ms. Wyld, welcome." Abara pointed around the table at the others.

"These are Detectives Molly Moy from Coeur d'Alene Police, and Mat Supon from the Kootenai County Sheriff's Department." Supon had a scruffy beard and sported a worn flannel with a greasy Idaho Vandals baseball cap. "Excuse Supon, he's been undercover." Abara chuckled. "Not that he cleans up very well anyway. Then we've got Trooper Robert Henderson from Idaho State Police." Henderson's nod was as sharp as his black uniform and the flat-brimmed hat sitting on the table in front of him. With a high-and-tight and impeccable posture, he reminded Zeke of the soldiers he'd grown up around.

"Gabriel," Henderson said, "like the archangel sent to destroy Jerusalem."

Molly Moy snorted. "You would know that, Robert."

Henderson ignored her and looked at Zeke. "That happens in the Book of Ezekiel, if I'm not mistaken."

"I'm gonna take that as a good omen," Abara said. "The four of us make up the Hate-Crimes Task Force. Moy and Supon went undercover on the Aryan Nations compound back when Butler was still kicking around in his red satin robe. Henderson joined us not long after the Aryans splintered. Gabe, tell them your nickname for Bruderschaft."

Gabe blushed. "Uh, Butler's Shaft."

Moy almost spat out her coffee and Supon burst into loud guffaws as he dunked a doughnut in his cup. Henderson's expression didn't change.

"I trust you've all read over the information I sent you last night?" Abara asked the rest of the Task Force. They all indicated they had. "Good. It seems the Shaft is trying to model itself after the Order, wouldn't you agree?" The other officers nodded.

"Excuse me," Gabe said, "but what's the Order?"

Zeke looked at him in shock. "You don't about know the Order? Those guys are legends!" He regretted saying it right away when the room went icy.

Heather leaned forward. "Please bear in mind that Zeke was raised in Bruderschaft and is just beginning to understand how much misinformation he's been taught. It's going to take him a while to acclimate to life on the outside." She smiled at Zeke, and it helped him to feel a little less like a criminal under interrogation.

The sloppy-looking Supon leaned forward, elbow on the table and fingers twined in his long beard hairs. "The Order was the most militant of the Aryan Nation's offshoots. Back in the '80s, they went on a massive armed robbery spree to pay for the weapons they were stockpiling for the race war they thought was inevitable. They had an assassination list a lot like the one you gave us, and they murdered a Jewish radio shock jock in Colorado."

"What happened to them? Did you guys bust them up or something?" Gabe asked.

Abara shook his head. "Not us. The Feds moved in, and it all ended in a shootout. The leader burned to death when they torched a cabin to drive him out. These things don't tend to end pretty. Fortunately, the Feds and Just Cause learned a lot from the Waco debacle."

Zeke shook as he imagined the neighborhood burning down. Shots ringing through the field, startling his sheep. Naomi gunned down and bleeding in the dirt. *What the hell am I doing?* Then he looked at the boy next to him and remembered—they were going to kill his best friend and turn Zeke himself into a weapon. *I just have to trust that the women will get out right away like they're supposed to.* As for the men, he supposed they'd be happy enough to see the law rolling in. It would prove them right and give them the war they'd always wanted.

The Task Force asked them how they came across the documents, what routines the compound followed, where the weapons were stored and what kinds they had. Heather encouraged the boys to be honest and reminded the Task Force the boys were not suspects, but victims. The boys answered as best they could, but Zeke had no idea what weaponry and explosives the off-limits buildings held. Then Detective Moy slid over an aerial photo and asked about escape plans. Gabe peered at it, then asked Zeke to help him find the route they'd taken. Zeke's ears buzzed so loud he couldn't think. *They want to cut off Naomi's escape route. And Mrs. Edwards' and her new baby.*

Words tumbled from his mouth before he knew he intended to say anything. "What will you do to them?"

"Do to who?" Supon asked.

"To whom," Moy corrected.

Supon rolled his eyes at her. "What will we do *to whom*?"

"If the law's at the gate, or trying to surround us . . . I mean, them . . . then all the women and children are supposed to get to trucks and go out the back ways." Zeke's eyes swung back and forth between the Task Force members, searching for confirmation they wouldn't just go in shooting and keep shooting until nothing else moved. "I know the group is bad, but there's a lot of good people there. The kids, the women . . ."

Moy held up her hand and Zeke fell silent. "I know you've been taught we're clamoring to get in there and slaughter you all. But here's the thing—Mat and I, we've been on the inside, like Sam mentioned. We know there are good people there, and even the ones who won't hesitate to shoot us down, most of them have been manipulated into doing it. We don't want bloodshed, on either side." She looked him square in the eye. "I promise you, Zeke, we want to protect the innocent people on that compound from the men who lie and manipulate them. And our best-case scenario? It's to arrest the leaders unharmed and see them stand trial, and to help the others get out safely so they can live their lives out from under the threat of violence. That's the best way to ensure we and our co-workers can go home to our families at the end of the day."

Zeke couldn't help feeling comforted by the woman with the pointed nose and small, prim mouth.

"C-can I get a glass of water?"

Detective Abara brought him one, and he gulped it down, then realized with a start that he didn't know what would become of his flock. "What about the animals? The sheep, and cows, and chickens?"

"In cases like this, they bring in people to take care of them pending trial," Abara told him. "Most likely, they'll eventually auction them off. Don't worry, we won't leave them to starve."

Zeke relaxed a little. "Okay. Good."

"Uh, there's something I need to tell you guys," Gabe said. "If you send your people onto the compound, they need to stay away from the explosives shed." He told them about the device he'd set up and turned to Heather. "Did I screw up by telling them?"

"Not at all." She eyed the Task Force members. "I'm certain they'll keep in mind that you're a minor, not under arrest, and helping protect law enforcement officers by giving you a friendly warning."

"Son, are you brave or just stupid?" Supon asked. "Lucky you didn't end up spattered all over the walls of that place."

Gabe shot a defiant look at the detective. "They were gonna murder me and I had no idea whether we'd actually be able to escape. I didn't feel like I had a lot to lose."

Zeke's glass empty, his throat still felt dry. *It's now or never.* He took a deep breath. "Okay. I'll show you the back ways out, and where they keep the trucks."

Saturday, July 29, 2017
Bruderschaft Compound, North Idaho

Preacher burst into the war room out-back just as Edwards pulled Tom Shepherd off of Barnabas.

"Lemme go, dammit," the drunken Shepherd demanded. "Thass my son you're talkin' about!"

Barnabas wiped the back of his hand across his lips and checked for blood. Fortunately for Tom, there was none. He pointed a finger in Tom's face. "Yeah, your freak son stole a truck and ran off with a faggot. So now we can add criminal to the list."

"If you children are quite through, I have important news." Preacher stared over his glasses at them until they settled down.

"Not quite yet, Preacher," Edwards said. "I make a motion to remove Tom Shepherd from the council, effective immediately."

Tom's face flared red. "What th' hell? My father founded this council! You got no right to kick me off it."

Barnabas snorted. "We got every right, Tom, according to the rules your father and mine set out. So long as there's cause, we got the right."

Tom spat on the floor. "Well then, what the hell cause do you think you got?"

Barnabas turned to Edwards. "Mark, you made the motion. State your cause."

"Oh, I got plenty," Edwards said. "For starters, being a damn drunk and lacking all the self-control and discipline of a true Christian soldier. Then let's add on having a freak of a son who's probably turned faggot to boot. And for that son stealing Bruderschaft property *and* leaving the compound without permission. That enough?"

"That ought to do." Barnabas looked to the other men. "Anyone second it?"

"I second the motion," Callahan said.

"Alrighty, then." Barnabas hooked his thumbs in his belt loops and stood up straight. "It's been moved and seconded that we remove Tom Shepherd from the council immediately, for the causes Mark Edwards listed, and I'd add attacking his rightful superior. All those in favor?"

"Aye," said all the men present save Barnabas and Tom.

"All those opposed?"

"Nay," Tom said.

Preacher sneered at him. "You don't get a vote, Tom, not when we're voting about you."

"Then it's unanimous," Barnabas declared. "That's that, Tom. Get out."

They all stared at Tom in cold silence. He turned tail and stalked out, giving the door a good hard slam behind him.

"Thank you, Mark, for bringing that up. It needed to happen." Barnabas turned to the Preacher. "What was you saying about news, Jethro?"

"That harlot senator from Boise will be in our territory soon. For the cursed parade." He slapped a newspaper down on the table.

Barnabas put on his reading glasses and peered down at it. "Well, I'll be damned. First, they put the freak slut on a float, and now they got this bitch coming to watch. Gentlemen, we need to forget about the runaways—we just found a way to launch *Operation 88* in style. I always hated that damn parade anyway."

"It's only a week away, Barnabas," Edwards said.

"Damn right it is," the leader replied. "And this has to go off without a hitch. Let's get to work."

Saturday, July 29, 2017
Coeur d'Alene, Idaho

"Wait, they're staying with you?"

Chloe had told Charlie, on the phone, about their surprise guests.

"Well, yeah. They don't have anywhere else to go." Chloe closed some open tabs on her laptop, where she'd been researching Bruderschaft and the other groups in the area. She'd never known much about them—those groups were the region's not-so-secret shame and most people preferred not to talk about it. "Especially if someone's out looking for them."

"So, lead the psychos right to you? Why would your parents put you in danger like that?"

She shook her head and suppressed a sigh. She supposed he was sweet to worry, but it still rankled her nerves. *What, is he jealous or something?* "Those guys have no reason to suspect Zeke and Gabe would come here. I'm perfectly safe."

Charlie sighed. "I hope so. Just watch your back, okay? So, are these guys like hideously deformed or anything?"

"Gabe's face is all bruised and lumpy. Why?"

"Hoping for something to put my mind at ease."

Chloe made a disgusted face. "Are you worried I'll cheat on you? With rando fugitives who showed up at my door? Wow, thanks for the trust."

"It's not that I don't trust you. Them, however . . ."

"Not that it should even matter, but Gabe is gay, and Zeke is so shy and scared he doesn't even look me in the eye when we talk." She chastised herself for indulging him but couldn't stop herself from going on. "He's all *sir* and *ma'am* and awkward, and he's not cute or anything. And the clothes, ugh. They make everyone dress alike on the compound, and it's not working for them."

"Okay, that's all good. Still, watch your back. I suppose the gay guy is probably safe, but you never know. Remember how fast Zayden got creepy."

Chloe cringed. "Not cool, bringing that up." She'd never forget how she felt when Zayden had grabbed her and refused to let her go. Even thinking about it made her feel gross, and now it was Charlie making her think about it.

"Hey, Wyld, I'm sorry. I'm being a dick. I guess I just really miss you, and with all the crap that's been going on . . ."

"I miss you, too. At least you'll be here in a few days."

"Sure will! Can't wait."

They said good-bye and hung up. Chloe had tried to act like nothing was wrong, but the whole conversation had rubbed her the wrong way. She told herself everything would be better when they could talk in person.

"We've notified the ATF and Homeland Security," Abara told the Wylds and the two boys over dinner. After he brought Zeke, Gabe, and Heather back to the house, he accepted Phil's invitation to stay.

"Won't they take the case away from you?" Gabe thought the detective seemed like he'd enjoy being the hero.

Abara took a moment to chew and swallow before answering. "This is a small town. We don't have the sort of funding, manpower, or equipment it takes to go up against a well-armed compound of a hundred and fifty people. We'll take all the help we can get."

"Is this something Just Cause would get involved with?" Chloe asked.

"Doubtful," Abara said. "They usually just deal with parahuman-related issues." He paused for a few seconds, looking thoughtful. "Although, you know, it might be smart to call in the ones who could help us cut down the number of casualties. I'll get a judge to designate them as a terrorist threat—shouldn't be hard with the evidence—and then the governor can ask for Just Cause involvement. Sure wouldn't hurt to have some guys who can take a bullet or eighty without blinking."

"Or the psionicists. Ment once put everyone in an office building to sleep," Chloe said.

The detective pointed his fork at her. "Now there's a brilliant idea. Imagine the bloodshed we could avoid with that kind of help."

"Sam, do you think it's dangerous for the boys to be out in public?" Heather asked.

"We've been monitoring the compound via satellite and haven't seen any vehicles leave, so it doesn't appear anyone is looking for them." He sipped the wine. "We know they have contacts outside the compound, but we have no way to track them. So, I'd say it's best to be cautious. Coeur d'Alene's not that big a town and it's an obvious place for the boys to come."

Phil poured more wine in Sam's glass. "They're welcome to stay here for a while, but there's got to be somewhere safer."

"We've contacted the witness protection folks. It's technically too early for them to get involved, but we wanted their guidance on how to proceed in the meantime. We don't want to create any records that could be used to find them."

Zeke started to say something, but his voice came out squeaky. He cleared his throat and tried again. "I, uh, I just wanted to say . . . I'm really grateful for how nice everyone has been. I can't even believe it. I was always taught the world was an ugly place and people who were . . . who weren't like us were the reason for that. I was raised to hate all of you and now you're taking better care of me than the folks I've known my whole life. So, um, thank you. Everyone." He stared at his lap, feeling conspicuous.

Heather wiped at a tear on her cheek. "You're welcome, Zeke."

Phil, sitting to his left, clapped Zeke on the shoulder. "The world can be ugly, it's true, but I believe there are more good people than bad people in it. Maybe I've got rose-colored glasses. I don't know. I'm just glad you got away from all that in time for the good inside you to still win out."

Zeke looked at Phil with watery eyes. "I'm sorry, Sir, can I please be excused? I . . . need a minute to myself."

Phil nodded and Zeke leaped up so fast he almost tipped over the chair then thundered up the stairs toward the guest room. Silence hung heavy in the dining room for several seconds.

"He's not okay with showing emotion," Gabe said.

Heather sighed. "I don't imagine he knows anything but toxic masculinity."

"Yeah," Gabe said, "I don't know how he managed to be pretty decent in spite of it all. He thinks the good stuff is weakness."

CHAPTER NINE

Sunday, July 30, 2017
Coeur d'Alene, Idaho

"Roomie!" Chloe ran down the stairs as her mom opened the door to reveal Lindsay. She threw her arms around the slender girl with long black hair. Lindsay's arms slipped between Chloe's dual sets of wings to hug her back. "Hi, Mrs. Malone," Chloe said over Lindsay's shoulder to the woman who looked just like her but for the auburn hair.

Heather chuckled. "Chlo, you want to back up so they can come in?"

"Oh, sorry!" Chloe grabbed Lindsay's hand and pulled her in, and Lindsay's mother followed.

Mrs. Malone and Heather drifted into the kitchen for coffee. The girls raced up the stairs so Lindsay could put her bags in Chloe's room.

"Wow, your room is huge!" Lindsay looked around with wide eyes. "Mine's way closer to the size of our dorm room."

Chloe shrugged, embarrassed. "We have an air mattress we'll put in here for you since I just have the twin bed. We're still not sure where Charlie's gonna sleep, with Zeke and Gabe in the guest room."

"Are they here right now?" Lindsay had told Chloe on chat she was kind of fascinated by the boys' weird story and looked forward to meeting them.

"Yeah," Chloe said. "They're out in the back yard. Come on." She led her friend back to the main floor and out the sliders.

Zeke's large frame looked awkward hunched over a croquet mallet. Gabe stood off to the side, mallet up on his shoulder like a baseball bat and an amused look on his face.

"What's up, guys?"

Zeke glanced up at Chloe's voice. "Why is this game so hard? It looks easy."

Gabe chuckled. "Lindsay, right? The infamous roommate with the famous mother?"

Lindsay's face went beet red. She was from a tiny town in Montana, where everyone had known about her mom, Katie Malone, for about a decade. She still wasn't accustomed to how other people reacted to her mom's notoriety. "Yeah, that's me, I guess."

"Gabe." He put out a hand, and she shook it. "And this big lug is Zeke."

Zeke dropped the mallet and wiped his hand on his jeans before offering it. "Uh, hi. Why's your mom famous?"

"Oh, she was a prison guard at Deep Six . . ."

"Ladies can be prison guards?" Zeke blurted out.

"Dude!" Gabe smacked him on the shoulder. "First of all, you interrupted. Totally rude. Second, I keep telling you, women can have any job. They're not all subservient and domestic like the ones you're used to."

Zeke ducked his head. "Sorry."

"That's okay," Lindsay said. "I interrupt a lot too when I get excited. But yeah, she was a guard, and she stopped the one-and-only breakout there. Now she's the deputy warden. So, a lot of people know who she is."

"Is she a f-, uh, parahuman?" Zeke asked.

"Yeah, but she can just light her fingertips on fire. It's kinda useful. Like, when you need a match or something, but it's not like a Just Cause kind of power."

They sat down around a table with an umbrella spread out over it to shield them from the sun.

"What can you do?" Gabe asked.

Lindsay grinned and held out her hand. The boys flinched back from it as flame sprouted from her palm. Using both hands, she rolled the flame into a fireball and tossed it toward the center of the yard. Zeke gasped, and Gabe's eyes went wide. Then, just as it began to descend toward the grass, she extinguished it with a thought.

"Sweet!" Gabe applauded.

"Whoa, that's way flashier than mine," Zeke said.

Lindsay grinned at him. "Show us what you can do."

His face relaxed as he focused. A bird chirped and several others chimed in. The neighbor's dog barked in a rhythm—*woof-woof . . .woof; woof-woof . . .woof.* Then a swarm of houseflies buzzed around them in a circle and flew off over the house.

"Awesome," the girls said at the same time, then laughed.

"Seriously, Zeke," Chloe said, "it's pretty cool. I've never seen anything like that."

He gave them a sheepish grin. "Really, you think it's cool?"

"He doesn't have the gene, you know." Gabe looked from Chloe to Lindsay. "The Musashi gene. No one on the compound has it."

"So, what, are you like the Divine Right guys?" Lindsay asked, referring to a former independent superhero team. They all tested negative for the gene and claimed their powers came from God.

Zeke shrugged. "Dunno. I just started being able to do it."

"He was always really good with animals, which got him a job tending sheep," Gabe told them. "But then he realized he could control them consciously just, what, a week or so ago?"

"Oh, wow, so it's really new," Lindsay said. "Still trying to wrap your head around it, right?"

"Yeah, for sure." He smiled. "It's so good being able to talk about it out in the open. I don't feel like such a freak here."

Chloe spread her wings and buzzed them. "There's way freakier than you around, believe me."

Heather and Katie came out with cookies and a pitcher of lemonade. "Anyone hungry for more than a snack?" Heather asked.

"I'm still stuffed from breakfast," Gabe told her. "You don't have to feed us constantly, Mrs. Wyld."

Heather laughed. "I'm used to Chloe. Flying burns a lot of calories, and when she's healing? She could out-eat a football team."

"Mom!" Chloe's face went red.

"What? Your boyfriend's not here yet. I've got to get my teasing in now."

Lindsay burst out laughing. "You can't embarrass her about eating in front of Charlie. After flight training? I've seen them compete for who can clean their plate first."

Chloe giggled. "What can I say? We have a lot in common."

"That's the moth kid, right?" Gabe asked. "I've been following the news reports. They didn't say you guys were dating."

"TMZ speculated based on a picture, but we intentionally didn't mention that in the interviews. It's bad enough dealing with the media stuff. No one wants them talking about your love life."

"I can't believe the whole moth love thing," Lindsay said. "I mean, Charlie's nice and all, but—sorry, Chloe—he's no Perspective. Or MetalBlade or Crackerjack, back in the day."

Chloe found herself not wanting to talk about Charlie, and especially not all the girls fawning over him across the country. She hadn't told Lindsay about his jealousy or her own feelings regarding Charlie's sudden popularity. She wasn't even sure she wanted him to come for a visit, but he'd be there in less than twenty-four hours.

Sunday, July 30, 2017
Bruderschaft Compound, North Idaho

"I need you to go scope out the parade route," Barnabas told Mark Edwards and Danny Ray Callahan. "Thing is, though, they're spying on us with a damn satellite. You gotta hike out to Clagstone and borrow a vehicle from someone. Try the Martins' farm first, and if that don't work, go to the Andersons or the Millers."

"Do we have a contact in Coeur d'Alene?" Edwards asked.

Barnabas nodded and took a folded piece of paper from his shirt pocket. "Here's his information. You remember how to use the laptop?"

Callahan nodded. "Yeah, well enough, I reckon."

"We'll go over it again before you leave," Barnabas said. "I don't want you contacting no one here after you leave, you gotta be self-sufficient out there."

"Why we being watched?" Edwards asked.

"Don't know." He tilted his head toward the piece of paper Edwards now held. "He could only get me a quick message, and it just said they'd know if anyone drove off the compound."

Edwards furrowed his brow. "Any word on where the stolen truck is? Or the boys?"

Barnabas shook his head. "Keep your eyes and ears open, though. They probably went east toward Milwaukee, or straight to the Spokane airport, but you never know. They ain't exactly the sharpest tools, those two."

Callahan nodded. "Zeke's even dumber than his pa. What if we do see them?"

"Shoot them if you can get away with it. Otherwise, bring them back, or at least figure out where they're staying." Barnabas looked from Callahan to Edward and back. "If you have to leave them there and breathing, let the contact know. We can trust him to take care of it almost as much as we can trust our own. Whatever you do, don't jeopardize the mission over them two."

He gave them a laptop and a printed map of the parade route. They also received some cash for food, gas, a hotel room, and to reimburse whoever let them borrow a truck. They went to their homes to pack, then headed up to the storage buildings—Edwards to grab the guns they'd need, Callahan to gather his beloved explosives.

As he selected a few choice pieces, his eye fell on a smattering of tools on a shelf. Out of place, like nothing should ever be—his guys knew he didn't tolerate sloppiness around explosives. He bent to pick up a device on the floor when the shed went dark and he looked up to see Edwards silhouetted in the doorway.

"Clean up your mess later. Let's get moving," Edwards said. "It's damn hot already, and we got a long walk ahead. Sure will be glad to get to a hotel." He raised an eyebrow.

Callahan's mouth twisted into a smile. "I hear that." Thoughts now distracting him from the out-of-place explosives, he closed up the shed and they headed out.

CHAPTER TEN

Monday, July 31, 2017
Bruderschaft Compound, North Idaho

Tom woke up, leaning against a tree trunk, at the southernmost point of his early morning patrol. The taste of beer and puke lingered in his throat and he cursed himself for being drunk enough to fall asleep on watch. No wonder they'd kicked him off the damn council—he deserved it. He was a disgrace to the order and to the memories of the great men who'd founded it. He wished he'd gotten himself and his son away from here before this humiliation.

The sound of approaching footsteps through the forest put him on alert. *An SIT training mission, maybe? Why wasn't I told?* Then he realized, for the first time in his adult life, he stood outside the inner circle. He didn't like that one bit.

Moving low and fast, he stalked toward the noise, then crouched behind a deadfall tree and listened. It was no training mission, but the actual soldiers, judging from the individual voices he could identify. He heard Olson and McCallum, and he was pretty sure Williams and Beck, too. Then a loud voice cut through the din— the newest soldier, Justice White. Tom felt old, realizing Justice was just two years older than Zeke.

They passed by him and continued on their trek, heading in the direction of Clagstone. No one saw him, and he didn't call out, either. After his expulsion from the council, he didn't much want to be seen. Tom counted thirteen soldiers, loaded with weapons and gear. The party comprised about half of the fully trained men in Bruderschaft.

It didn't make sense that they'd be going to town, but that was an odd direction to go for maneuvers. They usually did those to the north.

Hell, it ain't my problem no more, he thought. He turned around and went back north a bit, stopped to puke into a bush, and then resumed his miserable patrol. He couldn't figure out what those men could be up to and decided he'd better keep his ear to the ground.

Monday, July 31, 2017
Coeur d'Alene, Idaho

"What's wrong?" Lindsay asked the next morning as they stood next to each other in Chloe's bathroom, doing their hair and makeup.

"Nothing. Why?"

"Because every time I mention your boyfriend, your brows get all pinchy." She put down the flatiron and turned to face her roommate. "Spill the tea, sis. You might as well tell me now, 'cause you know I'll get it out of you eventually."

Chloe sighed and her shoulders drooped. She stared at the sink, her face blank, while she gathered her thoughts. "I'm probably making too big a deal out of it, but first, there's all these girls suddenly in love with Charlie. I know we agreed not to talk about our relationship with the media, but it kinda bugs me he hasn't put it out there. And now other girls are Photoshopping their face on my picture, and he still hasn't said anything publicly."

"I guess I can see both sides of that, but yeah, it would be annoying."

"And then, when I told him about Zeke and Gabe, he got all weird and possessive. Like he thought I'd cheat with one of them."

Lindsay's face twisted into a distinct *ew* expression.

Chloe laughed. "Right? Then he told me to be careful and brought up Zayden getting all creepy and aggro."

"Not cool!"

"Right? He apologized, but it just left me feeling weird. We haven't talked on the phone since then, it's just been messages. So now I don't know if I'm excited to see him or not."

Lindsay slipped between Chloe's wings and the counter to give her a side hug. "I'm sure everything will be fine. Long-distance is hard, and then you've got tons of crazy to deal with . . . I'm sure it'll be better when you're face-to-face."

Chloe leaned her head over against Lindsay's. "Thanks. I'm so glad you're here!"

Phil called up the stairs to let them know it was time to leave for the airport. Chloe put on some lip gloss and they headed out. Lindsay sat in the front seat of the SUV with Phil, and Chloe sat in the center of the middle row because of her wings.

Phil glanced at his daughter in the rearview mirror. "Still want to go to Riverfront Park before we take Charlie home?"

"Yeah, for sure."

"Where's that?" Lindsay asked.

Chloe couldn't help but grin, despite her trepidation over Charlie's arrival. "Downtown Spokane and the Spokane Falls are right in the middle of it. It's amazing to fly over it! Flying through the spray is my favorite thing ever. Of course, Charlie will have to stay higher, so his wings don't get wet."

"Does water mess up the powder on his wings, like with real moths?" Phil asked.

"Technically, it's scales, not powder, but yeah. That's why he had so much trouble getting me to safety after I opened the hatch, 'cause one wing tip dipped in the water."

A holdover from when the military stored chemical weapons in underground tunnels, the hatch was at the bottom of a man-made lake just off the Hero Academy campus. Chloe had opened it to flood the tunnels and take out Zayden's explosives. It took too long, though, and she inhaled water on her way up. She would've drowned, if not for Charlie.

"Wait, he had trouble?" Her dad eyed her in the mirror again. "You never told me that part."

Chloe shrugged, looking sheepish. "Oops?"

At the packed Spokane International Airport, Chloe's delicate wings kept getting bumped. She tried staying between her dad and Lindsay so she was more protected, but then someone's briefcase caught the tip of one and gave it a good yank.

"Okay, that's enough of this." She waited until a break in the crowd gave her room to spread out her wings, then buzzed them and flew up over their heads. In school, she'd learned to stagger her wing motion, creating less noise and wind when she flew. It made the sound imperceptible over the airport's din and kept people from getting blasted in the face. She spun toward the terminal and saw Charlie flying to her over the crowd. The look on his face—the unmistakable *I'm crazy in love with that girl* expression—melted away her worries and she zipped over to him. They met in the air and touched their palms together. They'd developed this greeting because it was impossible to hug or hold hands while they flew, due to the size of their wings.

"It's so good to see you, Wyld."

"You too, O'Neal."

She wanted to stay just like that for longer, but while hovering was effortless for her, it took a lot of wing power for Charlie. Amid curious and stunned stares, she turned and led him back to her dad and Lindsay. Charlie landed and shook Phil's hand. He gave Lindsay a friendly hug, but Chloe stayed above them. Lindsay gave her a questioning glance to see how she was, and she returned a smile and slight nod to let her know everything was good—now that he was here.

They all headed toward the baggage claim area, with Chloe still flying, and about halfway there a guard ran toward Chloe telling her to get on the ground. She found a place to touch down and apologized to him.

"There's no law against flying in a public building, is there?" her dad asked.

Chloe shook her head. The Academy required them to learn local laws regarding parahuman abilities, and she'd decided she should learn Washington's, as well since she lived so close—and no law said she couldn't fly in an airport. "It's good PR to avoid confrontations and play well with authorities, though. I don't want people to think I'm some entitled brat, plus if something happened, the security guard and I would need to work together."

Phil raised an eyebrow. "That school's doing a damn good job. You guys really know what you're talking about, don't you?"

They shrugged and went back to chattering about a spat some classmates had gotten into last week.

Once Charlie had his baggage, they returned to the SUV and put up the third-row seat since Charlie and Chloe each needed extra space. The three kids talked and laughed as Phil drove to downtown Spokane and parked.

"Where are we?" Charlie asked.

"Riverfront Park," Chloe told him. "Remember me telling you about the falls?"

The Spokane River ran through the heart of downtown, complete with a spectacular waterfall in the center of a sprawling park.

He grinned, and the moment they left the car, the two fliers took to the air. "Meet you there," Chloe called down. From their high vantage point, they could see the falls in moments. Charlie flew toward it in a straight line, but Chloe flew in loops and swirls around him, just for fun.

As they drew nearer, she led him up high to keep him out of the spray as the powerful river surged beneath them. With runoff at its peak, the water churned with a ferocity they could feel.

Charlie whooped as he felt the current caused by the water's drag on the air, and side-by-side he and Chloe flew down the river and over the falls. A dozen or so people lining the footbridge pointed and stared and several raised up their phones to get pictures and videos.

Chloe dove low and reveled in the cold spray against her skin while Charlie banked above her. She did a barrel roll to show off for the crowd, then flew straight up while keeping her body parallel to the ground, as only a dragonfly could. Charlie met her there, and they went back up over the falls. Straining against the air currents, they looked at each other and laughed. Chloe gestured back toward the falls with her head and he nodded. They turned and gave in to the current, and it propelled them back over the bridge and the hundred-foot drop beyond it. Then Chloe led him to where her dad and Lindsay waited. They touched down, red-faced and exhilarated, and collapsed on the soft grass.

Lindsay applauded. "That was awesome! I so wish I could fly."

Charlie looked up at the blue sky. "Amazing, Wyld. What a rush!"

"Isn't it? And it's so much better having someone to share it with." She looked up at her dad. "Do we have time for one more pass?"

Phil checked the time on his phone. "I want to get home and start dinner, but you guys can go again while

Lindsay and I start back to the car. As long as you're sure you can catch up." He winked at his daughter.

"Haha, Dad. Let's go, Meta Moth!" Chloe grabbed Charlie's hand and pulled him up.

"Ugh, I'm way too big a nerd for all this exertion," he teased. "How did I end up with an athlete?"

She laughed. "Same way I ended up with a geek, I guess."

He hauled himself up and glanced at Phil's back to make sure he wasn't looking, then gave Chloe a kiss. As he drew away, their eyes locked, and they lost themselves in each other for a while. He kissed her again. "I'm suddenly feeling better. Let's fly!"

They took off together and made another exhilarating dive over the falls, grinning at each other the whole time. This was a special thing they shared, and Chloe never felt more connected to anyone than when she flew with Charlie.

Then the wind shifted, and the spray washed over them both. Water droplets pelted against Charlie's wings, damaging the tiny, delicate scales.

In a panic, he changed direction and made a beeline for the riverbank, but she could see he struggled to maintain altitude. They'd practiced for this scenario after a rainstorm broke out during flight training. That time, she'd tried catching him from below, but his momentum overcame her wings' strength as he plowed into her. They'd both plummeted to the ground and been lucky to escape with no worse than bumps and bruises.

Chloe zipped down and positioned herself head-to-head with him, flying backward, and reached toward him. He clasped her hands and she yanked, pulling them both upright and slowing his downward momentum. She wrapped her arms around his waist in a tight embrace, her wings buzzing at full speed. She arched back and brought her legs up as he leaned forward. They ended up parallel to the ground with her beneath him, flying upside down on her back. Charlie continued flapping his damaged wings, so she didn't have to support his full weight. Ten feet above the grass, they again shifted their weight together so they could land on their feet.

"Are you okay?" Chloe asked.

A crowd of cheering people ran toward them, most with their cell phones out. Chloe smiled and waved, then turned back to Charlie.

"I'm great. Just great! That wasn't humiliating at all, and it's probably already on YouTube." He sighed, head hanging. "Thanks for the save, Wyld." He turned away from her and started walking back toward the car, wings limp behind him.

"Don't be like that," she said as she caught up. "It could just as easily happen to me. You've seen me clip the tip of a wing and go spiraling out of control."

"Yeah, but then you heal in like, minutes. I'm grounded for days now."

She tried to take his hand, but he crossed his arms. "And with just about anyone else, you can do your power-swap thing and *they* can heal fast. But no, of course, it doesn't work with me."

"Or any other physical powers. When I swapped with Ondine at the lake, sure, I could swim, but I didn't get her gills. Who saved me then?"

As Charlie climbed in the SUV's rear seat, everyone could feel the sulky vibe he put off. Lindsay caught Chloe's eye and gave her a questioning look.

Chloe grimaced. "We . . . had a little mishap."

"Is everyone okay?" Phil asked.

Charlie didn't respond.

Chloe told them about his wings getting doused. She didn't mention having to help him get back to the ground.

"What kind of superhero gets taken out by rain?" he grumbled. "I'm gonna end up with the Champions or stuck in a desert somewhere."

"You're a great leader, and your power is still more versatile than mine," Lindsay said. "Just Cause will want you for sure."

He shook his head and stared out the side window. Chloe slumped in her seat, feeling defeated and wishing she hadn't suggested the last pass. She tried to chat with Lindsay and her dad, but long stretches of uncomfortable silence punctuated the forty-five-minute drive back to Coeur d'Alene.

When they pulled into the driveway, a knot of dread settled in Chloe's stomach. It was bad enough Charlie was sulking over his wet wings, and now she had to introduce him to Gabe and Zeke. She took his hand and lingered in the driveway as the others went inside.

"Hey, I'm really sorry about the water. I should've realized . . ."

He looked ashamed. "Naw, I'm sorry. I just got here and already I'm being a huge drag." He wrapped his arms around her waist and pulled her close. "I should've watched out for myself better."

The hug helped ease her stress and she smiled up at him. They walked inside holding hands.

They found the guys watching TV in the family room, and Zeke looked like he was about to puke.

Chloe glanced at the screen and saw why—it was a documentary on hate groups. She grimaced. "Gabe, do you think maybe this is a little much?"

Zeke shook his head. "No, it's okay. I need to know this stuff."

"If you want, I guess. Can you pause it for a sec, though?"

Gabe hit the button and the screen froze. Chloe introduced Charlie to them, noticing her boyfriend seemed a little distant, but at least he was polite.

Phil and Heather ate inside while Chloe and their four house guests had dinner around the patio table. With

Charlie loosened up, the three Academy students told the boys stories about school, including their big moment of heroism and how Chloe nearly drowned to pull it off.

Charlie grinned. "After I saved her life, she decided she liked me back."

Chloe blushed. "Actually, I've never told you this, but I realized I liked you as I was flying to Zayden's house to talk to his mom."

"Really?"

"Yeah, I started thinking about how nice you always were and that I wished you'd come with me. And I was like *whoa, I think I like him.*"

"So, you mean I didn't have to risk my life to land you?" he teased.

She wadded up her napkin and threw it at him. "If you hadn't, I'd be dead, and that would be no fun for anyone."

Everyone laughed. "Nah," Charlie said, "Dax would've saved you." He turned to the other boys. "He's in love with her, too, but I don't think he's much competition."

"Yeah," Chloe laughed. "He's what, ten?"

"And now Moth Man's an internet heartthrob and a way better catch," Lindsay blurted out. Too late, she realized she'd brought up a sore subject and shot Chloe a "sorry" look. Chloe tried to laugh it off.

Charlie scoffed. "Yeah, I guess I owe that to the whole geek chic trend. We all know who I was really looking at, though."

"I wish someone would look at me that way," Gabe muttered.

Lindsay laughed. "Right?"

"So, is it Moth Man or Mega Moth?" Zeke asked.

"It's *Meta* Moth," Charlie corrected.

Zeke cocked his head and looked confused. "What does that mean?"

Gabe chuckled. "He's a moth, who's self-aware and naming himself as a moth, which is totally meta."

Charlie high fived him. "Thank you! Finally, someone gets it!"

"I still don't understand," Zeke said.

"Don't worry about it, man." Charlie sighed. "Almost no one does. It's a dumb name. I need to change it, but I can't come up with anything good. Chloe nixed Super Geek. Moth Man is cheesy, plus that's already a crypto creature. Mothra's a kaiju, and that's it, I'm out of ideas."

Lindsay tapped her fingers on the table, thinking. "Your name doesn't exactly lend itself to anything, like Chloe's does."

"Not unless I want to be O'Moth or The Irish Flyer."

"Have you thought of a code name yet, Zeke?" Chloe asked.

He shook his head. "Gabe calls me Plague Master Z, but that doesn't sound like a good guy."

"No, that's pretty villain-y," Lindsay agreed. "What's your full name?"

"Ezekiel Matthew Shepherd."

The three parahuman kids stared at him in disbelief. Chloe tittered. "You don't see the obvious one?"

Zeke's eyes narrowed in confusion.

Gabe smacked his own forehead. "Ugh! I can't believe I didn't think of that! Dude, what does a shepherd do?"

"Looks after sheep. Oh! He takes care of animals!" A smile crept across Zeke's face. "Shepherd. I'm The Shepherd. I like that! I always thought it was kinda funny I got put in charge of the sheep when that's my last name."

The sliding door into the house opened, and Chloe's parents came out, followed by Detective Abara, who'd arrived with news.

"We've been able to confirm a few key things you boys told us and we're close on the probable-cause. The judge gave us the terrorism designation, so the governor's putting in the request for Just Cause assistance, too. We're in good shape." He pulled an envelope from an inside pocket in his blazer. "Also, state troopers found your truck and did a thorough search, in case there were weapons or anything else of interest. They found this."

"Oh yeah, the boarding pass. I forgot about that," Gabe said.

"Boarding pass*es*," Abara said. "There's one in your father's name, Zeke, and one in yours. What do you know about these?"

Zeke blinked several times. "Nothing, really. I found the envelope as we was getting away. Gabe told me what that was, 'cause I ain't never seen one before, but I didn't realize there was two."

"Do you have any connection to Springfield, Missouri?"

"That's where my ma was from, but I don't know why we'd go there now." Zeke shrugged. "Unless my pa thought we could stay with her people or something."

"And you had no idea he was planning to take you off the compound?"

He shook his head. "No, if I had, I wouldn't have left like I did. As long as he was willing to get Gabe out of there, too, we could've just left together. I can't believe he'd leave Bruderschaft because of me, though. Never seemed to care enough to do something like that. Wish I could talk to him."

Abara put a hand on his shoulder. "I'm sure you have a lot of questions, but I need you not to contact him until all of this is over. Knowing he planned to leave, though, I'd sure like to see if he could be a resource. What's the best way to establish communication?"

Zeke shrugged. "Barnabas is the only one on the compound with a phone, and I don't even know the number. Mail's too dangerous—it all goes through the council first."

"Dude, what about a carrier pigeon, or something like it?" Gabe asked. "Use your abilities."

"Oh, yeah! I'm the Shepherd now." Zeke grinned.

"Excellent idea, Gabriel." The detective slipped the boarding passes back into his pocket and stood, resting his large hands on the back of the chair. "We're hoping this'll all be over soon, and if anything goes to trial, it looks like we will be able to get you boys into witness protection. So there's a lot of good news."

"Did you ask if we could go in as brothers?" Gabe asked.

"I passed your request along, but that's all I can do. I have no control over what they do, and they'll do what they think is safest for the two of you. They're working with a local organization to get you a temporary placement until you're officially named witnesses. You could hear as soon as tomorrow, and don't expect any notice. Once plans are solid, they'll work fast and say as little as possible to anyone, so expect it to be a bit of a whirlwind. I gave Phil and Heather a password to let them know it's legit when it happens. Zeke, I'll be in touch about getting a message sent." He said his good-byes and left.

CHAPTER ELEVEN

Tuesday, Aug. 1, 2017
Coeur d'Alene, Idaho

Chloe awoke to her mom's soft knock on her door. "Come in," she croaked. Lindsay groaned and pulled her pillow over her face.

Heather opened the door. "The boys are about to leave, if you want to say good-bye."

Chloe leaped out of bed. "So soon?"

Her mom nodded. "Hurry—they're giving us five minutes."

Chloe threw her backward robe on over her t-shirt and boxers while Lindsay pulled on leggings under her short nightgown and they hurried downstairs.

Charlie sat on the couch, where he'd slept, still half under the covers. Two men who looked too *Men-in-Black*-ish for comfort stood near the door talking to Phil as Heather hugged first Gabe and then Zeke.

Chloe didn't feel comfortable hugging them, especially with Charlie watching. Lindsay rushed forward, though, and gave Gabe a big hug and then, appearing not to notice the fear on his face, wrapped her arms around Zeke, too. He gave her an awkward pat on both arms.

Chloe hung back. "I'm really glad you guys came here. It's been awesome getting to know you."

"Thanks, me too," Gabe said. "I hope we get to see you guys again."

Zeke, still uncomfortable, just nodded and thrust his hands in his pockets.

Charlie mumbled some good-to-meet-yous from where he sat, and the MIBs whisked the boys away.

The five who were left stood in silence for several seconds. Then Charlie stood up and, through a yawn, told them he was going to take a shower.

"I'll make waffles," Phil announced. "Do we have any huckleberries left?"

"A few, in the back of the freezer," Heather said.

"Perfect! Lindsay, get ready for the best breakfast of your life." He went into the kitchen.

"Okay, morbid curiosity here." Heather leaned in toward the girls with a conspiratorial tone. "With the whole water issue, I have to wonder how Charlie showers."

Chloe blushed. "Not that I've actually seen it or anything, but he has to stand with his wings outside the shower and he puts a rain poncho over them to be extra safe."

"That doesn't sound comfortable. I hope he never cared about long, hot baths."

Chloe laughed. "You know, mom, not everyone considers that the best way to spend a Sunday afternoon."

Heather scoffed. "They just don't know what they're missing."

Twenty minutes later, they all sat around the kitchen table. Phil hadn't just made huckleberry waffles. He also served up bacon, hard-boiled eggs, and hash browns. They all dug in.

"I know they were only here for a couple of days," Chloe said, "but it's weird having Zeke and Gabe just . . . gone."

Her parents nodded in agreement.

"They seem like decent guys." Charlie helped himself to more bacon. "Are you sure Gabe is gay, though?"

Lindsay laughed. "Uh, yeah. He told me he kinda had a crush on you."

Charlie choked on his orange juice. "I guess so, then."

"So, should *I* be jealous now?" Chloe asked. She intended it to sound like a joke, but it came out a little bitter. Heather's right eyebrow went up.

Charlie's energy diminished and Chloe chastised herself for saying the wrong thing. Again. Then she got angry with him for making her feel that way.

Her mom got up, filled her to-go cup with coffee, and kissed Chloe on the head. "Don't forget you've got a parade meeting at two. See you kids at dinner, unless I'm stuck in depositions for way too long."

Tuesday, Aug. 1, 2017
Kootenai Boys' Ranch, Near Coeur d'Alene, Idaho

They started with a circuitous ride in the back of a van with blacked-out windows, and then switched to a different van for the rest of the trip. Eventually, Gabe and Zeke found themselves on a ranch that seemed in the middle of nowhere. A wooden sign proclaimed it *Kootenai Boys' Ranch,* with crosses on either end of the name and a Jesus fish below it.

Gabe had watched the road signs, though, and knew they'd ended up just a little east of Coeur d'Alene. He figured the route had been designed to ensure they weren't followed.

He sighed. "So much for getting back to civilization."

Zeke took a deep breath and let it out with an *ah.* "Back to someplace that makes sense, you mean."

The men who'd picked them up at the Wyld's house had given them information packets to memorize on the way. They were posing as runaways from a group home in Spokane. Zeke's name was Joe Simpson and Gabe's was John Gray. Gabe told them John was his dad's name, and he'd rather have anything else, but they said he had to stick with what was on the documents.

"Maybe . . . Johnnie?" Zeke suggested. Gabe thought that would be okay.

Pastor Ken had driven the second leg of the journey and seemed nice enough. He ushered them into a large farmhouse. Inside, it had plain white walls, fake hardwood floors, and old office furniture. A woman at the front desk introduced herself as Julie. She checked them in with crisp efficiency and gave them the keys to their rooms, then handed them each a manila envelope with *Work Schedule* written on the front.

"What, are we sentenced to hard labor or something?" Gabe asked. "We're the witnesses, not the criminals."

Julie smiled. "It's just to keep up appearances. We take in troubled boys, but you're here because it's a secure facility where no one's likely to look for you. The jobs you've been assigned will help fill your time and make it look to everyone else as if you're just two more residents. Don't worry, we're not going to work you to death. Joe, I hear you're experienced with animals, so I've assigned you to help with the horses."

Zeke's face lit up. "Yeah, that sounds good. Thank you, Ma'am."

"Johnnie, you're working in the kitchen. Both of you just do what you're told and keep your heads down."

"Got it," Gabe said.

"You'll be given placement tests, but we don't anticipate you staying long enough to start classes. Again, it's just for appearances. No one other than Pastor Ken and I know the truth about you. Let's keep it that way, okay?"

She issued them baby blue coveralls with *Kootenai Boys Ranch* stenciled on the back on crosses on the front pocket. Gabe held his up and gave it a sour look. "These are just as fashionable as Butler's Shaft clothes. What I wouldn't give for a graphic tee and a pair of Vans."

They went into a small curtained area off the front office and got changed. A mousy boy dressed in identical coveralls took their clothes, tagged them with their names, and hung them in a closet. He then showed them to their rooms, which were next to each other and at the end of a long building that looked like a run-down, '50s-era motel.

Gabe opened his door and went in. He'd been pretty sure no living conditions could be worse than the Butler's Shaft barracks. He'd been wrong.

"Well, isn't this cheery," he muttered to himself as he regarded the cinder block walls painted a dingy white and metal-framed bed so narrow he doubted it was even a twin. A classroom-style desk with an attached chair and no drawers sat against the other wall. In the corner, a short wall jutted out a few feet to conceal with toilet and sink. The single tiny window sat just below the ceiling and had bars over it. *At least in a prison cell, you can see out.* As scared as he'd been about the witness protection program, it had to beat the hell out of this.

He answered a knock on the door to see Pastor Ken, and Zeke behind him. Zeke looked excited and Gabe couldn't fathom what in the world he had to be happy about. "It's time for your tour," the pastor said with a smile.

Zeke grinned. "We get to see the horses!"

Tuesday, Aug. 1, 2017
Coeur d'Alene, Idaho

Chloe stepped out of the car at the fairgrounds, and a woman rushed over to meet them. She wore a vest with kittens appliquéd in little panels all over it and mom jeans. Her smile showed a lot of gums and sent her eyebrows to the upper reaches of her forehead.

"Hello, hello! You must be Chloe! Or should I call you WyldWing? I don't know what's proper in this situation."

Chloe felt trapped between this over-enthusiastic person and the car. "Uh, Chloe's fine."

"Oh, good, good! I'm Minnie. And this must be Charlie and Lindsay. Oh, I'm just so thrilled to meet all of you! Look at all these fabulous wings!"

Phil came around the car and introduced himself. "Can you show us to the float, Minnie? We don't have much time."

Chloe knew they had all afternoon, but she also knew her dad had a talent for handling annoying people and appreciated that quality more than ever.

Minnie led them into a vast, hangar-like building where crews worked on several floats. "These are all of the city's official floats. That one's for the mayor, this one's for the city council, and here we are with yours." She stopped at a flower-and-tissue-paper explosion with a large blue area representing Lake Coeur d'Alene and replicas of buildings along the shore, plus a big arch with bright blue letters that read, *Super Heroes for a Super Future!*

A single chair on the float's deck had an over-sized back featuring paper flames for Lindsay, and Chloe wondered where she and Charlie were supposed to sit. Then she noticed the poles on either side of the chair and looked up.

Oh, no! She thought. Eight feet up, atop the two poles, sat bird-like perches.

Minnie prattled on to Phil about something, so Chloe interrupted. "I'm sorry, but are you expecting us to sit on perches? Like we're pet birds or something?"

"Are those even sturdy enough to hold a person?" Charlie asked. "I sure don't want to risk falling."

Minnie's smile collapsed. "I'm sure they're strong enough. And how can you fall? You can fly!"

Charlie's nostrils flared. "It takes a few seconds to get my wings moving and plummeting to the ground is a lot faster."

"Plus, how will it look, if we're clinging on for our lives?" Chloe shook her head. "I think it's a lot better to have us on the float itself. Then people can see us better, and if we want to fly, we can take off from somewhere safe and stable."

Minnie foundered. "B-but the perches were the mayor's own idea . . ."

"You know," Phil cut in, "I'm sure it's perfectly safe. My wife's worked with most of the city attorneys. I'll have her contact them about drawing up some extra indemnity clauses . . ."

Chloe wanted to burst out laughing at her dad's not-so-subtle reminder of his wife's profession.

Minnie gaped as she tried to collect herself. "No, no, we'll come up with another design, if there's time. The designers wanted me to ask if the two of you, Chloe and Charlie, can wear green."

"My regular costume is green and purple," Chloe said, "but I also have a blue Hero Academy uniform. We all have those, so if you want us to match . . ."

"We'd prefer the green. What about you, Charlie?" Minnie asked.

"My costume is brown tones, to go with the orange and tan in my wings."

Minnie looked disappointed. "That's a shame. Chloe, can you do your hair like Tinkerbell? The designers can provide a wand . . ."

Charlie put his hands up. "Whoa, whoa, whoa!"

"What? No, way." Chloe's hands went to her hips. "I am not playing pixie."

"Oh, but we thought it would be fun for the children . . ."

"We're training to be law enforcement, not circus performers," Charlie said.

Phil stepped between Minnie and the teenagers. "How does this sound—replace the perches with benches. The kids will all wear their Hero Academy uniforms, and Chloe and Charlie will fly over the crowd now and then and hand out candy."

"But hey, so we don't lose that circus vibe, I can do some fire tricks," Lindsay said.

Minnie's eyes went huge. "Fire? On a tissue paper float? Oh, I don't know about that . . ."

"I can put it out at will, so there's no danger. And think what fun it will be. For the *children*!"

Chloe couldn't bear Lindsay's taunting, all in her sweetest voice, and had to turn away so Minnie wouldn't see her holding back laughter.

"Oh, there's the designer now." Minnie hurried toward a tall man in his late twenties wearing sunglasses, a beret, and scarf despite the dim interior and heat. Chloe thought he tried too hard to look like an *artiste*. As Minnie talked to him, with her hands waving all over the place, he grew angrier and angrier. Then he put a hand up to Minnie's face, dismissing her, and marched over to them. Chloe braced to take the brunt of his artistic temperament.

"My dear heroes!" He sounded more exasperated than mad. "That silly woman has wasted I-don't-even-know how many hours with her ridiculous ideas. Of course, we will excise those horrible perches! We'll build you beautiful chairs—thrones!—that match your gorgeous wings . . ."

"Actually," Chloe said, "it's hard for us to sit in chairs. Maybe benches or stools?"

He placed a hand on each of her cheeks. "Of course, dear one, anything for you. Oh! How rude of me, I haven't even introduced myself. I am Raul, and I've adored you ever since I saw your wings emerge. I'm a sucker for a dramatic reveal!" He turned to Charlie. "And you—what bone structure. Cheeks to die for! Have you done any modeling?"

Charlie looked on the verge of panic. "Uh, no."

"I'm a fashion designer. If I design some garments that accommodate your wings, would you grace the runway for me?" His focus switched to Lindsay before Charlie had a chance to answer. "And this one—the drama of the white skin and black hair. Is it natural, or are you trying to look less like your mother? It's not working. Fortunately for you, she's gorgeous!"

By the time they left, everyone feeling dazed, Raul had changed the entire float design. He insisted they wear their costumes instead of the HA uniforms and—upon learning Lindsay didn't have one yet—promised to design something to accentuate her coloration and *scrumptious proportions*. Minnie stood off to the side the whole time, fuming in silence.

"This parade will be an interesting experience," Phil said as they climbed into the car.

Chloe laughed. "Way to understate it, Dad."

Lindsay couldn't stop smiling. "I'm just excited to get a real costume. Blue is so not my color. Plus, my grandma always called me *gangly*. I like *scrumptious proportions* a whole lot better."

Edwards and Callahan, in a borrowed farm truck, pulled into the Mo-Z Inn parking on the outskirts of Coeur d'Alene. They'd changed out of all their Bruderschaft clothing in favor of jeans and cowboy boots. Edwards wore a flannel shirt and baseball cap, and Callahan had a Western-style button-down and straw hat. They paid cash for their room in advance and hung the Do Not Disturb sign on the outside doorknob first thing.

"It feels weird not letting Barnabas know we made it," Callahan said. They sat at the room's small table, the laptop in front of them.

Edwards shrugged as he stuffed a wad of chew in his lip. "We do what we're told, and that's what we was told."

"Yeah, I know." He opened the laptop and pulled up the secure messaging program. "I'll get word to Jeremiah, anyway."

"We stink to high heaven," Edwards said. It had taken them twenty-two hours to get from the compound to Clagstone, and they'd had next to no sleep along the way. They didn't find a vehicle they could use until they reached the third farm. Mr. Miller had just bought himself a new truck and the old one sat on the road with a for-sale sign in the window. They paid him to borrow it and took turns driving and napping.

"I'm gonna get in the shower, Danny Ray." Edwards raised an eyebrow and looked Callahan up and down, an appreciative glint in his eye. "Once the message is sent, you want to join me?"

A lascivious smile crossed Callahan's face. "You sure we got time for that?"

"Long as it's been, I'll be quick."

"You get the water going, then. I'll be right in." He one-finger typed the username on the piece of paper Barnabas had given him and sent a single word message: *Here.*

CHAPTER TWELVE

Wednesday, Aug. 2, 2017
Kootenai Boys' Ranch, Near Coeur d'Alene, Idaho

After praying and eating breakfast in a big dining hall with all the other boys, Zeke was headed out toward the stables when Julie called after him. "You have a visitor," she whispered, then led him to a small conference room off the front office.

"How are things here so far?" Detective Abara asked.

"Not too bad. The rooms are kinda bleak, but I get to work with horses and be outside a lot, so that part's good."

"Good. I recommended this place, so I hope it works out for you." Abara reached under the table and pulled up something tall and rectangular, covered in a cloth. With a flourish, he pulled off the cloth to reveal a large black bird in a cage. The bird cawed at Zeke and cocked his head.

A smile spread across Zeke's face. "Cool, I like crows! Does he have a name?"

"*She's* a raven, and her name is Lenore. Clever, don't you think?"

Zeke squinted at the detective. "How so?"

"Have you ever read Poe's The Raven?"

"What's Pose the Raven?"

Abara snorted. "You're gonna have some catching up to do once you get into school. Anyway, Lenore here is going to be our messenger. She's been trained to carry things, and she's quite the talker."

Zeke's eyes went wide. "Sweet, what does she say?"

"Lenore," Abara said to the bird, "who is your message for?"

"Tom!" the bird squawked.

"Whoa! How'd she know that?"

"Her trainer drove me out here, and we worked on it the whole way." He stuck a treat between the bars of the cage, and she snatched it up. "How does your power work? Can you get her to your house at a time you know your dad will be there?"

Zeke hadn't considered all the complexities of getting a creature to the right time and place. "I . . . I think so. The best time would be early in the morning. His patrol shift starts before hardly anyone else is up. If she was on the porch when he came out, there shouldn't be anyone to hear her." He stopped and thought hard for a minute. "Can I test her? See if she can go find Gabe?"

"Be my guest." Abara lifted the cage door and Lenore hopped out onto the table.

"Hey, Lenore," Zeke said. He stared at her, intent, and thought about Gabe's face, then mentally walked the route from the back door to the kitchen window. *His name is Johnnie. Can you say that?*

She stared at him in the way he'd become familiar with but didn't say anything. He sensed intelligence coming from the bird, though, in a way he hadn't with other animals. "Johnnie," he said out loud. The bird croaked two syllables that didn't sound right at all.

"Maybe that's too complicated. Try John instead."

Zeke nodded and looked Lenore in the eye. "Can you say John?"

"John! John!"

"Atta girl!" Zeke grinned, and Abara tossed a treat that Lenore plucked out of the air.

The detective then pulled out a dollar and folded it up. "Here, tell her to give this to him and to bring something back from the kitchen."

Zeke thought the instructions at her and stuck out the dollar. She wrapped a claw around it. They took her out the back door and she flew off toward the kitchen. A minute later, she came back around the corner and landed at their feet. She now clutched a spoon instead of the dollar bill. Just then, Gabe came around the same corner.

"You send this to me?" he asked, holding up the dollar bill.

"We did," Abara said. "It was a test for the bird."

Gabe nodded, smiling. "Sweet. I'm gonna hang on to this, if you don't mind." He pocketed the dollar and walked back the way he'd come from.

Abara chuckled. "Should've seen that coming. Glad it wasn't a twenty."

"So how are you gonna deliver the message?" Zeke asked.

"*We* are going to drive up near the compound tonight. That way, you can be there to give her the best instructions possible. We can talk about what the message will say on the way up, but for now, I supposed you'd better get to the stables."

Zeke said good-bye and headed to work. He felt anxious about going back up toward the compound. Spending hours alone with Detective Abara made him nervous. Could he give Lenore solid enough instructions to pull this off? He couldn't even consider what could be happening on the compound just a few days from now. How many deaths would he be responsible for? Deaths of people who'd been like family to him his whole life?

Wednesday, Aug. 2, 2017
Coeur d'Alene, Idaho

Raul called the house as they cleaned up after lunch and asked if they could come to the fairgrounds to see how the changes to the float were coming. "Also, I need measurements for Charlie and Lindsay, and I've got some sketches I'm dying to show them."

They told Raul they'd be there in an hour.

"Can we still go to the beach afterward?" Lindsay handed Chloe clean dishes from the bottom dishwasher rack. "I don't want to miss out on the lake."

"Yeah, for sure. We don't have anything else planned for the afternoon, so I'm sure you'll still get in your beach time, Miss Scrumptious Proportions."

Lindsay stuck out her tongue. "Gee thanks, Dragonfly Detective."

Charlie sighed at that pot he scrubbed. "What am I supposed to do while you guys swim?"

Chloe bristled inside and turned to put a bowl away so he wouldn't see her pinchy expression. "It's an awesome place to fly, and you can wade in with us—I doubt we'll do any real swimming, anyway."

"I'll see if my wings are recovered, I guess."

Chloe met Lindsay's eye and they shared a moment of annoyance. She'd started wondering whether she wanted to keep going out with him.

With the kitchen clean, swimsuits on under their clothes, and Chloe's and Charlie's costumes in a bag, they piled in the SUV and headed to the fairgrounds with Phil once again playing chauffeur. Raul met them at the door to the float hangar and gave them all air kisses on both sides of the face.

"I can't wait to show you how far we've come in just a day." He clapped to get the attention of the half dozen people working on the float. One of them painted a backdrop while others hung streamers from the side and two attached large wire frames, shaped like moth wings, to a saddle on their right that had taken the place of a perch. "Clear off so our heroes can see!"

They stopped working and hopped down.

Lindsay gaped. "Wow, Raul, it's amazing!"

"Yeah, it is." Chloe couldn't believe the transformation. The backdrop now bore the outline of the Hero Academy logo—a gold **HA** lined in red, inside a blue circle.

"You're too kind! It's rough still, but the ideas are beginning to be realized. You brought your costumes?" Chloe opened the bag and pulled them out. He took hers and held it up. "Swatches!"

One of his assistants hurried over with a large ring holding hundreds of small cards, each bearing a square fabric sample. She sorted through until she found similar greens and held them up for Raul to compare. "No, too yellow. Not yellow enough. That's close—one more. Yes! Perfect!" They repeated the process until they'd matched the purple, as well, then did the same with Charlie's but also held swatches up to his wings.

"Now, let me show you a few things," Raul said to the three heroes. He climbed up onto the float deck and pointed to a spot under the gold H. "You see there, that hole? It's for the driver to see through. Chloe, I put you on this side because your wings will obstruct his view a lot less than Charlie's. If you do block it, though, it's not the end of the world—he's got an observer who will sit up front here." He turned toward the front and gestured to a raised area with their code names on it. "He'll watch through here." He reached over it to indicate an area just above *Fireball* in the center, and they noticed a small window there. "Make sure you don't ever block this one. Now, since even the observer can't see a lot, they'll both be watching a spotter, who will be walking backward off to the side giving them directions. So, you can spread your wings—to show them off or to take off flying—and it won't be a problem."

"Yeah, we'll see if I can even fly," Charlie muttered.

"Why wouldn't you be able to, darling?" Raul asked.

"My wings got wet Monday, and they get damaged stupid easy by water." He looked miserable. "It's totally embarrassing."

Raul put a finger to his lips, looking thoughtful. "Hmm, I'll have to give that some thought. I'm sure I can find a solution." He snapped at an assistant, who rushed over. "Show them the chassis."

The assistant raised up the curtain circling the bottom and exposed a complex wire framework over a chassis. It had three sets of wheels, a seat in the front, and a seat and steering wheel set up in the back.

Phil peered at the setup. "Fascinating!"

"Whoa, I had no idea all that was under there," Charlie said.

Raul then told them he'd have Chloe and Charlie's saddles covered by the next day. He whisked away first Lindsay, then Charlie so he could get their measurements. When he came back, he showed them all some sketches of the costume he planned to have ready for Lindsay by Friday. They would have a fitting then and make adjustments before Saturday's parade.

"Oh my God, it's so perfect!" Lindsay stared in amazement at the red bodysuit with yellow swirls all up the sides.

"I'm delighted you think so." Raul blushed. "I kept the arms bare, both because your long limbs are so extraordinary and so we wouldn't have to worry about you setting them ablaze."

Minnie came bustling along just as they were leaving, a man in grease-stained overalls trailing behind her. Minnie wore a flowy button-down shirt covered with turtles in every color of the rainbow. "Oh, oh my! How lovely to see you all again. Phil, this is my husband Jerry. He's so excited to meet our little heroes!"

Jerry gave them blank stares and Chloe doubted he got excited about anything. Then again, with Minnie around, he didn't have to.

She looked over the float and clucked her tongue. "I do hope you're not disappointed in the float. So many changes!"

"I assure you, we're quite happy with it," Phil told her. "It's much improved."

She clenched her jaw and tried to force a smile that looked more like a grimace of pain. "The mayor will be annoyed, to say the least, that his ideas have been discarded. But, of course, we hire designers for a reason, now, don't we?" She looked toward Raul, but he made a show of ignoring her as he directed his assistants to get back to work and sent one out to buy fabric. Minnie turned back toward Phil, but he'd turned to admire another float in the works. "Well, Jerry, come see how it's all put together!" She led him around the back to show him the inner workings while everyone ignored them.

Wednesday, Aug. 2, 2017
Bruderschaft Compound, North Idaho

Tom Shepherd sat alone in the community room, staring down at his plate without seeing what was on it. He'd lost the right to sit up front with the council and instead found himself paying attention to a conversation between Naomi Jones and her mother at the next table.

"How are we out of bread?" Naomi asked. "I thought the supply run was on Tuesdays."

"It's supposed to be, but they didn't go yesterday and we're clean out of flour," her mother said.

"Why not?" the girl asked.

Mrs. Jones humphed. "Barnabas wouldn't let them. Said no one can leave for a while, not for food, not for nothing. Don't ask why." She cut off her daughter before the question was out of her mouth. "It ain't for us to ask, it's for us to obey."

"Yes, Ma'am. Sorry for being impertinent. What are we gonna do for food, though?"

"We still got all the beans and carrots we was gonna trade, and the early potatoes should be ready soon. Not that those work for sandwiches, mind you, so we'll have to get creative for a while." Mrs. Jones sighed. "We'll make do, and trust God to provide."

"Yes, Ma'am. Praise be to God."

Tom sighed to himself. That Naomi was a good girl. She'd have been a good wife for his son. Would he ever know his future daughter-in-law, now? Or his grandchildren? He pushed his half-full plate away. He just didn't have an appetite.

As he left the community room, he realized he'd passed more empty benches than usual and that the empty ones belonged to the soldiers. He thought back and realized he hadn't seen a single one who'd headed south two days ago.

Soldiers leaving the compound on foot under cover of darkness. Supply runs canceled. *What the hell's going on?*

Wednesday, Aug. 2, 2017
Coeur d'Alene, Idaho

"It's pretty empty today, even for a weekday," Chloe said when she saw the beach. A handful of people lounged in chairs and a few others waded out into the water.

Lindsay gasped. "Whoa, it's gorgeous."

Lake Coeur d'Alene glistened in the sunlight and reflected the towering Coeur d'Alene Resort on their left and wooded hills to the right. A sailboat drifted off around the bend in the distance.

Phil chuckled as he set up a chair. "Once people spot you and Charlie in the air, it'll get more crowded, I'm sure."

"Hope not." Chloe eyed Charlie to see how he'd reacted to the flight comment, but he didn't seem grouchy.

Lindsay dropped her towel in a heap and stripped down to her suit. "Come on, Chloe!"

Chloe kicked off her shoes and reached back to unhook her shirt's harness-back. "Go ahead, Scrumptious, I'll catch up."

Lindsay took off, sprinting across the sand and wading in thigh deep. She whooped and turned back to motion her roommate to follow.

"Are you coming?" Chloe asked her boyfriend.

He sighed. "Even to wade, I'd have to hold my wings up the whole time. It gets uncomfortable pretty quick, and I want to be able to fly Saturday."

He looked so miserable that she felt bad for being annoyed. "I'm sorry. I'll stay here with you if you want."

"No, you go ahead, Wyld." He gave her a wistful grin. "I'll see if I can get any decent altitude and cruise over the lake."

"Cool. Good luck!" She jogged off to join Lindsay. When a shadow passed over them seconds later, she looked up and smiled. Charlie's wings were performing pretty well and were gorgeous with the sun shining through them. She did notice, though, that he didn't stay up there for long, and the left wing seemed to drag as he headed back to where her dad sat, reading a book. She tried not to think about it as she and Lindsay laughed and splashed around, but she did hope this didn't put him in a bad mood. *I feel like a babysitter.*

CHAPTER THIRTEEN

Thursday, Aug. 3, 2017
Bruderschaft Compound, North Idaho

Tom Shepherd stepped out onto the little front porch of the house where he now lived alone. At least losing status didn't also mean losing the house. Not yet, anyway. The sun wouldn't rise for another hour, and he was grateful for the dark. His head hurt enough without the sun in his eyes.

"Tom!"

He startled at the odd voice, which was loud enough to make his head throb. He looked around but didn't see anyone.

"Tom!"

He jumped again as he realized it came from under the porch swing. He bent over and peered underneath. "What the hell?"

A raven hopped out and flew up onto the railing. "Tom! Message. Zeke!"

Tom shook his head to clear it, then regretted the motion when a stabbing pain pierced his temple. The pain confirmed it for him—he really was awake and wasn't dreaming. Also, not still drunk, since then he wouldn't have the hangover.

The bird held out a talon toward him with a pouch wrapped around it. Tom untied it, slow and steady, expecting the bird to take off at any moment. Instead, it stood still and stared at him as if a bird talking to a man on his porch an hour before sunup was perfectly normal. Tom untied the strings holding the pouch in place pulled out a folded-up note.

Mr. Shepherd,

Your son is safe. He realized too late you'd planned to take him off the compound and wants to talk to you. Before that can happen, though, I need your help. Zeke and his friend got some information to me and my associates and we will be acting on that information soon. If you help us out, it'll save the lives of a lot of people, especially those on the compound.

If you choose not to help us, you'll be among those in harm's way and may never get to say good-bye to your son.

I hope you'll decide to do the right thing. If so, attach a message to the bird and tell her 'Car.' She'll understand. Let me know how I can get you a phone.

On the back, Zeke had scrawled a short message. Tom recognized the sloppy penmanship right away.

Pa,

I'm sorry I left and messed up your plan. Sure wish I could see you right now. I'm staying someplace I like well enough and got plenty to eat and keep me busy. Please say you'll help. This guy's real nice and don't want to see no one get hurt.

Zeke

Tom slumped down onto the porch swing, note clutched in his hand. What information could Zeke have, he wondered, to be able to pass it along to the cops? Or was it the Feds? *No way he could've known about Op 88. Is there?* He knew Zeke could never get on a computer, but that Gabe kid sure could, he was damn certain of that. If that information was in the hands of law enforcement, things were about to get real damned ugly.

But here it was, a chance at redemption. He knew he could never be forgiven for all his terrible, hateful acts, but here was an opportunity for him to do just one thing right. Most people never got a second chance.

He told the bird to stay where it was and went into the house for paper and pen. A few minutes later, the raven took off with a brief message in the little pouch.

I'm in. Drop a phone by the gate you left from. Camera still ain't working.

Thursday, Aug. 3, 2017
Kootenai Boys' Ranch, Near Coeur d'Alene, Idaho

"How'd it go?" Gabe asked.

"It went fine." Zeke was dead on his feet, having slept precious little in Abara's back seat, then returning just in time for his morning shift. Mucking stalls demanded a lot more physically than minding sheep ever had. He'd just gotten back to the room, looking forward to a nap before dinner, when Gabe came over.

He yawned and stretched his legs out on the bed, hoping his friend, who sat at the desk, would get the hint. "Lenore did just like she was supposed to, and my pa sent back a note saying he was in. We dropped off a phone for him and everything. The camera you took out still ain't working."

Gabe smirked. "I'm not surprised. I cut the wires and threw rocks at the lens until it shattered."

Zeke laughed. "Well, it's a good thing, 'cause it gave us a spot we know ain't being watched." He grew quiet and serious. "Gabe, are we doing the right thing? I mean, I know it's right to stop *Operation 88*, but helping the cops take down the compound? People are gonna get killed, and it's all because of us."

Gabe leaned forward. "Look at it this way. Those guys on the compound, the leaders and the soldiers, they know it's illegal to have the weapons they have, and the explosives they have. They're stockpiling those so they can start a freaking war with the United States government. That's treason, dude. My father knows it. Your father knows it. They all know it. They also know about other groups who've been taken out by the Feds, and that's why they have evacuation plans for the women and children. If we don't take them down, with what we know? Then every damned thing they ever do is on us. Everyone they assassinate, every business they rob. Every kid they beat and publicly humiliate, too. Every member they execute. Every drop of blood, on our hands. I know I don't want to live with that. Even if it means I get my own father killed or thrown in prison for the rest of his life. 'Cause see, he knew what he was doing, and he knew what the consequences could be. So that's on him. The people who will have better lives because Butler's Shaft is gone? That's what's on us. That's the way I see it, anyway."

"Yeah. Yeah, I suppose you're right." Zeke didn't quite buy it, but the reasoning made sense. Maybe, in time, he'd feel the way Gabe did. "At least maybe my pa will get out of there okay. And Naomi."

Thursday, Aug. 3, 2017
Bruderschaft Compound, North Idaho

"Something's up, but I don't know what," Tom said into the burner phone. He leaned against the pole where the broken camera was still mounted. With the soldiers all gone, everyone had to fill in on extra jobs, meaning no one would get around to camera repair for a while. Not that anyone talked about the soldiers being gone—they all knew better. People accepted the extra work assignments and kept their heads down.

"Why do you think that?" Detective Abara asked.

Tom recounted the soldiers' deployment and lack of supply runs. "Nothing about *Op. 88* was supposed to happen for weeks, so something changed after I got kicked off the council. Two council members are gone, too. Edwards and Callahan."

The sounds of a keyboard clacking came through the phone for a few seconds. "Wait, do you mean Mark Edwards and Danny Ray Callahan? The sniper and the explosives expert?"

"Yep, that'd be them."

They went over how all those people could've left the area undetected and then arranged a time for their next phone call. "You'll slip away and alert me if anything changes, correct?"

"Yep. Now you be sure to tell my son I'm doing everything I can."

"I will, Tom. He's a good kid, your Zeke. You should be proud of him."

The call ended and Tom hung his head. He knew whatever good Zeke had in him had nothing to do with his father.

Thursday, Aug. 3, 2017
Coeur d'Alene, Idaho

Abara assembled the Task Force. As they filed into the conference room, they found him with his head in his hands.

"We got a problem, Boss?" Supon asked. He wore a wrinkled button-down shirt and a novelty tie sporting a coffee stain.

"Problems, plural. Big ones." He looked up at them—Supon with his bedraggled look, Moy always sharp and crisp, Henderson like a kid fresh from Basic Training. "The first problem is, the compound leaders know they're being watched. So how did word get out?"

Moy gasped and Henderson's eyes opened wide. Abara caught Supon's eyes dart toward Henderson and back. While Abara didn't want to suspect his people, he'd be foolish not to. On the other hand, they might know of potential leaks he hadn't considered. He might be tipping his hand by telling them, though, so he'd developed a contingency plan.

"Sir," Henderson began. "We had to get authorization and make arrangements for the satellite surveillance. My guess is that someone involved in the process is either compromised or sloppy."

Did he glare at Supon when he said sloppy? Abara wasn't sure, but he'd seen something. He supposed it was possible Henderson just considered his colleague a slob. In truth, Supon could look schlumpy in a tailored tuxedo. It made him perfect for undercover work, though, because he didn't look like a cop even when he tried.

"Molly, you follow up with everyone involved. Background checks, interviews, the works. See if anything about their lifestyles has changed recently, too." Abara pulled a piece of paper with side-by-side mug shots from a folder on the table. "About half their soldiers have left the compound and so have these two men. I need to know why. Edwards was a military sniper, and Callahan has expertise in explosives. Both men have extensive criminal records, but so far nothing that's earned either of them serious time. Henderson, you get all eyes looking for them. They don't have fuck all for traffic cameras up near Blanchard and Clagstone, but I want you to track down every bit of surveillance cam footage you can from between here and there. If we can find out where Edwards and Callahan went, we'll likely know where the soldiers are headed. All these men should be considered armed and extremely dangerous."

"How many soldiers are we talking about?" Moy asked.

"Thirteen. Fifteen if those two are with them."

Supon leaned forward. "I'm assuming they left the compound on foot, through the forest?" Abara nodded, and Supon gave him a shrug in return. "So, shouldn't we be looking for a big group traveling together?"

"Certainly, keep an eye out for that, Henderson. From what my contact told me, they'll likely borrow vehicles from sympathizers in the area and leave town at different times in different directions, two or three in a vehicle. I've got a list of names. Mat, I need you to pull up backgrounds and photos on them."

"When are we moving in, Sir?" Henderson asked.

"We're still on track for early next week." He wished they could go in right now, but the Feds wouldn't budge on their timeline. "ATF and Homeland Security should be in place Monday afternoon. State and both counties will be ready to move the second we get confirmation from the Feds, and I'm still waiting to hear yea or nay in regard to Just Cause."

Moy cocked her head. "But if a bunch of soldiers are off the compound, this would be the best time to strike."

"If it were all up to me, we'd move now," Abara said. "Then again, I don't know that it's wise to take my contact's intel at face value. If we go in without confirmation, we could be walking into a trap. That's part of why I need you to verify those men are off the property. Moy, Henderson, you're dismissed. Mat, stick around for a minute."

Moy and Henderson left the office.

"What's up, Sam?" Supon asked.

Abara sighed, leaning forward on his elbows. "Do you trust Henderson?"

"If I'm being honest, no, I don't. Not entirely."

"Any particular reason?"

Supon loosened his tie's messy knot. "I can't put my finger on it, exactly. Maybe it's 'cause he reminds me of the guys on the Aryan compound, how they were all about military precision and discipline. Maybe it's 'cause he's new and young and in great shape and I'm jealous. Like I say, I don't have a specific reason. I just don't trust him."

"I need you to keep an eye on him for me. Let me know if there's anything suspicious about him."

Supon nodded. "Will do, Boss."

Next, Abara drove over to the ISP headquarters and found a tidy office where a tidy Henderson sat behind a tidy desk, talking on the phone. He motioned for the detective to come in and have a seat. Abara smiled to hear he was arranging a sweep of gas stations to see what security camera footage might be available. *The kid's efficient, no doubt about that.*

Henderson hung up the phone. "Detective, this is a surprise."

"I need to ask you a question, and I don't want anyone to overhear."

The trooper looked concerned and waited.

Abara leaned forward, studying the trooper. "Do you trust Supon?"

Henderson sat in silence for a few moments, then swallowed. "No, Sir. I do not."

"Any particular reason?"

"Permission to speak freely, Sir?"

"This isn't the military, Robert. When I ask you a question, you damn well better speak freely."

Henderson gave a curt nod. "Very well. A few months ago, I went into a dive bar looking for a missing person, and Supon was there, playing pool with some rather . . . unsavory characters. One of them had a swastika tattooed on his neck."

Abara snorted. "That's it? You know he does undercover work."

"Yes, but he spoke to me. Called me by name."

"So, he wasn't working."

"That's correct, Sir. I asked around for the names of his companions and looked them up. Nothing came up on the one with the tat, but the other . . ."

"What about him?"

"He had ties to the Aryan Nations and two splinter groups from after Butler's death." Henderson got a file from his drawer and handed it to Abara. "Recent ties, Sir."

Abara opened the file. He sucked in a breath when he saw the face on the printed-out rap sheet. He'd know those eyes anywhere. "Holy hell. That's Jeremiah McNash."

"Yes, Sir. His list of crimes is extensive. And disturbing."

"You're damn right it is." *Why would Mat associate with McNash? Digging for information? Was McNash a snitch, maybe for a case unrelated to the Task Force?* "I need you to pull some strings for me—get a trooper to tail McNash and another one for Supon. I want to know if they talk, and if so, what they say."

"Hey, Fly Girl, can I talk to you for a minute?" Heather stood in the doorway to Chloe's bathroom, where her daughter stood in her backward bathrobe with a towel around her hair.

"Yeah, sure, Mom. What's up?"

"A couple of days ago, at breakfast, you made a crack about whether you should be jealous now, and dad and I have both noticed Charlie acting a little sulky. What's going on?"

Chloe sighed. "He's been all moody over his wings not working when they get wet. Even before he got here though, when I told him about Zeke and Gabe, he got all possessive."

"Has he acted like that before? Like, back at school?" Heather leaned against the door jamb, eyebrows pinched together in an expression Chloe had seen plenty of times on her own face.

Chloe shook her head. "Not since we've been together. At one point, early in the school year, we were out flying, and he asked if I was going out with Zayden. When I told him I was, he got really distant and then made an excuse to leave. I think he was just upset, though, and that's totally understandable, right?"

"Yeah, if he liked you and found out you were with someone else, that's pretty normal," Heather said. "How did he act toward you after that?"

Chloe took the towel off her head and brushed through her hair. "He was totally sweet. That's why I started liking him in the first place. Why?"

"Jealousy and possessiveness are red flags." She put a hand up when Chloe started to object. "Just hear me out. I like Charlie. He usually seems like a good kid. Jealousy stems from insecurity, and we all feel insecure sometimes. If he's acting possessive, though, like he owns you or wants to control you . . ."

"Yeah, that's a deal-breaker, for sure." Chloe put the brush down and turned to face her mom. "The jealousy bugged me, but he seems to be over it. He's never tried to tell me what to do or anything like that, and if he does . . . Well, you know how stubborn I get."

Her mom chuckled. "That I do. Promise me you'll dig in your heels, just like you always did with your coaches even though we told you not to."

Chloe grinned. "Deal! The sulking, though. Honestly, I don't know if I can handle much more of it."

Phil knocked and called through the bedroom door. "Chlo, how soon can you be ready to go? Raul called and says he has some outfits ready for Charlie and Lindsay."

Lindsay jumped up and down and squealed as she looked at herself in the boutique's three-way mirror. "It's so perfect and amazing! I never want to wear anything else again!"

Raul beamed at his creation—a red bodysuit that hugged Lindsay's willowy frame, with yellow swirls like stylized flames climbing up the sides. It was sleeveless and featured a collar that should've seemed out of place on a supersuit yet looked perfect on this one.

"Wow, Linds, it's awesome." The color set off her black hair and pale complexion like nothing Chloe had ever seen her roommate wear. "Well done, Raul!"

The designer fanned himself with his hand. "Oh, thank you so much. 'Twas my honor to create it." He turned to Charlie. "I haven't had time to finish the runway piece I'm designing for you, but I have come up with a remedy for your water problem." He motioned for Charlie to follow him into the back room. A few minutes later, Charlie emerged with his wings covered in holographic clear plastic. He looked skeptical.

"Oh, those are cool." In truth, Chloe didn't like them, but she wanted to keep things positive. "Can you fly with them on, do you think?"

Charlie shrugged.

"I hope so, but I can't promise that on such short notice," Raul said. "These will, at least, keep them dry when you're out walking around. And don't they look divine?"

Lindsay cocked her head. "You look way more . . . *butterfly*-ish."

Charlie winced. Raul beamed again, as if her comment were exactly what he wanted to hear.

A skeptical Charlie studied them in the mirror. "I guess they look pretty good. Better than the rain gear I usually throw over them, anyway. Let's go outside and see if I can fly."

They all followed him out to the parking lot. He gave his wings a test flap, then beat them harder. The plastic made a loud crinkly noise.

Charlie shook his head, deflated. "I don't think it's gonna work. They're cool, though. Thanks."

Raul looked disappointed but promised to keep working on it and bid them a warm farewell. He then turned with a flourish and went back inside. Charlie asked Chloe to help him get the wing covers off, but Lindsay wore her costume home.

CHAPTER FOURTEEN

Friday, Aug. 4, 2017
Coeur d'Alene, Idaho

"Madam Senator, it's a pleasure to speak with you. I'm sorry to interrupt your work," Abara said into the phone. With the Bruderschaft threat and *Operation 88*, his gut told him he needed to keep her as far from his town as possible.

"What is it you need, Detective, that my assistant can't handle?" Nancy Simmons asked, voice curt. "I'm busy."

"It's about Bruderschaft . . ."

"Your police chief spoke to my assistant, and she briefed me thoroughly, I assure you."

"Yes, Madam Senator. We have new information, though, and it directly concerns you. I'll be frank—I want you to stay away from Coeur d'Alene."

She sighed. "I'm listening but make it quick."

She remained silent while he gave her a synopsis of the group's plans and how they appeared to have changed after Zeke and Gabe left the compound. He wasn't at all sure she paid attention until he finished the briefing and she proceeded to grill him on every detail.

"Has the parade been canceled?" she asked at last.

"No, Ma'am. The chief and the sheriff urged the mayor to cancel it, but he refused. He said it wouldn't look good for the city to cave to a mere possibility of a threat, given what this parade represents."

"I agree with the mayor," Senator Simmons said. "I'll be arriving early in the morning, along with my security detail. You needn't worry. They are quite competent, and I'm sure I'll be just fine."

"Please, Ma'am, if you could take a moment to reconsider—"

"Thank you for your concern, Detective. Perhaps I'll see you tomorrow."

The line disconnected, and Abara swore under his breath. He wished he had something concrete to give the mayor and the senator, but the Task Force hadn't come up with anything. No one could find the missing Bruderschaft soldiers. He didn't blame anyone for not listening to his gut, but he knew better than to ignore it himself.

The phone rang and he recognized the Washington, D.C. area code. He snatched it up on the first ring. "Detective Samuel Abara."

"Detective Abara, this is James Forsythe from the Parahuman Resources Agency. I wanted to let you know I've approved your governor's request for backup from Just Cause Seattle. I also put Just Cause Denver on standby, in case things get too crazy up there."

Abara breathed a sigh of relief, despite the adrenaline burst he got from talking to his long-time idol. "Thank you, Sir. That's the first good news I've had today. What's the timeline?"

"The Seattle team is yours as of Monday. I understand that's when the Feds are sending you help, as well."

"That's correct, Sir. If we have any developments before then, can I call them in sooner?"

Forsythe paused. "*Have* things changed?"

"We've had some strange developments, and my gut says something's up. Something big. In case I'm right, I want to know what my options are." He knew Forsythe's reputation from his Just Cause Denver days. He'd been known as a maverick who got good at asking for forgiveness due to what some people—including a lot of elected officials—considered recklessness. Abara had always considered his actions sensible and proactive.

"I'll send you a list of Seattle and Denver team members who are available right now, along with how long it'd take them to deploy, plus the Champions and independents in your area. The rest of Seattle will be trickling in over the weekend. I'll have someone there keep you in the loop."

"I'll send you the contact information for my second in command." Abara copied Molly Moy's information into an email and sent it off to the PRA director. "I'm heading up toward the compound soon to confirm a hunch, so I may not be reachable."

"Be careful, Detective. I've read up on Bruderschaft. Like you, I've learned to trust my gut, and I've got a bad feeling about this one."

Friday, Aug. 4, 2017
Kootenai Boys' Ranch, Near Coeur d'Alene, Idaho

Zeke sat on the white horse and looked at how far off the ground he sat. His head spun with exhilaration.

"You never been on a horse before?" Tyler, the boy teaching him to ride, looked up at him from the ground.

Zeke shook his head. "No, I was raised with sheep and chickens and cows, but no horses."

The boy spat on the ground. "I never seen no one so good with horses who ain't never rode one."

"Yeah, I guess I'm good with animals." Zeke tried to pass it off as casual but wasn't sure it worked. "I always wanted to ride a horse. This is pretty cool."

While Tyler got his own horse ready and mounted, Zeke concentrated on getting his horse, Comet, to stamp his hoof. At first, the big animal just shifted a little. Zeke tried to give his mental words a soothing tone and tried again. *Paw the ground. Twice.* Comet pawed once, then tossed his head and nickered.

"Comet, you stay calm now, damn you," Tyler said. "He's pretty chill most of the time, but now and then, he gets stubborn AF. You gotta be tough with him, let him know who's boss."

Comet, paw the ground twice. Now!

The horse went stiff for a moment, then pawed, and pawed again. Zeke grinned.

Tyler taught him the basics of horseback riding and declared Zeke a natural. By the time he took off Comet's tack, Zeke felt like he had a good bond with the horse. He almost regretted that he couldn't stay at the ranch long-term.

Friday, Aug. 4, 2017
Boise, Idaho

Jeffrey hurried to complete the logistical preparations for the senator's trip north and pack everything they'd need for a mobile office. Senator Simmons didn't believe in taking time off from her senatorial duties, and that translated into additional work for all her staffers.

"What's up with you today?" Tamara asked. "I expected you to wrap this up before lunch, not rush around until we have to leave for the airport."

"Sorry, Tam. I'm just . . . distracted, I guess." He grabbed for a stapler and knocked over a pen cup, spilling ballpoints all over the floor.

Tamara dropped down on her knees to gather them while he continued packing.

"Damn, I'd say you're distracted. Is it the marching band again?" She stood and put the pen cup back on the desk, but farther from the edge.

Jeffrey sighed. "It is, but I can't make sense of it yet."

"Tell me what you're forecasting."

Jeffrey eyed her, considering. Tamara worked closer with the senator than anyone. Maybe she'd know something he didn't that could help fit the pieces together. "Okay. I keep seeing a boy. Not a little kid, a teenager. He's on a ranch somewhere, and there's horses and a raven—it's named *Lenore*. How ridiculously on-the-nose is that? Anyway, I feel like he needs to be at the parade."

"Why would some random kid need to be there?"

"I don't know yet, but it's important." Jeffrey picked at his bottom lip, willing another vision to come even though that never worked. "It feels . . . Tamara, it feels like a life-and-death moment."

She looked concerned. "You don't think the senator is in danger, do you?"

He shrugged. "I wish I knew. It's possible, though."

Tamara tapped her foot as she thought for several seconds. "Tell me everything you *do* know. What does this kid look like?"

Jeffrey closed his eyes and focused. "Tall. Husky. Short hair, like in a buzz cut."

"Do you see anyone else?" she asked. "Or is he alone except for the animals?"

"I caught a glimpse of another kid with him. Shorter, skinny. And I don't know why, but I get the feeling he's . . ."

"He's gay?"

Jeffrey looked her in the eye, stunned. "Why did you guess that?"

She raised an eyebrow. "Am I right?" He nodded, and she gave him a crooked smile. "I think I know who they are. The Coeur d'Alene police are worried about a situation up there, and these two boys are involved."

Friday, Aug. 4, 2017
Bruderschaft Compound, North Idaho

Tom slipped into out-back after jimmying the lock. He pulled a bandanna from his pocket and wiped the knob the way Detective Abara had told him, then mopped his sweaty brow.

The next part would be harder because it would require Tom to touch a computer for the first time in his life—or so he and Abara had expected. Once he entered the office, it became apparent he wouldn't need to use the computer at all, for the council had lain everything out in the open.

A map of Coeur d'Alene hung on the wall with a route traced in red. Tom knew from previous plans that a large black **X** on a building meant a sniper, and the smaller **X**s along the streets would be gunman locations.

Tom took pictures with the phone, swearing at it when the first ones came out blurry. Then he got some clear images, but how would he send them? He didn't know. He'd have to wait for the bird to contact him and then arrange to get the phone itself to the detective.

He took one more look at the map and noticed a yellow **X**. That meant an explosive. He took a picture of it, too.

Time to leave. Opening the door was the most dangerous moment of the operation since he had no way to know who might be on the other side. He couldn't risk opening the window shutters, plus he couldn't see much of the danger zone from there, anyway. Hand on the knob, he put his ear against the door and listened. Nothing. He turned the knob and cracked the door the tiniest bit.

Someone yelled, just an unintelligible sound. From nearby.

Certain he was caught, Tom debated between throwing the door open and putting his hands up and grabbing a gun from the office and going out Ruby Ridge style.

Then the scream came again, only this time, he realized it was a bird's caw. Not a raven's, though. He wished he could ask the damned thing if the coast was clear, then wondered if his son could do that.

Fuck this, sneaking around! He was a man, dammit, and men didn't act this way. He flung the door open and jumped back when he found himself face-to-face with Barnabas' wife, Charity Clark, who carried a caddy of cleaning supplies.

She yelped in surprise. "Tom Shepherd, what in Heaven's name are you doing out here?"

"What, like I never been in this building before?"

"That was when you were on the council." Her hands went to her hips. "You have no more business being in here now than Judas had at the foot of the cross."

Tom drew himself up to his full height and stepped forward, so he loomed over her. "I'll never set foot in here again, I promise you that, and you'd best never say anything about this time."

"You don't scare me, Tom. You think after being married to Barnabas for twelve years and teaching school for ten, I'm still that meek little girl you used to pick on?"

He put his hands on either side of her waist and yanked her up against him. The caddy fell to the ground, spilling bottles and sponges at their feet. "Oh, no. I know very well how much woman you are. You ain't forgot that night, have you, after my wife got sent away? When you came by to drop off dinner and . . . comfort me?"

She struggled but he held her tight. "I'll scream, Tom, I swear I will."

"No, you damn well won't, Charity. Not unless you want your husband to know all the dirty things you did with me. 'Cause I know you ain't done half those things with him. He'd've cast you out like the whore of Babylon."

She paled. "You wouldn't. He'd kill us both."

Tom smirked. "Oh, trust me. I'll be ready to shoot first, although I just might let him beat the holy Hell out of you before I kill him."

"Fine, I won't say nothing." She managed to break his hold on her and step back, smoothing her rumpled dress. "But I know how to fire a gun, too, and I'll drop you dead if I find you anywhere near my house again."

"Deal." Tom swatted her on the rear. He tried to saunter away, but his nerves wouldn't allow him to do anything but rush back into the woods where he was supposed to be on patrol.

Before long, he realized he'd slipped his flask out of an inside pocket. He needed a drink something fierce but didn't dare. If he fell asleep before the bird came, it'd mess everything up and he'd never see his son again. He looked at the flask for an eternity, then went to slip it back into his pocket.

With it halfway in, he paused and withdrew it again. He had his chance for redemption. He couldn't screw up. Not this time. After a longing look, he chucked the flask off into the dense trees and walked away.

Friday, Aug. 4, 2017
Coeur d'Alene, Idaho

"Did Jeremiah get the job done?" Edwards asked.

"He's bein' paranoid again, said someone was tailing him," Callahan told him as he cut through an alley, gloved hand holding on to the burner phone. "So, I met his lady there and put it on the float myself."

Edwards sighed. "That ain't no good. You could've been caught on surveillance cams."

"What, you think I'm some kinda idiot? His lady turned those off. Damn, but she's ridiculous in her kitty sweater and that ugly-ass gummy smile."

"You sure got that right. You comin' back now?"

Callahan paused at a dumpster. "Yep. Gotta pick up some dinner and then I'll head back."

"Hurry up," Edwards said. "I'm hungry and I ain't got time to go out."

Callahan knew his partner would be going over the guns all frigging day. He couldn't understand why it took so long to prep an M14 and three Skorpions, but then Edwards was the firearms expert, not him. Callahan thought he could rig up all of Coeur d'Alene to explode in the time it took Edwards to clean and load a single weapon.

He said he'd make it quick, hung up, and tossed the phone into the dumpster. He was glad to get the glove off—it made his hand all sweaty, and it looked pretty damned suspicious to walk around in the middle of summer with a glove on. He stuck to the alleys as much as possible and kept his head down.

It was almost time.

CHAPTER FIFTEEN

Saturday, Aug. 5, 2017
Near Bruderschaft Compound, North Idaho

As the sun rose over the mountains, Sam Abara watched for Lenore's return and marveled that such beautiful land could be home to so much hate. He'd found an old shed to hole up in just a few miles from the compound's rear entrance. He peered through the ragged hole where the wood had rotted away.

Staking this whole operation on a bird and a barely literate racist. He sighed and shook his head, certain this would be the time Lenore got distracted by some male's impressive tail feathers. Just moments later, though, she burst through the trees and headed right for the shed as instructed. He went out to meet her.

She landed on his arm and held out the talon with the message bag attached. He pulled it out, recognizing Tom Shepherd's juvenile scrawl.

Ditective,
I got pichers of a map but I don't no when they gonna hit it. Black Xs are gunmen, the yellow one is where they'll blow something up. I'll put the phone at the drop sight. Thought it mite be to heavy for the bird.

Sam cursed in frustration. *A map of what, you inbred hick? Why didn't you just send them to me?* He realized he'd made an error, though—he knew how un-tech-savvy Shepherd was and didn't plan accordingly. *So now I get to make a long hike and hope I'm not spotted along the way.*

He turned to Lenore, who tilted her head and gave his shirt pocket an expectant stare. Abara chuckled and withdrew a treat for her. "Who'd have guessed you'd be the more reliable one, eh?"

Saturday, Aug. 5, 2017
Coeur d'Alene, Idaho

Jeffrey shifted from one foot to the other and glanced at the time on his phone. The Coeur d'Alene Resort and streets around it were nice enough, but the rest of the town had a tired air to it. He mentally urged the detective to hurry, so the senator wouldn't notice his absence.

Beyond all the desks where officers sat over their keyboards, a door opened and a tall, severe woman in professional attire strode toward him.

"I'm Detective Moy," she said. "You have a question for the Task Force?"

"I do. Thank you for seeing me." Jeffrey handed her a business card. "Senator Simmons would like to meet the boy who brought you the information on Bruderschaft. Can you tell me where he's staying?"

The detective's brow creased. "I'm afraid I can't, for his safety. Give the senator my apologies."

Damn it, damn it, damn it! His mind spun. He didn't know why this boy was so important, and Tamara refused to bring it up to the senator until he did. He knew his forecasts well enough, though, to know something bad would happen if he didn't get that kid to the parade. He had to make it happen in just a couple of hours. His mind hit on something from his vision and, for some reason, being in this woman's presence helped him understand it.

"Of course, we wouldn't want to compromise his safety, especially after all he's been through. What about the messenger bird, though? The raven, Lenore? The senator is a big fan of birds and would love to see it while she's in town." He had to work at keeping a straight face—Nancy Simmons hated anything messy, and that meant animals. The thought of a raven on her arm, it's talons digging into her tailored suit jacket . . .

Moy smiled. "Lenore's pretty amazing, I gotta say." She grabbed a business card and scribbled a name and phone number. "I'm the one who got her involved—her trainer's a good friend."

Jeffrey thanked her and left, then stopped at the coffee stand and raced back to the hotel. He got to the senator's room just behind the room service cart.

"We have excellent coffee. You didn't have to go out for it," the waiter said.

Jeffrey flashed a weary grin. "The senator is particular about her brand." At least it had given him an excuse to get out. Now he had to find another one so he could get close to that bird and its trainer.

Saturday, Aug. 5, 2017
Kootenai Boys' Ranch, Near Coeur d'Alene, North Idaho

Zeke, Gabe, and the rest of the boys sat on the floor in the common room, which housed the sole TV on the ranch. It hadn't been on yet during their stay.

They'd been called here to watch a movie—a post-Saturday-morning-chores tradition—and then the parade. As he did anytime the boys were all in one room, Pastor Ken took the opportunity to read from scripture. In the four days since he'd arrived, Zeke had heard several new passages and some new interpretations of familiar ones, but nothing had prepared him for what Pastor Ken read that morning.

"When a stranger resides with you in your land, you shall not do him wrong. 'The stranger who resides with you shall be to you as the native among you, and you shall love him as yourself, for you were aliens in the land of Egypt. I am the Lord your God.'"

Pastor Ken closed the Bible.

Zeke raised his hand. "Pastor, Sir?"

"Yes, Joseph?"

"Can you read that last part again, the part about the stranger?"

He nodded and recited the line from memory.

Zeke scowled, trying to reconcile this new bit of scripture with his upbringing. "So, does that mean God wants us to treat foreigners like they're . . . not foreigners?"

"That's exactly what it means, and it doesn't apply just to foreigners—it refers to anyone who's an outsider, anyone who's considered different from you or most of society."

An older boy with a crew cut snickered. "Yeah, except for faggots. God hates them." Several boys laughed.

Pastor Ken clapped his hands to get their attention. "The people who say that don't understand God or his word. God hates no one. He created us all and he loves us all, and Jesus died so each and every one of us might find salvation. As it says in Romans 2:11, God does not show favoritism."

With a final admonishing look at Crew Cut, Pastor Ken turned on the TV and started the movie.

"Dude, you okay?" Gabe asked Zeke. "You look pale."

"If God loves everyone, even people who are different," he whispered, "then . . . that means He loves me, too."

Saturday, Aug. 5, 2017
Coeur d'Alene, Idaho

"I'm sorry, but Lenore is . . . not available right now," the raven's trainer, Janine Martin, said on the phone.

She had one of those North Idaho accents with an incongruous Midwestern bent. "I might be able to arrange something in a few days, but—"

"No, it has to be now!" Jeffrey winced at his outburst and worked to calm himself.

"Excuse me? Some things are more important than your boss's curiosity. If you know the service she's provided lately, you should understand that."

"I'm so sorry, of course. I understand." Jeffrey paused. Did he dare just tell this woman the truth? *Not much to lose,* he decided. Worst-case scenario, a stranger would think him crazy. People far more important to Jeffrey had called him worse. "Ms. Martin. This is going to sound ridiculous, but please hear me out. I'm a parahuman and I have premonitions. They always come true."

She fell silent for a moment, and Jeffrey feared he'd lost her. "Go on," she said at last.

"I . . . I don't understand all of it yet, but my visions are telling me I have to get Lenore to someone in particular so she can deliver a message. It's vital."

Another pause.

Jeffrey's heart pounded. "Please, Ma'am. I'm begging you."

"Who's this *someone in particular?*"

He felt so relieved he thought he might faint. "Oh, thank you! Tell Detective Abara I need the heavy-set boy and his skinny friend to get to the parade. ASAP."

She repeated it as if she were writing it down. "Is that it? The whole message?"

"It's enough."

Saturday, Aug. 5, 2017
Near Bruderschaft Compound, North Idaho

Abara stashed his backpack under a distinctive cluster of fallen trees. He didn't want it weighing him down. A quarter mile further, the trees thinned, and he saw the road marking the compound's border.

Staying concealed, he stopped to peer through the binoculars. The surveillance camera on the tall post still bore the cracks in and around the lens. Abara listened and looked both ways on the road for the rising dust cloud that would signal an approaching vehicle. All was clear.

In a crouch, he crossed the narrow road and looked through the foliage at the base of the post. Nothing. Riffling through the leaves and grasses, he didn't feel anything, either. He started to suspect Tom had set him up when his hand landed on a small canvas bag.

He crossed back to the safety of the not-Bruderschaft land and hurried through the trees until he knew he couldn't be seen from the road. He pulled out the phone. The screen still displayed one of Tom's pictures, and he recognized it right away—Front Avenue on Lake Coeur d'Alene. His gut clenched as instinct became certainty.

Abara swiped to the next image and reeled. A red line started in the shared parking lot of city hall and the public library, wound through a neighborhood to Sherman Avenue, the main street through downtown, then circled back along the waterfront to end at the library. He recognized it at once—the parade route.

His eyes flicked to the top of the phone screen. No service. He checked his own phone. No luck.

He took off at a dead run.

Saturday, Aug. 5, 2017
Coeur d'Alene, Idaho

"Expecting something?" Tamara asked.

Jeffrey looked up from his phone. Again. He checked it every few seconds. They were almost ready to usher the senator down to the Front Avenue bleachers where she'd watch the parade. He gave her a tense nod. "Still trying to get that kid here."

"Any more forecasts?"

He shook his head, then startled as the phone vibrated in his hand.

"Jumpy much?" Tamara asked.

He unlocked the screen to see a text from the bird trainer. *Texted the detective. Haven't heard back.*

Saturday, Aug. 5, 2017
Near Bruderschaft Compound, North Idaho

Abara reached the falling-down shed where he knew he had a signal and unlocked his phone. He almost clicked on a message notification, but then the phone connected to a 4G signal and he speed-dialed the chief. Lenore cawed at him from her cage, annoyed at her continued imprisonment. The phone rang several times, then clicked to indicate it had gone to the front desk. A retired cop who volunteered answered the phone—Abara would know that raspy old voice anywhere.

"This is Abara. I need the chief right away."

"Sorry, Detective, but the chief's out escorting the senator to her seat for the parade."

Abara clenched his jaw. "Transfer me to his cell, now. I have urgent news about the senator's safety."

The volunteer transferred him. The phone rang and rang and rang, then went to voicemail. "Chief, it's Detective Abara. I need you to call me back right away." He turned on Tom Shepherd's phone to transfer the images to his own phone, but the damn burner still had no service. He had to get those pictures to law enforcement.

He grabbed Lenore's cage and ran for his car.

Saturday, Aug. 5, 2017
Coeur d'Alene, Idaho

Chloe and Charlie flew up onto the float while Lindsay climbed the ladder up the back. The city hall parking lot held a long queue of floats, marching bands, mounted First Nations riders, and the usual parade fare. Their float was number seventeen, and Chloe had heard they had more than fifty entries this year.

Minnie stopped fawning over the mayor and hurried over. "Oh, good, you're here! I was so worried the float wouldn't come together. The crew just finished it this morning. You know, because of all the changes."

"It looks really good." Chloe wished the obnoxious woman would scurry off.

Minnie, showing no intention of scurrying, scanned the growing crowd for someone. "I'm pleased you like it, even though it's not to the mayor's specifications."

"Jeez, get over it, lady," Charlie muttered.

Chloe snorted. "Right?"

A trio of college-aged people arrived a few minutes later. Minnie flashed them an enormous fake smile and introduced everyone. "Lanae will walk along in front of you and communicate with David as he drives, and Erik will be his second set of eyes inside the float. Now, does anyone need anything from me? This is probably your last chance to ask."

They all stared at her until it got awkward.

"Very well, then. I must go attend to the mayor." Minnie turned and scanned the crowd. "Jerry! Jerry!" Her grim-faced husband stood several yards away talking to someone and seemed not to hear her. Chloe wouldn't have blamed him for tuning her out. Minnie's hands went to her hips. "Jeremiah McNash!" she bellowed. At last, he looked her direction, and she motioned for him to follow her.

"Damn, that lady's annoying," David said once she was out of earshot.

They all laughed.

"Right? The poor mayor!" Lindsay said.

"How long until we start?" Charlie asked.

Lanae flipped open her phone. "We've got twenty minutes. Which probably means more like forty until we move. These things never start on time, and it takes forever to get the line going."

"We're gonna get in and make sure everything's set up just right." David gave Lanae a peck on the cheek and he and Erik went underneath the deck. Lanae climbed up on the float and the four of them sat down to wait.

"How'd you learn to do this?" Chloe asked.

"The guys are in the welding program at North Idaho College. They built all the undercarriages, and the city offered to teach them how to drive. They needed spotters, and I thought it sounded kinda fun."

"Cool," Chloe said. "Do you go to NIC, too?"

"Just graduated. Are you gonna go there?" Lanae asked.

"No, I'm hoping to get an internship with Just Cause after graduation."

Lindsay laughed. "*Hoping*. Yeah, right, sister! If anyone in our class gets one, it'll be Chloe."

Chloe blushed. "Flying's not *that* great a skill. You're way more useful in combat, Scrumptious."

Lindsay smiled at the dig but continued. "Yeah, but you're a proven leader and investigator. Plus, you can get a bird's-eye view of the scene. You and Charlie will get snatched up by Just Cause right away, I'm sure."

Lanae went pale. "You guys sit around and casually talk about combat? Holy crap, I'd be terrified."

"Kinda weird, right?" Charlie chuckled. "You get used to it, though, when you have a class called Combat Training three times a week."

"I never thought about that. I don't think I could do what you guys do," she said.

"I didn't think I could, either," Chloe told her. "When I started at the Academy last year, I was in awe of the students who'd already done heroic things. But it's amazing what happens when you're put in a dangerous situation. You just respond, and then later you're like, 'Whoa, how did I do that?'"

The other paras nodded.

Lanae shivered. "I hope I never have to find out."

Edwards emerged onto the roof of the four-story brick building overlooking Front Avenue and the bleachers where the bitch senator would soon be sitting, according to Jeremiah McNash's wife. He heard the noise of the gathering crowd below but stayed out of sight.

He stretched his legs, cramped from hours spent hiding in a janitor's closet. Jeremiah had broken him in before dawn to minimize the risk of being seen by crews cordoning off the parade route. The closet was supposed to be locked when not in use, and the cops who did the security sweep of that floor didn't have the key—Jeremiah's friend's cousin, who worked for the cleaning company, made sure of it. Besides, with the door locked from the outside, how could anyone be hidden inside?

Stupid people were the conspirator's best friends, even if they didn't know it. Dumb ass cops had no idea a smart man with the right tools could get through a locked door, no problem.

Edwards pulled a padlock from one of the myriad pockets on his hunting vest and secured the door to the roof. He settled in where he would be hidden from below, and even from the twenty-story condo building on the next block, and assembled his weapon. After loading and triple checking it, he looked at his watch. Fifteen minutes until the parade was supposed to start.

Their plan was simple. Simple and elegant. He just had to get the bitch in his sights, wait for the explosion, and fire.

Then he'd break down the weapon, join the pandemonium in the streets, and run to the getaway car.

Easy as pie. The M14 ready, he looked out over the glistening lake and smiled.

Saturday, Aug. 5, 2017
Near Bruderschaft Compound, North Idaho

Abara kept one eye on the road and one eye on the burner phone's service indicator. The moment it showed bars, he skidded to a halt and transferred the pictures to his phone. Soon as he had them, he forwarded them on to Molly Moy and then called her. She picked up on the first ring.

"Molly, thank God," Abara said. "Bruderschaft is attacking the parade. I sent you pictures of their plan."

"Holy shit. I'm on it, Sam."

He hung up and opened the text message from Lenore's trainer, planning to let her know he'd have the bird home soon. When he read her message, his heart skipped a beat.

A parahuman psi on sen. Simmon's staff says she is in danger and needs the heavyset kid and his skinny friend. Needs you to send Lenore to him. Hope that makes sense to you.

Why would they need the boys? Was Bruderschaft going to somehow try to use animals in their attack or was something else at work? Whatever the reason, Abara had encountered too many parahumans to question their abilities. If a psi said they needed Zeke, then he'd get the boy there.

Lenore would never make the trip in time, so he called the Kootenai Boys' Ranch and got Julie at the reception desk.

"I'm sorry, Detective. I can't let the boys leave unattended, and we don't have an authorized driver here right now," she said. "Even given their special circumstances, I can't. I'm sorry, I wish I could help."

Time to take a page out of Juice Forsythe's playbook, he thought. "Look, I'll take the heat. This is an emergency. Isn't there even a bike or a horse or something? I'm too far away to get there in time."

She hesitated. "I suppose they could take a horse, but—"

"That'll have to do. Julie, please. Tell Zeke I need him in Coeur d'Alene as fast as he can get there and let him go. On my authority."

"Okay." She sighed. "But if I lose my job, you better have a position for me on the force."

"Consider it a promise. And thank you." He checked his watch. It wasn't long until the parade started.

He called Just Cause Seattle.

CHAPTER SIXTEEN

Saturday, Aug. 5, 2017
Coeur d'Alene, Idaho

A little girl squealed and pointed at Chloe from the sidewalk in front of modest older houses. Chloe grinned and waved at her, then tossed a handful of salt-water taffy from the barrel between their saddles. Kids scrambled after the candy.

"Okay, this is more fun than I thought it would be," she told Charlie. He grinned back and flew over above a knot of kids who'd been too far away to get the candy Chloe threw. He dropped his right in the middle of them. They dove for it.

Detective Molly Moy stood before the other officers not already on parade duty.

"Everything we know about Bruderschaft says the explosive will be remotely detonated. We can't afford to tip anyone off that we're onto them until we get the bomb handled, or they're likely to set it off early. Our best guess is that it's on the float with the parahuman kids. We have to assume Bruderschaft is monitoring our radio frequencies, so it's cell phones only. Get the word out and let's find those shooters."

Just then, Trooper Robert Henderson came on the radio. "One-delta-two-four, on scene."

"Copy. One-delta-two-four, switch to the secondary channel." A moment later, her phone buzzed with a text message from Henderson. *Copy.* She was grateful for the reliable trooper's presence but cursed Supon for not having called in yet. *Unprofessional ass. I'm done covering for him.*

Saturday, Aug. 5, 2017
Outside Coeur d'Alene, Idaho

"On Comet, on Cupid, on Donner and Blitzen!" Gabe yelled as they galloped over a hill just off the ranch.

"Would you be serious for once?" Zeke asked over his shoulder. Detective Abara's message didn't make a lot of sense, but Zeke had a bad feeling in the pit of his stomach. He knew how much Bruderschaft hated the Diversity Day Parade. With Chloe and Senator Simmons there, it was no wonder they'd decided to attack it. If anything happened to Chloe, Lindsay, or Charlie, he'd never forgive himself for not realizing what a huge target the parade represented.

Gabe had insisted on coming and neither Zeke nor Julie could dissuade him. The only way Comet would agree to such an arrangement was if the smaller boy rode behind the saddle to better distribute weight. Zeke just hoped the extra burden wouldn't slow them down and make them late for whatever they were supposed to do when they got there.

Saturday, Aug. 5, 2017
Coeur d'Alene, Idaho

Kids and adults alike oohed as flame sprouted from Lindsay's palm and vanished. Chloe and Charlie laughed at a little boy who put out his hand just like Lindsay and stared at it as if he expected it, too, to burst into flame.

Then Chloe's eye landed on a man who glared at her from under a straw cowboy hat. A swastika tattoo filled the front of his sunburned neck. He turned to say something to the man next to him, and she felt a weight in her gut as she realized who it was. Neck Tattoo's buddy was Minnie's husband. Glaring at her, he raised a phone to his mouth. She felt the hairs raise on the back of her neck.

"Charlie, I think something's wrong."

A communications tech relayed the float spotters' frequency via the radio app. Trooper Henderson, who'd traded his uniform for pressed and tailored civilian clothes, talked into his phone. "One-delta-two-four, confirm float number, over."

"Float number is seventeen and it's approaching Fifth Street now," a voice confirmed.

Henderson switched to the spotter frequency. "Float seventeen spotter and driver, can you hear me?"

"This frequency's reserved for spotters," a young female voice said.

"This is Trooper Robert Henderson of Idaho State Police and we have an emergency regarding your float. Act like nothing's wrong and listen carefully."

The head of Senator Simmons' security detail, in a poor-fitting sport coat and mirrored sunglasses, stepped across the raised platform and lowered his head. "Senator, the local PD says there's a problem. A car is coming for you."

Jeffrey overheard the warning and looked around, hoping to see two boys galloping in on a white steed.

Nothing yet. Whatever. As long as the senator got somewhere safe.

Simmons huffed. "These local cops are too twitchy for my taste. Did they say what the problem is?"

Her security head whispered in her ear. The blood drained from Nancy Simmons's face.

"Why do you say that?" Charlie asked.

She told him what she'd seen, trying to smile and wave as she did it. "It's probably nothing, just my nerves over the whole Bruderschaft thing . . ."

"I don't know, I've learned to trust your gut." Charlie tossed some candy. "Didn't Zeke say something about Bruderschaft hating this parade?"

Lindsay came back from the front of the float. "Um, guys? Lanae was just talking into her radio and got a panicked look on her face. I think something's wrong."

Charlie turned and knocked on the backdrop, which concealed Erik from view. "Is something going on?"

"Act normal," Erik said. The heroes did their best to turn toward the crowd and smile while listening to him. "At my signal, grab your friend who can't fly and get out of here."

"Why?" Charlie asked.

"Just do it."

Chloe looked back at the viewing slit. "No way, not unless you tell us why."

"The cops radioed that there's a bomb on the float. Remote detonator. I confirmed—it's under David's seat."

"How will you guys get out?" Lindsay asked.

"After we turn the corner on Third," Erik said, "we'll go straight instead of turning onto Front."

Charlie and Lindsay looked at Chloe, confused. She nodded. "There's a boat launch there. They can drive right into the lake."

"How do we know they won't blow us up before then?" Charlie asked.

Erik swallowed hard. "We don't. The cops think they'll wait until we're on Front, but I don't know why."

"Can you jump out before the float hits the water?" Charlie asked.

"I can't get out before David," Erik said. "No room back here, and he's got to keep his foot on the gas or the float will stop."

"How well do you guys swim?" Chloe asked.

"Um . . . okay-ish."

"Here's what we'll do," she said. "We'll bail right at the last minute. Charlie will carry Lindsay. And then . . ." She took a deep breath, "I'll come in the water to get you and David out." Fear blossomed in Charlie's eyes, but he nodded. He knew better than to ask her not to be a hero. "We just passed Fourth. One block to go."

"Hey, guys?" Erik called. "The cops say there are gunmen in the area. Four, they think. Once you bail off the float, they want you to find cover and stay there."

Chloe turned to look at Charlie and Lindsay. Their exchanged looks told them they all agreed—that was the last thing they'd do.

The float began to turn left onto Third.

Callahan's earpiece squawked. "Target's turning."

"The kids all ready to go?" he asked into the slender mouthpiece well camouflaged by his beard. Using kids with firecrackers, both as a signal and to confuse people, had been his idea and he was mighty proud of it. He watched the corner, so he'd be able to see the target the moment it came around.

"One, kid's ready."

"Two, kid's ready."

"Three, kid's ready."

"All right. You'll hear the signal." Callahan's finger itched to push the button that would blow up them damn freak kids. Waiting would give Edwards the best chance of getting away clean, though. If it had been anyone else on that roof, he might've gone early anyway.

Molly Moy's phone crackled and an officer's voice came over the app. "Two men on a horse are approaching the barricade, Ma'am. What should I do?"

Moy hadn't considered outside attackers moving in, but what else could it be? "Order them to stop. If they refuse, stop them by any means necessary. What's your location?"

"Sixth and Sherman," the officer replied.

Moy whirled around. A traffic cam monitor showed the horse galloping up Sixth Street a block north of the parade route. "Don't let them past the barricade under any circumstances."

A pause. Two officers stepped into view, one on each sidewalk. The taller one raised a bullhorn to his mouth, the other had his gun trained on the rider, who didn't slow. The horse came into clearer focus and Moy gasped.

"Hold your fire, hold your fire!" she yelled into the phone. Unable to breathe, she watched the scene play out. The first cop dropped the bullhorn and raised his weapon. She expected to see twin muzzle flashes, but then the two officers lowered their weapons and watched as the horse bearing Gabe and Zeke barreled past. Choking down the gorge in her throat, Detective Moy got on the phone once again. "No one's to interfere with the two boys on the white horse. Repeat, do not interfere with the boys on the horse."

Despite the ready confirmation on the radio seconds before, Edwards knew the jig was up when the security guard

whispered in the senator's ear. *Should I take the shot now?*
He couldn't stand the thought of the bitch walking away
alive. *No, that ain't the plan, and for good reason.*

Cops and security officers flanked the bleachers and
the senator herself. If she took a bullet to the head right
now, even with his silencer, at least one of them would
figure out pretty quick where the shot had come from. No,
he couldn't risk it. Waiting would give him the best chance
of getting away. He steeled himself for the explosion.

"Be safe, Wyld." Charlie squeezed her hand as the float
approached the corner where it wouldn't be turning
onto Front Street.

"Be safe, O'Neal. You too, Linds." Chloe took a deep
breath and yelled at the few people in their path, "Get
out of the way!"

People screamed and jumped aside as the float hit
the intersection. Charlie grabbed Lindsay around the
waist and took off, veering away from the parade route.
Chloe buzzed her wings and lifted off a second later,
hanging a left and staying low above the descending
slope toward the boat launch. She knew David was
accelerating, but the float lumbered along at far too
slow a pace.

Somewhere behind her, she thought she heard a gunshot.

CHAPTER SEVENTEEN

Saturday, Aug. 5, 2017
Coeur d'Alene, Idaho

Justice White glared at the back of a man with one of them towel things wrapped around his head and thought how good it would feel to take that man out of the chosen race's homeland forever. That man and a few others stood behind a row of lawn chairs. In front of the chairs, kids and a few adults perched on the curb. Everyone watched the stupid marching band and the cheerleaders passing by in their slutty outfits.

Justice was fresh out of training, antsy to prove himself to Barnabas, his father, his superior officer, and God. He just needed the go-ahead.

Callahan gave everyone a standby on the radio. It was time.

Justice got up off the cooler he'd been sitting on and crouched behind it. He glanced around. Nobody paid him any mind when they had a parade to watch instead.

His hand slipped beneath the blanket in the cooler and found the Skorpion Evo 3, his favorite gun in the world. He unfolded the stock and took off the safety, the weapon concealed behind the cooler lid. He glared again at the turbaned man, hatred seething, and longed for the signal.

Then some cops stepped in front of the next float and stopped it. Two other officers started ordering people to please exit the parade route.

No! Justice screamed inside. *They can't stop us!* He wanted to jump up and start shooting right then and there, but he remembered his training. He would wait for the signal.

Zeke thought he'd pass out from the terror of those cops pointing their weapons at him. He had no idea why they lowered their weapons and let him pass.

Once on the parade route, he veered the horse around a decorated pickup truck full of kids with different colored faces and the same color t-shirts. The truck's driver yelled at him for going the wrong way, but Zeke ignored him. Abara had told him the senator's assistant wanted him there real bad, so he went toward where the detective said the senator would be.

He turned right from Sixth Street onto Front Avenue and knew just what was happening. Across Front Street and at a slight angle from the bleachers stood a four-story brick building—the tallest on that block or the one beyond it. The perfect vantage point for a sniper.

If he was right, the woman in the business suit was the senator. Her security people blocked her at the moment, which was good—no decent sniper would shoot when his target wasn't clear.

The target would be clear at some point, though. Someone, probably Edwards, would be ready to take the shot.

With the full force of his powers, Zeke called to every bird and bug around and directed them at the roof, telling them to attack the man up there. In moments, swirling clouds of creatures moved that way en masse.

Callahan saw the front of the float and grinned. It was almost time. He told his men to stand by.

Then the moth boy grabbed the girl in red and swooped off, and the dragonfly girl flew off down the hill toward the lake.

"What the . . ."

He realized the float wasn't turning, it was going straight. Toward the water. Where his bomb wouldn't detonate.

"Ah, fuck!" He thumbed his radio. "We're found out. Abort! Abort!"

Jeffrey watched the horse round the corner and stop a block away from the bleachers. Moments later, swarms of flying insects and a flock of birds made a beeline for the roof of the building across the street. His vision clouded and smeared, and in the next moment he peered down at the bleachers—at himself and the senator. Through a scope. He saw Nancy Simmons rising, her head just starting to poke up above the security guard in front of her, felt his finger start to move . . .

And then he saw through his own eyes again, saw the senator rising. He threw himself into her and knocked her down onto the riser. The bullet cracked against the lamp post behind where her head had been.

"Sniper!" He pointed up at the roof of the brick building across the street, where dense clouds of bugs and swooping birds must have made another shot impossible. Officers streamed that direction. Simmon's security detail pulled her off the risers and rushed her down the slope behind them to a waiting police car.

The crowd erupted in panic.

Callahan said something on the radio, but Justice couldn't hear it for the drums and trombones in the street. A sound cut through the band music—a firecracker. The signal he'd been waiting for.

Justice leaped to his feet, pulling the Skorpion from under its cover. The man in the turban had startled at the firecracker and turned his head to the left. Justice opened fire and saw shock and pain as his bullets tore into the man's back. Blood sprayed everywhere.

Deafened by the gunfire, high on adrenaline, Justice swung his weapon. A woman fell, then two men. A teenager with blue hair and a rainbow beanie. He swept back the other way. Through a red haze, he yelled in triumph as bodies jerked and twisted and fell to the pavement. Two cops drew their weapons just before he cut them down.

He wished he could hear all the screams as they fell in a fan shape with its nexus at his feet.

The float hit the water just as Chloe heard multiple shots fired. She wanted to go stop whatever was happening, but first, she had two people to save.

She looped around and dove, entering the water with enough force to keep her moving toward the sinking float. The paper decor of the upper deck fell apart in moments and sodden streamers filled the water around her.

She got beneath the float, so she could come up into the undercarriage. David had managed to extricate himself already and swam toward the surface. He pointed back at Erik, tangled in waterlogged paper, struggling to get out. She gave David a thumbs-up and swam to help the trapped spotter.

Charlie dropped Lindsay on a lawn and flew over the fleeing crowd, looking for gunmen. A little boy stood alone on a sidewalk, crying. A man looking back over his shoulder ran into the kid, knocked him down, and kept running. As Charlie headed for the child, another man stepped on the boy's leg and the child screamed. The man tried to help but the swelling throng knocked him down and surged right over the two of them.

"Out of my way!" Charlie yelled as he swung low and his wings knocked people aside like bowling pins. Civilians recoiled and swerved around him as he scooped up the bleeding boy and got him above the throng. The man who'd tried to help regained his feet and took off running.

Charlie cradled the shrieking boy and realized he had no idea what to do with him. In a strange town, he didn't know where the hospital was. All the police officers below them scrambled to help people and find the shooter.

Then he remembered seeing a fire station in the neighborhood the parade had wound through to reach the main street. He headed that way.

Lindsay froze beside a hedge on the lawn of the hotel where Charlie had left her. She wanted to help all these people, but how could she do that?

As she scanned the crowd fleeing away from the lake, a loud pop caught her attention. A stern-looking man hit firecrackers out of a ten-year-old boy's hands and dragged him toward her. He looked far too calm and purposeful amid pandemonium. "You wasn't supposed to do that," he scolded the boy. "He said *abort*."

Lindsay had heard firecrackers just before the shooting started. *Was it a signal?* She sprouted flame from her palms.

The stern man spotted her in the red-and-yellow costume, stopped, and pushed the boy away.

He drew a gun.

Heart pounding, Lindsay flung out her hands and sent twin jets of flame streaking toward him. Fire engulfed him and he shrieked in pain. His gun fired once and the bullet flashed past Lindsay's ear to splinter concrete behind her. The man then collapsed onto the street in a smoldering pile, no longer resembling anything human.

Lindsay cut off her flame and gaped in shock at the results of her power. Her ears rang from the gunshot and as her hearing came back she realized the boy was screaming at her.

" . . . punish you, you murdering freak! God will punish you!" He swiped an arm across his tear-streaked face and ran.

Trooper Henderson ran against the streams of people fleeing from the parade ground. His height gave him a distinct advantage as he scanned for signs of danger.

He spotted a man crouched in a doorway, opening a cooler. He wore a cap pulled low over sunglasses and, most significantly, wasn't trying to get away. Henderson drew his weapon and pushed through the crowd, approaching the man from the side.

"Police! Let go of whatever's in your hand and stand up, nice and slow," he yelled over the din as he leveled the gun at the man's head.

The man paused, then pulled empty hands out of the cooler. With a measured calm, he stood and put his hands up.

"Leave my papa alone, you commie pig!" a kid yelled behind him.

"If your son has a weapon, tell him to drop it now," Henderson told the man.

"He don't. Just firecrackers," the man said.

"Good. Tell him to come where I can see him and sit on the ground."

The man relayed the order and a boy of about nine came into view. He appeared to be complying but then darted forward. Henderson thought he meant to hug his father, but the boy spun around with a pistol in his hand.

"Do it, son," the father ordered.

Henderson froze. He couldn't bring himself to turn his weapon on a child.

The boy pulled the trigger. Henderson dove to the left, hearing the gun's blast and feeling white-hot pain in his side. The trooper landed hard, barely keeping hold of his own weapon.

He heard fresh screams over the buzzing in his ears as a black woman recoiled from the kid with the gun. The kid swung the weapon toward her and this time, Henderson couldn't hesitate. He fired.

The boy's father drew a gun and shot himself in the head.

Edwards hurried down from the roof, swatting at flies and bees and wasps still buzzing around and praying he didn't get stung. Last thing he needed right now was anaphylactic shock. He ducked in the janitor's closet and closed the door.

The sniper jumped and stifled a yelp at a sharp stabbing pain on the back of his neck. He slapped at it and his hand came away covered in squashed wasp. "Son of a bitch, don't that just figure!"

He reached for the EpiPen in a vest pocket, but then he heard footsteps and a cop barking orders. He clutched his beloved M14, but he knew there were too many of them. He'd get a few, by God, but then they'd take him down well before the wasp sting could kill him.

Surrender? No, that wasn't an option.

The sounds receded and he thought, just maybe, they'd be dumb enough to bypass this closet twice. His throat swelled, and he considered reaching for the EpiPen, but then the door opened, and he found himself face-to-face with a service revolver. Two more officers in the hallway trained weapons on him as well.

Edwards raised his weapon, welcoming his blaze of glory.

Zeke's ears rang from the repeated blasts, and he couldn't hear the screams anymore. Through the panicked throngs of people, Zeke spotted—and recognized—the shooter, even with his back to them. Mercy White's older brother, Justice. For the first time, Zeke wished for a gun in his hand. He looked around for a police officer but didn't see any.

After a moment of feeling helpless, Zeke realized he did have a weapon. He could end this.

Comet, run him down.

Comet started forward at a trot, hesitant amid the screams and people running in every direction. *Run him down. Run him down, now! That noise will go away if you do!*

The horse took off on a run, right for Justice White's back. As they got closer, Zeke saw the sprawled mass of blood-soaked bodies. He heard wounded people scream in pain and fear, just audible over the chatter of Justice's gun as he pulled the trigger again and again.

Zeke shut his eyes as Comet bore down the boy he'd known his whole life, felt the impacts as Justice went down beneath the hooves. He turned his head to the side and vomited.

Envisioning the spot where they'd entered the parade route, where the two officers had almost shot him, he sent the mental image to the horse. *Go here, but don't . . . don't hurt anyone else. Don't step on any . . . people.* He couldn't bear to think the word "bodies," even though they littered the street.

Callahan crouched down behind a bench and waited until most people had run away. Once the shooting stopped, he took off down Third Street toward the first getaway car. He prayed Edwards would be there, but he'd seen the unnatural plague of creatures, and he'd seen the cops stream toward the building.

How had this gone so wrong? All their careful planning, all their training, and not only were they thwarted, but some damn fool started shooting after he'd told them to abort. He wanted to know who'd blown it.

"One, what's your status?"

Screams came through the radio as the channel opened. "One, heading for rendezvous point beta."

"Copy, One. Two, status?"

Silence.

"Three, status?"

Silence. He swore under his breath, cold sweat on his forehead.

"Four, status?"

Four was that idiot Justice White, and Callahan was pretty sure the first shots came from his location. He was the one who botched this more than anyone. This was all his fault.

At least, that's what he'd tell Barnabas.

Chloe managed to tear through most of the materials holding Erik in place, but he still couldn't get free and she needed air. Pushing off from the metal frame, she shot upward, bursting through the surface and gasping for breath. She couldn't take long, though. After three good lungs full, she dove back down and found Lanae working to free the now-unconscious Erik. The young woman must have dived in after the float. She had his upper body untangled and went for a leg, so Chloe worked on the other leg. In seconds, they had him free.

From the desperate look on Lanae's face, Chloe knew she needed air. She motioned for Lanae to go and grabbed Erik under the armpits. Lanae shot up toward the surface as Chloe struggled, pulling the limp man against the water's drag.

Halfway up, seeing spots, lungs on fire, Chloe wondered if she'd make it. Then a hand closed around her arm. Moments later, she broke the surface, and someone hauled her into a little fishing boat. Lanae hung onto the side while David and another man pulled Erik in and started mouth to mouth.

"Get him to help," Lanae called. "I can get back to shore on my own."

Amazing what happens when you're put in a dangerous situation, Chloe thought as she watched her swim away.

Firefighters geared up to head toward the scene as Charlie arrived with the little boy. He left him with the battalion chief and flew back along the parade route.

A few people still fled from the area. Others hid in terror. Some stood and stared in shock. Charlie didn't hear any gunshots as he approached, then saw why—bodies lay in a fan-shaped swath on the sidewalk and street, and at the base of the fan, a mangled body still clung to an assault rifle. Blood pooled in tire ruts and trickled toward the gutters.

Charlie trembled all over and felt sick. Tears clouded his eyes.

Who could do this? But he knew. He knew, without a doubt, it was Bruderschaft.

Uniformed police moved in from all directions, and a few eyed him. He spread his hands to show he was unarmed.

He blinked away tears, intending to head toward the lake and check on Chloe. Then he saw it—three blocks away, down a side street, a man ran toward a waiting car. A motorcycle cop tried to head him off, but he drew a gun and fired. The bike went down and skidded into a parked car.

"Officer down!" Charlie yelled over his shoulder as the getaway car sped away and he flew after the shooter. The man looked over his shoulder and saw Charlie barreling toward him. In a panic, he flung his right arm back and fired. Charlie saw the muzzle's high angle and dropped low, then swerved up high on the left.

The shooter swung around to get a better angle and Charlie flapped hard to lift himself above the trajectory. The bullet missed—barely, its wind skimming his leg.

Screw this! Charlie arched up over the building to get out of the line of fire. He'd keep an eye on the guy for police, but he wasn't going to risk apprehending an armed man by himself.

He gained altitude and veered back over the alley, where the gunman ran up a fire escape. *Does he want a better shot at me, or does he think he scared me off?*

As Charlie kept his distance and scanned the area for cops, the man reached the roof and whirled around, searching the sky. Charlie moved back and up, trying to get out of range. The shooter raised his gun and fired, but the bullet went wide. He angled up to try again and . . . nothing happened. He threw aside the empty weapon.

Seeing his chance, Charlie dove to tackle the guy. *I got you now, Butler's Shaft asshole,* he thought.

He didn't have time to pull out of the dive when the man whipped out another gun from inside his shirt and fired.

David and the fisherman got Erik breathing and awake before they reached the shore. Chloe thanked them and buzzed off to see how she could help. From the air, she saw a few stragglers running from the parade route and a mother behind a hedge, huddled down over a stroller.

Then she noticed something smoking and swooped down to investigate. Lindsay called her name as she touched down, and Chloe looked over to see her roommate kneeling on the ground with tears streaming down her face.

Chloe ran to her and gave her a hug. "What happened?"

Lindsay stammered so much Chloe couldn't make sense of it. She comforted her roomie until Lindsay could give her the gist. Chloe struggled to conceal the revulsion that seized her when she realized her friend had burned a man alive, no matter how justified.

"Did you see where Charlie went?" she asked once her roomie had calmed down a little. Lindsay pointed the direction he'd gone. Chloe was torn between staying with her friend and finding her boyfriend.

A shadow fell over them, and she looked up to see a horse and two riders silhouetted against the sun.

"What are you guys doing here?" she asked, shading her eyes.

"We got a message that Zeke was needed." Gabe's voice was somber, and Zeke looked stunned.

"Gabe, can you keep an eye on Lindsay for me? I need to go to find Charlie," Chloe said.

He nodded and asked Zeke to help him dismount. Chloe gave Lindsay a quick hug. "Hang in there. I'll be back." She took to the sky.

As sirens wailed in the distance, she went high and flew in a random zigzag in case shooters lurked on rooftops. When her path took her out over Sherman Avenue, the scene below shocked her so bad she froze and plummeted toward the ground. The rush of air snapped her out of it enough to buzz her wings and stay aloft, but tears blurred her vision. Her mind shrieked that it wasn't real, this couldn't be happening.

She struggled to clear her mind and her eyes, so she could find Charlie. Only then, once she knew her teammates were safe, could she look for her parents.

A single gunshot sounded from a few blocks away, and she thought it had come from a rooftop. She dropped low to use buildings as cover and headed there at top speed. She heard a scream and recognized the voice. *Charlie, I'm coming!*

She shot straight into the sky beside the building, trusting her speed to keep the gunman from getting a lock on her before she could survey the scene. Below her, Charlie lay in a pool of blood, face down atop a man who wasn't moving. Cursing her inability to loan Charlie her healing power, she landed next to him and felt for a pulse. Faint, but there. She let out a ragged breath, and her eyes fell on the other man. His head lay unnaturally flat against the roof. He wouldn't be hurting anyone again.

Remembering the sirens she'd heard, Chloe took to the air and scanned for a paramedic. A fire truck had just stopped, and the crew ran toward the carnage on Sherman, laden with emergency medical gear. She swooped down and hovered in front of a shocked woman whose name tag read *O'Sullivan*. "Come with me. There's a shooting victim on the roof."

The woman looked toward the bodies in the street, now surrounded by cops and her fellow firefighters, then back at Chloe. "Lead me there."

"I'm not leading you. I'm carrying you." Chloe hooked her arms under the firefighter's and hoisted her into the air. O'Sullivan screamed and closed her eyes and didn't open them again until Chloe set her down on the roof.

O'Sullivan triaged Charlie. "He needs evac, probably to Spokane. Can you carry him like you did me?"

Chloe shook her head. "Not all the way to Spokane."

O'Sullivan nodded and called for a chopper. She then examined the other man and confirmed he was dead.

"I'll be right back." Chloe took off toward where she'd left Lindsay. She found her friends not far from there, talking to a police officer. She landed, and Lindsay ran over to her.

"Did you find him? Is he okay?"

Chloe nodded, a lump in her throat making it hard to talk. "He's alive, but he got shot. You don't have your phone, do you? Mine got soaked."

Lindsay shook her head. "No pockets. Dammit, Raul." She laughed too loud for a moment, verging on hysteria.

Chloe hugged her friend, then hurried over to the cop. "Excuse me, do you have a phone I could borrow? I . . . I need to get a hold of my parents."

"Uh, yeah. Stay close with it, though." He handed it to her.

"I will. Thank you." She stared at the keypad for a moment, unable to remember their numbers. Then her mind managed to put her dad's number together and she dialed.

On the first ring, her dad picked up, sounding terrified. "Hello?"

"Daddy?"

"Oh, thank God, Chloe! When I saw the police number, I thought . . ." His voice broke.

"I'm okay. Are you guys?"

"Yeah, baby, we're fine. We were well away from the shooting and got out of there quick."

Legs buckling with relief, Chloe collapsed onto the grass. "Daddy, Charlie's hurt."

"Baker three-eight. Affirmative, it is Danny Ray Callahan," said the officer's voice over the radio app.

Molly Moy stood over the dispatcher's shoulder, listening. Just before the shooting started, a motorcycle unit had radioed in about a suspicious car parked nearby with the engine running. She'd ordered the officer to stay hidden and keep an eye on it, and sure enough, it paid off. They'd found Bruderschaft's top explosives expert.

John Beck sat in the getaway car, lips pressed together and hands clenched around the steering wheel as Callahan climbed into the passenger seat.

"Where the hell's everyone else?" Callahan asked over the din of the police scanner.

Beck gave a tight shake of his head.

Callahan gaped at him. "How can I be the only one? Edwards should've . . ."

"I'm sorry, Danny Ray. I know you and him was close, but I heard on the scanner . . ." His eyes flicked away as he put the car in gear and pulled away from the curb. "They got him."

"What, arrested?" Callahan's ears rang. As bad as Edwards getting arrested would be, he prayed that's what the driver was talking about.

Beck swallowed hard and shook his head again. "He never got out of the building."

Callahan's vision swam as the realization sank in. "Fuck. Fuck fuck fuck *fuck!* No. He ain't dead!"

Beck's eyes widened as he looked in the rear-view mirror. "Oh, shit!" He hammered down the accelerator, and the car leaped forward, tires squealing.

Rage welling up, Callahan whipped around and saw the motorcycle's flashing lights. He fumbled for his pistol. "I'll fucking kill you, pig! I'll fucking kill you!"

"In pursuit, northbound Eighth Street from Lakeside," the cop radioed. Moy's heart leaped to her throat as scenario after scenario went through her mind. Baker three-eight survived this encounter in too few of them.

The dispatcher's hands flew over the keyboard as he talked into the headset, getting backup en route.

The detective looked up at a traffic cam pointing straight north up Eighth Street. After a few pounding heartbeats, the car flew through the frame, motorcycle on its tail.

"Adam one-four, en route to intercept at Boyd," the radio said.

Hurry up, Adam one-four, she urged in silence. In a few seconds, they'd be joining the chase rather than heading them off. Those Bruderschaft assholes were too savvy to allow a chase to continue for long. They knew the regulations prohibiting high-speed pursuits in populated areas and how to exploit them. *Get those assholes, come on!*

As Callahan's car continued, she ticked off the street names in her head. *Pennsylvania, St. Marie's, Montana . . . almost there . . .*

A police cruiser streaked into view just yards ahead of the fleeing sedan, which swerved and skidded to a stop. Two uniformed officers leaped out. They and Baker three-eight took up defensive positions. *Good work, boys. Keep it up,* she thought, trying to smother the voice in the back of her head saying she was about to watch someone die.

Beck had just got the car under control and stopped when Callahan leaped out, gun drawn, screaming in wordless fury.

"Gun!" somebody yelled. A bullet displaced the air inches from Callahan's face before he heard the gunshot. An instant later, he knew he was falling but didn't understand why. He smelled the stink of hot asphalt and felt gravel press into his cheek. *Am I shot?* He didn't feel pain, just pressure on top of him. He could see his outstretched hand on the ground, his gun a few feet beyond it. He reached for it in vain as black-booted feet pounded into view.

Moy saw the muzzle flash in the background of the blurred black-and-white image on the screen, but she couldn't tell if Callahan was hit. Then the getaway driver dove out the open passenger-side door and tackled Callahan.

As the three officers moved in, she cursed the camera angle for not providing a view of the two men on the ground. A semi-truck pulled out of a side street just then and slowed down. *Damn rubbernecker! Move!* Radio silence stretched on.

Then—a burst of static. "Two in custody."

Moy let out a breath and clapped the dispatcher on the shoulder. She allowed herself to take a moment and celebrate the victory, then checked her phone for the dozenth time. Supon still hadn't responded. Everyone was supposed to be on-call—he should be reachable and sober. She feared neither was true.

"Detective Moy," the dispatcher said. "We just got a report of two state troopers found dead."

Her brow furrowed as she whipped around. "How is that possible? Henderson was the only statie on scene."

"This isn't at the shooting scene, Ma'am. They were found in a dumpster behind a dive bar over on Government Way and Sunset."

"You tackled me," Nancy Simmons said to Jeffrey as the car sped away from the scene and into a residential neighborhood.

"Yes, Ma'am. I'm sorry."

She scoffed. "Why are you apologizing? I saw where that bullet hit. You saved my life, Jeffrey. You had a vision, didn't you?"

"I did, Senator."

"Ma'am, he went to great lengths to make sure nothing happened to you," Tamara said.

Senator Simmons gazed out the window, looking thoughtful. "I want to hear the whole story sometime, but for now, just know that I'm grateful."

Chloe watched the paramedics load Charlie into the helicopter before flying to where her parents waited, just outside the police perimeter.

Lindsay, Zeke, and Gabe talked to a Coeur d'Alene police officer who took a break from his notes to wipe away tears. Heather had an arm around Lindsay.

Chloe touched down and Phil threw his arms around her. She could feel him shaking.

"Lindsay told us about the bomb. When I think how close we came to losing you . . ."

Heather appeared at her side and they all hugged. Chloe cried, her face buried in her dad's shoulder.

"How's Charlie, sweetheart?" her mom asked when they separated. The others had all gathered around them.

"Not good. They took him over to Sacred Heart in Spokane, so I need to get there fast and see how he's doing."

"We'll drive you over," Phil said. "They can't tell you anything, anyway. You're not family."

Chloe's eyes fell shut. "Oh, my gosh, I didn't even think about his parents!"

"I called them already," Heather said. "They'll be on the next plane out. I had them send medical consent before he came, so the hospital can give us information. But only to Dad and me, so there's no use flying off without us." She looked around and spotted the police officer. "I'll go make sure it's okay for us to leave. They'll want your statement, Chlo, but they should be able to wait."

As much as she itched to be in the air and beat the car to Spokane, she decided it would feel good to be with her family and friends.

"Excuse me, young lady," a deep voice said behind her. Chloe turned to see a white-haired old man with a bushy mustache. He looked familiar, but she couldn't place him. "I'd like to shake your hand, if I may." He extended his hand and Chloe accepted it. "I've always said hate and racism were the deadliest plague of the modern era. I hate being proved right, but I'm grateful for heroes like you."

Her face got hot and she stammered a thank you.

With a nod, he turned away, then looked back. "Excelsior, WyldWing."

The familiar catchphrase jogged her memory. She thought his name was Stan . . . Something.

Chloe turned back to her friends and family as they tried to figure out what to do with Zeke's horse.

"I figured we'd ride him back to the ranch," Zeke said. "But I'd sure like to go to the hospital with you and see how Charlie's doing."

"We'll need to talk to Detective Abara about where you should stay. If he thinks it's safe, you're welcome to stay with us if you'd rather not go back to the ranch," Phil told him and Gabe.

"I don't know about Zeke, but I'd way rather stay with you guys," Gabe said. "If I have to go back to that dingy little cell of a room right now, I'll freaking lose it."

"You'd still take us in, after Bruderschaft . . ." Zeke gestured toward the scene and swallowed hard.

"You're not one of them." Heather put a hand on his shoulder. "That's the whole reason you're here, isn't it?"

He nodded, looking pale and lost.

"But yeah, I'm not sure what to do about the horse," Phil added.

"Hey, Zeke," said a scruffy man who approached them. "I have a friend with horses. I can call him to come get this guy." He patted Comet on the neck.

"That'd be great. Thanks, Detective Supon."

Heather introduced the Task Force member to Phil and the girls.

"Can you let Sam know the boys are with us?" Heather asked him as he typed a message with clumsy fingers.

"Actually, he just messaged me," Supon said, still buried in his phone. "He needs me to bring Zeke up to the compound right away."

Zeke went pale, and Heather put a comforting hand on his back. "D-did he say why?"

"He found something. I can't go into specifics, but we gotta get going." He glanced down at the phone. "My buddy's bringing his horse trailer." He turned to the uniformed officer. "Take charge of the horse until my friend gets here." He gestured to Zeke. "Let's go, kid."

"What about me?" Gabe asked.

The detective narrowed his eyes. "You know the compound, too, I suppose. So sure."

Zeke and Gabe followed Supon to his car. Zeke looked back and Chloe and Lindsay waved at him before they headed off in different directions.

CHAPTER EIGHTEEN

Saturday, Aug. 5, 2017
Near Bruderschaft Compound, North Idaho

A shaken Detective Abara sat on a roadside stump and watched a live newscast on his phone. He ached to talk to someone in the department, especially Molly Moy, but he couldn't distract them in the aftermath of the worst mass murder in Idaho history.

Twenty-three people were confirmed dead, including a rookie officer from his department. No one had a good estimate on the number of wounded, but a live shot from the hospital showed medical staff triaging people in the driveway. He fought to keep an emotional distance, so he could handle what still lay ahead.

Next, a grim-faced reporter interviewed the CPD's public information officer, Captain Wolf. He said the shooter appeared to be part of an organized group that had planned the attack. Additionally, an attempt had been made to assassinate Senator Nancy Simmons. Both the shooter and sniper were confirmed dead. "An additional two suspects are in custody, and an Idaho state trooper was shot while attempting to apprehend another suspect. He is currently in surgery."

Abara's blood ran cold. It had to be Henderson. *Damn it, poor kid!* He felt a twinge of guilt for questioning Henderson's loyalty.

"Was that suspect apprehended, or did he get away?" the reporter asked.

"The trooper's body-cam footage shows that the shooter and, uh, an alleged accomplice are both dead. The trooper shot the gunman to protect a civilian and the other took his own life."

"So at least four suspects are dead."

Wolf shook his head. "No, actually. At this time, the confirmed count is six."

Several reporters talked at once, but one shouted over them all. "Were they all killed by officers?"

"No, we had two shot by officers, the one suicide, and three killed by, uh, civilians."

"Civilians with guns?" asked the reporter.

"Um, no . . ."

"If the civilians weren't armed, how did they take down men with assault rifles?"

Abara cringed. *Don't say it!*

"They appear to have used, uh, parahuman abilities to protect civilians and stop the attackers."

"You mean superheroes? The kids in the parade?"

"No further comments at this time." Wolf stepped away from the podium, ignoring the eruption of questions from the reporters.

Abara grimaced. Wolf knew better than to include that detail. He wondered which of the kids would now have to live with being killers. He'd had a hard enough time as a twenty-seven-year-old soldier.

He received a text from his contact at Just Cause Seattle and paused the news. The jet would be landing nearby in thirty minutes. Abara got in the car and headed that direction.

On his way, he got a call from Moy. "Sam, you're a hero," she said. "If you hadn't gotten those pictures sent out when you did, things would've been much worse."

"Worse." Abara felt sick. "Twenty-three dead is bad enough. But damn, it's good to hear your voice."

"Wish I had good news."

"Tell me Henderson's not dead."

"He's not. The bullet's in his side, but the doctor said it didn't hit anything vital." Her voice shook. "Sam, it was a nine-year-old kid who shot him. Then Henderson shot the kid when he turned the gun on a civilian."

"Holy Christ, what a goddamn nightmare." Abara pulled to the side of the dirt road and leaned back against the headrest. "What about the para kids? How were they involved?"

"Fireball torched one shooter. He got a shot off at her but missed. She's with the Wyld family now. The moth kid took down another, but he got shot in the process. He's at Sacred Heart, and I don't know how he's doing." She paused. "Zeke took out the primary shooter. He made a horse trample the guy. Jesus, Sam, it was ugly."

"Any idea where Zeke is now?"

"No, none. I'm assuming he and Gabe are also with the Wylds."

Sam took a deep breath and got the car moving back down the road. "Do me a favor and confirm that with them. We could really use his knowledge of the compound. Can you have someone bring him out here?"

"You got it. Hey, you haven't heard from Supon, have you?"

"No, why?"

"I can't reach him. He better not be on another bender —when the Sheriff finds out, his career is over." She paused. "Just got a message that Henderson's out of surgery. I'm gonna head up there—I'll text you how he's doing."

Saturday, Aug. 5, 2017
Blanchard, Idaho

Zeke stared out the sedan's rear window at the washed-out mascot on the local fast-food joint's sign and imagined himself opening the door and running off. He wanted to be anywhere in the world other than where they headed. Even now that he'd seen the worst of what Bruderschaft could do, he didn't want to see the compound attacked. The ever-present fear of it had loomed over him for as long as he could remember, and now he had to not only see it, but help it happen.

Detective Supon came out of the restaurant and handed the boys bags filled with burgers and fries. Zeke didn't think it would've been dangerous for him and Gabe to go inside. If they'd been in Clagstone, where he'd be recognized, it would've made sense, but no one in Blanchard knew him. Still, the detective had insisted they stay in the car.

"I got you guys milkshakes, too," Supon said. "Hope you like chocolate."

Supon's casual manner rubbed Zeke the wrong way. After all that violence, all that death, how could he act like it was just any other day? He took the milkshake and sipped it without enjoyment while Gabe picked mechanically at the fries.

Country music blared as Supon started the engine. They got back on the road and headed toward Bruderschaft, Zeke's dread growing with every mile.

Saturday, Aug. 5, 2017
Spokane, Washington

"He's unconscious, and he's lost a lot of blood, but the surgeon said the damage to his shoulder was minimal," Charlie's nurse told the Wylds. They'd had to Skype in a specialist from Paris to advise them on the abnormal physiology.

Chloe hugged her dad while Heather texted the update to Charlie's parents. An alert sounded on Chloe's phone, then another, then three more. Lindsay's blew up, too, As they got messages from numerous Hero Academy classmates.

"Oh, man." Lindsay grimaced. "Someone said on TV that parahumans killed some of the suspects, so everyone wants to know who it was." Her eyes teared up once more.

Phil groaned. "Damn. Wish they hadn't done that."

"Right?" Chloe thumbed in a message to Rhiannon, one of her closest friends at school, telling her about Charlie and that she'd fill her in on the rest later. She sent it, then added: *Tell everyone to leave Linds alone for a while. She's going through some stuff.*

Chloe worried about her roommate. She hadn't said much, which wasn't like her at all, and her eyes looked haunted. Chloe's stomach churned when she tried to imagine what it would be like to burn someone to death.

Lindsay stared down at her phone as it dinged over and over, but she didn't respond to anyone. Phil put a hand on hers. "Why don't you let me hang on to that? You don't look like you're up to much conversation right now." Lindsay blinked at him and handed over her phone with a slight nod.

Rhiannon messaged Chloe back and said rumors were already flying online about her—as the only known local parahuman—either performing heroics or being reckless and getting people killed. Chloe shook her head, then noticed the reporter who'd ambushed her from her neighbor's backyard, standing across the waiting room. Jenna Holt looked uncomfortable and guilt flashed across her face when their eyes met.

Chloe approached her. "Thanks for hanging back, but I want to do an interview now, so I can get the truth out there. I guess a lot of rumors are already going around."

Jenna's brow furrowed. "Are you sure you're up to it?"

Chloe looked at Lindsay and back to the reporter. "Yeah. I think it will help everyone in the long run."

The reporter nodded. "Let me check with your parents first, but if it's okay with them, we'll go find somewhere quiet to talk."

Saturday, Aug. 5, 2017
Coeur d'Alene, Idaho

Molly Moy's heart ached as she walked through the triage area at the hospital. Shooting victims, family members, and hospital staff alike appeared shell-shocked. She struggled to stay focused on what she needed to do. She knew Abara was struggling, as well. She'd heard it in his voice. He had enough to deal with, so she didn't tell him about the two murdered troopers.

She realized she'd forgotten to call the Wylds to see if Zeke was with them. She texted someone at the station to take care of that for her, then went to find Henderson's parents.

Saturday, Aug. 5, 2017
Near Bruderschaft Compound, North Idaho

The VTOL jet with *Greta* painted on her side touched down on a dusty private airstrip. Not that the Just Cause plane needed an airstrip—it could land anywhere a helicopter could. But with Bruderschaft sympathizers in nearby towns and dense forest everywhere else, this spot made the most sense. Four Just Cause Seattle members filed out.

First came Eagle Eye in his distinctive brown and white costume. He had the ability to manipulate air currents, which allowed him both to soar and to guide projectiles to their targets with a high degree of accuracy. He was a short and slender white guy who bristled with guns and grenades.

Behind him came Topaz, an enormous, muscular woman with faceted golden-orange skin invulnerable to bullets of all calibers. Abara'd been damn glad to hear she was available.

Next in line, Black Ice, a young Korean-American who could freeze anything within a certain range. The second to use the name, he'd chosen it as a tribute to the first, who'd died defending New York City from the Hind invasion.

Bringing up the rear and cutting an impressive profile due to massive, black-feathered bird wings, came the young man Abara had followed since he was just an inner-city Chicago kid. Corvid was almost as tall, broad, and black as Sam himself. The detective felt an almost fatherly pride watching the young intern stride toward him, dressed in head-to-toe black spandex and aviator sunglasses. Abara returned the hero's up-nod of acknowledgment.

Just as the group reached him, another jet drowned out their words of greeting. It was the *Dorothy*, all the way from New York. Abara exhaled in relief at the arrival of the hero he'd most wanted on his side: Ment, the psionicist, who could put entire buildings full of people to sleep. Now he just needed Zeke to complete the plan.

While Detective Abara introduced himself to the team, a half dozen military vehicles arrived. "The National Guard out of Spokane," he said. "Right on time."

He texted Moy to have Zeke meet them at the back road out of the compound. They couldn't afford to wait around, especially if the kid wasn't even on the way yet.

Saturday, Aug. 5, 2017
Bruderschaft Compound, North Idaho

Barnabas stood at the desk in the small out-back office, slumped forward with his hands on either side of the speakerphone. Preacher stood beside him with a large hand splayed over the bottom half of his face.

Neither could believe what they heard from one of the back-up getaway drivers, in place just in case the primary drivers were compromised.

They wouldn't have believed the number from the news reports—six suspects dead?—except that it meshed with the number who weren't reporting in. That meant Edwards, all four gunmen, and even one of the firecracker kids weren't coming home.

Barnabas ran a hand through his hair. "How the fuck is this happening?"

"Someone snitched," Preacher said behind him.

"No way. Only the council knew about the bomb." Barnabas shook his head. "Well, and Jeremiah. No way he turned on us."

"We need to prepare. They know Callahan's one of ours and they'll come for us."

Barnabas narrowed his eyes. "You're right. It'll take time for them to mobilize, though. We'll be ready."

Gabe didn't trust the situation. Supon seemed . . . off in a way he couldn't pinpoint. He'd grilled Zeke on how to get onto the compound even though they'd be with him when he got there.

And then there was the thing with the shakes.

Gabe didn't think his stomach could handle much more than a few fries, but Supon kept looking back and telling him, "Drink that shake!"

After the third admonition, Gabe put the straw in his mouth now and then without drinking any of it. He wasn't sure if it was keen observation or paranoia, but he thought Zeke's eyes looked heavy-lidded, and his friend seemed duller than he had been even right after the shooting. He grew more and more certain the detective had drugged the shakes.

"Where should I pull off?" Supon asked as they trundled down the dirt road the boys had used to escape.

"Just up here," Zeke slurred. Gabe studied Zeke's face and tried to mimic the vacant, saggy expression.

The detective nosed the car behind a thick stand of trees with heavy underbrush and told them to get out. "We need to get deep in the woods, where no one's likely to see us."

Zeke nodded and trudged across the dirt road. Gabe followed, shuffling and letting his hands hang limp, the same as Zeke.

Supon followed as they wound down an almost invisible path Zeke could follow with his eyes closed. They walked for several minutes before Zeke stopped and looked around, confused.

"Where was we going, again?"

"This ought to do," Supon said. "You boys stand next to each other, right there. What's that, up there in that tree?"

Zeke looked where Supon pointed. Gabe turned his head but kept the detective in his peripheral vision. The scruffy-looking man reached up under his flannel shirt, toward his holster, and Gabe knew he had moments to act or they'd both be dead. He whipped his head to look beyond Supon's shoulder and screamed. Startled, his hand on the butt of the gun, Supon reeled around and saw . . . nothing but trees.

"Call the animals!" Gabe yelled to Zeke as he tackled Supon, knocking down the stocky man face-first into a bush. The gun fired off to the side and Gabe went deaf. As he'd seen in movies, he grabbed Supon's gun arm and slammed it into the ground. Supon clung to the gun and it was all Gabe could do to keep the stronger man down. He didn't dare turn to see if Zeke was doing anything to help.

"What the hell?"

To Gabe's traumatized ears, the deep voice sounded as if it came through water. He recognized Abara's voice.

"Help!" he yelled. "He drugged Zeke and tried to shoot us!"

Someone grabbed Gabe and pulled him off Supon. A moment later, crackling ice appeared over the gun and hand, then raced up Supon's arm and across his back, freezing him to the ground. Supon screamed, and then a block of ice formed in his open mouth and stifled him, leaving only his nose and eyes uncovered.

Abara approached and looked down at him, hands on his hips. "Damn it, Mat. I really hoped it wasn't you, you son of a bitch. How'd you slip the surveillance?"

Gabe recognized Eagle Eye and Black Ice from Just Cause Seattle, and Ment from the New York team, but not the big guy with the black angel wings. He realized he'd been pulled off of Supon by Topaz, another agent he recognized right away.

"Whoa, sweet! The heroes are on the case, eh?" He yelled, ears still ringing from the gunshot.

"I managed to pull some strings," Abara said as he zip-tied Supon's ankles. "A National Guard force is heading to the front entrance."

"Nice!" Gabe turned to Zeke, who stood unmoving with tears streaming down his cheeks.

"It's time, isn't it? It's the war they always told us was coming."

Tom Shepherd staggered toward the community room when the bell tolled, a half-full whiskey bottle dangling from his hand. He ached to drink it, but it was just for show. He hadn't touched a drop since throwing away his flask.

All of Bruderschaft gathered inside the community room and Barnabas stood before them.

"The day has come. We've prepared for the corrupt lawmen to come for us, and now they're coming. In our surveillance cameras, we seen military vehicles heading this way on the road and figure they'll be here in about twenty minutes." He paused for a few seconds to let it sink in. "You all know your role in this. We're short a few soldiers, but we still got plenty of men who know how to use a gun, especially with the boys who are trained up. Any questions?"

Tom swayed and raised the hand holding the bottle.

Barnabas sneered at him. "What do you want, Tom?"

"I ain't in no shape to hold a gun. I'll lead the women and children out, make sure they're safe."

Their leader shook his head in disgust. "Fine, but for God's sake, put down the bottle already."

Tom saluted and set the bottle down on the nearest table. "A'right, women and children, this way." He staggered outside. They followed, with pale faces and anxious chatter. As they reached the schoolhouse, Tom looked back, half expecting to turn to salt. No men had exited the building yet. He smiled and straightened up, no longer needing the charade, and walked past the barracks, then the schoolhouse. As they came upon the barns, he told a few of the women to make sure no stragglers were inside. While they were distracted, he grabbed his duffel bag, which he'd concealed behind a shed.

Once the women and children cleared out, Barnabas led the men north past his house and toward the woods, to the weapons depot and the explosives shed beyond it. He'd have preferred having all of his soldiers, but every man on the compound knew how to shoot. They were still a formidable force. Barnabas had no doubt they could keep the National Guard from even getting through the gate.

As per their long-practiced plans, five men went into the depot to start issuing firearms, and two went into the shed to bring out and dispense grenades. He, Preacher, Doc Jones, and the ranking commander huddled up to talk strategy.

"I want six good shooters on the gate," Barnabas said. "Another five—"

The world went blindingly white. Pain flared as his eardrums ruptured. A blast threw him twenty feet, and he landed hard. Barnabas couldn't catch his breath. Something heavy landed on his chest. He groped for whatever it was and found several thin, hard, protrusions covered in sticky liquid.

. . . *bone?* Gasping for air that would never inflate his punctured lungs, Barnabas' last realization was that he was touching his own exposed ribs.

Zeke and the others watched from the trees as the women and children hurried into the woods south of them. He didn't see whether Tom was with them like he was supposed to be, but he had seen Naomi and breathed a little easier.

"The front gate is due east of us." Zeke struggled to focus despite the remains of Supon's drug. He pointed across the field where he used to graze his sheep and to the low hill separating the fields from the main compound. "Right now, everyone's probably getting geared up right over—" As he pointed northeast toward the weapons depot, an explosion tore into the sky. They all hit the ground.

No one moved or made a sound. Zeke looked at Gabe, whose face went from startled to satisfied.

Abara spoke into a radio, letting the National Guard know they weren't involved in the explosion. Eagle Eye motioned to Corvid and the two fliers took to the air. Topaz and Black Ice raced across the field and up the hill to survey the scene.

Zeke envied their ability to communicate with each other. He and Gabe were the only ones not on headsets. Abara told them in no uncertain terms to stay with him and Ment, well away from any combat. They moved south until they could see the sheepfold. Zeke felt a pang of sorrow as he remembered all the good times in the field and wished he could go back to that life.

"So how is this supposed to work?" Ment asked, Zeke reflected double in his mirrored lenses. The signature black trench looked as alien in the woods as the man himself.

"I'll get Eleanor to come where you can see her," Zeke told him.

Ment peered at him over his glasses. "It has a name?"

"Of course, *she* has a name!" Zeke wished he didn't have to work with this guy, but then, he wished none of this was happening. He focused on his favorite ewe and a few seconds later, she appeared at the fence, alert and looking off in the distance toward him. Zeke smiled. "There's my girl!"

"Hold on. This will be disorienting," Ment said. Zeke closed his eyes and felt a tug in his brain. *Open your eyes,* Ment's voice said inside his mind.

Holy crap! Zeke opened his eyes and experienced a weird sense of vertigo as he stared at himself, Gabe, Abara, and Ment across the field. Ment had done it—he saw through Eleanor's eyes.

The ewe shook her head, seeming to sense something strange, but Zeke calmed her with a few words. *Come on, old girl, let's run wild again.*

Eleanor reared up and kicked at the fence. The rest of the flock followed her lead.

From above, the flying heroes reported the effects of the explosion. The metal building had been reinforced to contain an accidental blast, so much of the force had been directed through the door. It left behind a gaping wound lined with gnarled metal fingers. Several men who'd been in its path lay dead, and certainly, no one inside survived. Several people along the edges of the path appeared wounded, but no one tended to them.

Men rushed around on the ground, putting out small fires caused by the explosion. Many had assault weapons slung on their backs. The weapons depot didn't appear damaged, and fifteen to twenty men remained functional.

The rest of the compound was deserted.

"Come on," Abara told Gabe. Zeke and Ment stood stock still, their minds elsewhere. "Let's get where we can see this go down." They climbed the hill and lay on their bellies, watching through binoculars as armed men made their way down from the depot and toward the front gate.

The sheep broke out of the fold in no time and streamed north on the compound side of the hill, moving as a unit behind Eleanor.

By the time they reached the weapons depot, the last of the men had moved away from it. *So far, so good,* Zeke thought. He directed the rest of the flock to follow the men, then poked Eleanor's head into the depot. No one had stuck around, and few guns remained inside. Zeke knew they'd each take multiple guns. It was way more efficient than having to reload all the time.

The damage to the shed made it unnecessary for Zeke to check inside it—no way could anyone have survived in there. He had to know who the dead men were, though. He still couldn't believe his father had turned against Bruderschaft.

"Hey, what are you doing up here, Eleanor?" asked a weak voice from the fringes of the explosion. Zeke recognized a farmhand who applied pressure to a gaping wound in his thigh. His pant leg had burned away, exposing red, puckered skin. Zeke wanted to help him but how could he? Eleanor wanted to bolt, get away from the smell of blood and charred flesh, but Zeke made her go to the man and nuzzle his arm. He reached up and petted the woolly animal, looking comforted. "I don't suppose I'm gonna make it through this, am I?" Then his head lolled, and he slumped over onto the ground.

Zeke steeled himself and moved on four legs over to the bodies. He came upon Preacher first. His face remained intact, but not much else. He identified Doc Jones by his iron cross wedding ring. He'd seen that thing at every exam he'd ever had and would've known it anywhere. Then he came to the third body. He first thought it could be his father—the build was right, but when he forced himself to get closer, he recognized what was left of the hair. It wasn't Tom. It was Barnabas.

The only man moving tried to pull himself up onto a leg with the thigh bone exposed. His dazed eyes didn't seem to register the sheep wandering past. Some others appeared alive but unconscious.

Give her instructions and then we're pulling out, Ment told Zeke. Moments later, Zeke's head reeled as his vision shifted from Eleanor's body to his own, and he ran off into the woods to throw up.

Gabe watched as the armed Butler's Shaft members gathered around a confused-looking man giving commands. "That guy's a nobody," he told Abara. "The council must all be dead."

"Let's hope so."

Just then, the flock ran into view and swarmed the men, knocking several down and causing confusion. Eleanor joined them, and Gabe knew Zeke had completed his reconnaissance. She ran in a circle around everyone and the other sheep joined, tightening their circle as they went. Forced into a tight knot, some of the men looked about to start shooting the sheep.

"Some guardsmen just neutralized the injured men at the shed," Abara reported.

Gabe didn't ask if that meant killing them or taking them into custody. As proud as he'd been of sabotaging the shed and had fantasized about it blowing up as many Butler's Shaft men as possible, he now understood the reality of killing was nothing like he'd expected.

"It's about to go down." Abara pointed skyward.

Gabe watched as Corvid flew over the men penned in by the sheep, holding Black Ice below him. Gabe's gut clenched, sure the heroes would get shot down, but the sheep appeared to be a sufficient distraction. A handful of men stopped moving as ice engulfed their heads. Deprived of oxygen, they collapsed on the ground and convulsed.

Corvid swerved away and ducked behind Barnabas' house before anyone managed to take a shot.

The flock scattered, and Gabe heard Zeke's voice just behind him. "She better not hit the sheep!"

Gabe lowered the binoculars as Topaz ran up—carrying a thirty-foot lodgepole pine, roots and all, above her head. A few men got off shots, but the bullets just bounced off her gem-like skin. She stopped and threw the tree, giving it a little spin, and it took down a half dozen men who couldn't dive out of the way in time. Blood flew.

One of the few survivors tried to run away, and Topaz took off after him.

Two men bolted for the barracks and Eagle Eye opened fire from a roof and cut them down. The hero lowered the gun and tossed a grenade at the front gate. It hit the keypad on the post and blew it away. Three more grenades turned the gate itself into twisted metal fragments. The National Guard vehicles came into view just then and the front one plowed through it, scattering shards everywhere.

Three Bruderschaft soldiers managed to gain their feet. Two put their hands up in surrender, but a third pointed his gun at the vehicle. Eagle Eye shot him just above the ear and he collapsed in a heap. Guardsmen hopped from the vehicles and took the other two into custody. Moments later, Topaz came back with the runner over her shoulder, hands and feet bound.

"Damn, that was over fast," Gabe said.

"No casualties on our side, either. That's why they're the pros." Abara stood and brushed himself off and spoke into the headset. "Well done, team. Let's go talk to the commander and see how we can help."

As the detective and the heroes made their way to the Guardsmen, Zeke plopped down on the hill, exhausted. Gabe sat beside him and wasn't surprised to see Eleanor wander up and lay her head in Zeke's lap.

Zeke stroked the ewe's head and stared at the ground. "That's it. There's no more Bruderschaft."

"That's a good thing, dude."

Zeke nodded. "Yeah. I know it is. But damn, that was awful. First the parade, then this?"

Gabe put an arm around his friend's shoulders. "I don't imagine life will feel any kind of normal for a while."

"No matter how fucked up it was, this place was my home. My entire world, and now it's just . . . gone."

"Did your father get away?" Gabe's voice broke.

"I think so. I didn't see him anywhere."

"What about mine? Did you see him?"

Zeke's eyes fell shut. He hadn't even thought about Gabe's dad, and that made him feel even worse. "No, man, I didn't see him."

"Maybe he was at the parade. Or maybe he was in the shed." Gabe wiped a tear from his cheek. "Zeke, what if I killed my own dad?"

Zeke had no answer for his friend.

CHAPTER NINETEEN

Sunday, Aug. 6, 2017
Coeur d'Alene, Idaho

State police transported all the Bruderschaft refugees to a college dormitory that was empty for the summer. Zeke thought, with all the guards, it looked more like a prison. Abara took him to a nearby building, and they waited in a small lounge until a trooper brought in Tom Shepherd.

"Hey, Pa." Zeke scuffed the toe of his boot on the floor.

Tom hurried to Zeke, threw his arms around him, and sobbed on his shoulder. Zeke never expected to see that and didn't know what to do. After Tom let him go, they sat down on a couch amid an uneasy silence.

Zeke cleared his throat. "Are they treating everybody okay?"

Tom nodded. "Yeah, real good. Better than I ever imagined. When I first saw cops, I thought we was all dead, or going to prison, but they say none of us who left will face charges."

"You were a big help, Tom," Abara said. "Without you, I'm sure a lot more people would've died."

Tom rubbed a hand over his mouth and chin, the way he always did when he was uncomfortable or needed a drink. Or both. "How many died on the compound?"

"A lot, Pa."

Abara sighed. "Most of those who were left, I'm sorry to say. We took three into custody. Four went to the hospital. We've got twenty-one confirmed dead, possibly a few more. Do you happen to know how many men were on the compound when you left?"

"Twenty-nine. I counted when Barnabas gathered us all together."

"Likely twenty-two dead, then."

Tom rubbed his face again. "Did Barnabas or Preacher survive?" Abara and Zeke both shook their heads. Tom let out a breath. "Good. I won't have to spend my life looking over my shoulder."

"Any idea what you're going to do now?" Abara asked.

"I was planning to take us to Missouri, so I guess we can still go there." He looked at his son and swallowed hard. "I got something to tell you, Zeke. I been lying to you all these years. Your mama . . . she ain't dead."

Zeke gaped in disbelief. "What?"

"God *damn* it, I could use a beer!" Tom hung his head, elbows on his knees. "I ain't at all proud of this, son, I want you to know that. Your mama wanted us to leave the compound. She never liked it much, and she didn't want you growing up to be . . . well, to be like me, I guess. She didn't want her son to be a soldier. I didn't want to go, and she said she was taking you and leaving no matter what I did. I told Barnabas." Tom's eyes flicked up to Zeke, then back to the linoleum. "He and some others barged into the house that night and dragged her out. Took her to town and put her on a bus. Said they'd kill her if she came back, and you, too."

Zeke's hands shook as it sank in that he'd been without her for all these years when he didn't have to be. Memories of her flooded his mind, and he didn't even notice the tears rolling down his cheeks. "You let me think she was dead all these years? Why didn't you tell me?"

Tom just shook his head, eyes trained on the floor.

"Have you talked to her?" Zeke asked.

Tom nodded, still unable to look at his son. "I snuck off to town and called her before I bought the plane tickets."

"How is she?"

Silence hung heavy as Zeke waited for an answer and Tom stared at the tile. At last, Tom sighed. "She sounds real good. Living on her papa's farm, helping out. Said she found a good man and they want to get married, and I agreed I owe her a proper divorce, finally. They, uh . . . they got two daughters together."

Zeke gasped. "I got sisters?"

Tom shrugged. "Half-sisters, but yeah." After several more seconds of silence, he looked up at Zeke. "Ezekiel, saying I'm sorry sounds just dumb as hell to me right now. I know it ain't near enough, but son, I regret this like I didn't know I could regret nothing. What I done to you . . ." His voice cracked and he hung his head.

Zeke sat motionless, still crying. "Do you ever wish you'd just picked up and left, all of us together?"

Tom put a hand on Zeke's shoulder and looked him straight in the eye. "Every day, son. Every damn day."

"Is that your father?" Molly Moy asked.

Gabe stared at his father's face through the glass. "Yep, that's him. John Beck."

"Do you want a minute to say good-bye?"

He shook his head. "I've got nothing to say to him." Gabe turned his back and left the room.

Moy pushed an intercom button to talk to the guard in the lineup room. "Take John Doe . . . oh, excuse me, John *Beck* back to his cell. Nice try, Johnny boy. Told you we'd figure out who you were."

"What will happen to him?" Gabe asked when she joined him out at her desk.

"I'm not sure what all charges he'll face. If they can prove he was in on the conspiracy—even as just a getaway driver—he could go to prison for a very long time. And then there's the child abuse charges, too."

Gabe nodded. "Good."

"I have some more good news for you." Moy opened a file and handed him a piece of paper. "This explains why your aunt hasn't been responding to emails."

Gabe's heart accelerated as he scanned the document. "This is all bullshit. She never abused me. How can they get a protection order for me that I don't even know about?"

Moy shrugged. "You're a minor and legally in their custody."

"So, can you let her know it's okay to talk to me now?"

"I can't tell someone to violate a legal order, but your mother could ask the court to remove it, if she wants."

Gabe's gaze fell to the floor.

Moy put a hand on his shoulder. "Have you talked to your mom, Gabe?"

"No, and I don't want to. Ever. Why should she get any say over what happens to me, after what she let my fucking father do?"

"I'm no expert in emancipation or custody issues, but it just so happens you know a good attorney who'd probably help you out."

Sunday, Aug. 6, 2017
Spokane, Washington

"You can go in and see him now," the nurse said. Chloe jumped up and ran in so fast she almost forgot to go through the door at an angle, so she didn't knock her wings against the jamb. Charlie looked up and tried to smile.

"Hey, Wyld. At least you stayed safe, eh?"

Chloe picked up the non-IV hand and kissed it. "You scared the crap out of me, O'Neal."

Behind her came his parents, then Lindsay, Phil, and Heather. After tearful greetings and careful hugs, the doctor came in and told them he should be able to leave the hospital in two or three days.

"How soon can I fly?" he asked.

The doctor grimaced. "Now, there's a question I've never been asked, and I don't know how to answer it. I'm afraid I don't understand your anatomy well enough."

"Just Cause has already said they'll get you in with one of their doctors for rehab," Charlie's mom told him. "We'll get you back to Denver as soon as we can, okay?"

He nodded, glum. "I guess that's as good as I can hope for. I just wish I'd seen the gun in time to dodge." Brow furrowed, he cocked his head. "Did they catch the guy who shot me? I hope it hurt when I plowed into him. That's the last thing I remember."

The room fell silent and everyone exchanged looks.

"What?" Charlie asked.

"I found you on top of him," Chloe said.

"I knocked him out?"

She hesitated long enough that he knew without her having to say it.

"Wait, he's dead? Did I kill him?"

Chloe swallowed hard and Phil stepped in. "It looked like he bashed his head pretty hard when you, uh, flew into him. He bled out."

Charlie's eyes went wide. "Wow. That's . . . that's a weird thing to wrap your head around, isn't it?"

"You've got company." Lindsay's voice was strained.

Their eyes met and neither of them spoke for a while. "Maybe we can borrow a Just Cause therapist, too," Charlie said.

Chloe's phone rang and her face lit up when she saw the caller ID. It was Mustang Sally, former Just Cause superstar and current combat instructor at the Hero Academy. Chloe stepped out of the room as she answered.

"Chloe, what's going on? Is everyone okay?"

"We all survived," Chloe said, a vocal tremor revealing how hard it was to think about what could have happened. She briefed Sally.

"Good work, all of you," Sally said. "Let me talk to Charlie. I have some news that might help cheer him up."

Chloe went back into the room and gave him the phone. Charlie listened for a bit and his face broke into a huge grin.

"Seriously? Thanks, that's awesome!" When he hung up a short time later, they all looked at him, expectant. "So Just Cause has been working on the wing problem. You know, with water? Sally just found out they came up with a spray, some kind of silicone thing, that'll waterproof my wings without gumming them up. I'll be able to get wet without being grounded!"

"Cool," Chloe said. "Next time, *you* get the underwater heroics."

"You got it, Wyld. As long as that doesn't mean next time *you* get shot."

Sunday, Aug. 6, 2017
Coeur d'Alene, Idaho

Zeke reeled from the bombshell his father had dropped on him. As Detective Abara led the confused and angry boy back out toward the car, a girl's voice called Zeke's name.

"Naomi!" Zeke whirled around. She leaned out of a third-story dorm window, waving at him. "Can I go see her?"

"I don't think you want to be surrounded by Bruderschaft folks right now. I doubt you'd be welcome."

Zeke considered that. "I just want to see *her*. We was gonna get married."

Abara looked from him to the girl in the window and back again, then called over a trooper and asked him to escort Naomi out. "No one has been notified of any deaths yet, so don't say anything."

"What if she asks?"

"She won't know you were on the compound unless you tell her."

Zeke realized he was right. Still, it felt wrong not to tell her that her pa was gone.

When the trooper brought her out, she ran to him but stopped short. Zeke held out a hand and she took it in both of hers.

"It's so good to see you, Ezekiel."

"Yeah. You, too. I missed you."

They blinked at each other for a while, not sure what else to say.

"Are you . . . are you doing okay here so far?" Zeke asked.

She nodded. "Well enough, I suppose. How have you been?"

He told her a little about the ranch and how he got to work with horses. He didn't mention the parade.

"That's good. I know how much you love animals." She paused. "Have you heard anything about the compound? They haven't told us anything."

Zeke glanced at the detective, who gave him a warning look. Zeke stammered, trying to think of what he could say, then blurted out the truth. "Naomi, I'm so sorry, but the explosives shed . . . it blew up and your pa was caught in the blast. He . . . he's gone."

Abara sighed and shook his head. The troopers moved in closer but he motioned them back.

Tears welled up in Naomi's eyes. Then she blinked several times, and a resolute look stole over her face. "Good. He'll never hit me again. Or Ma or Jemima."

"He hit you? I thought Doc was one of the few good ones."

She hugged herself and shook her head. "He just knew how not to leave marks." She stood on her toe and kissed Zeke on the cheek, making him blush.

"You're the only good man to come from that place, Zeke. I hope you'll come see me again."

He nodded, and she beamed at him through watery eyes before turning to go back inside.

CHAPTER TWENTY

Saturday, Aug. 12, 2017
Coeur d'Alene, Idaho

Jeffrey looked out from a high balcony of the Coeur d'Alene Resort at the street where so many people had died in just a few awful moments the previous week. The town looked so peaceful now. It was hard to believe it was the same place. Or, at least, it would have been if not for the ribbons, crosses, flowers, and stuffed animals making up impromptu shrines on the sidewalk.

The senator and her staff had flown up for a ceremony honoring the law enforcement and parahumans who'd stopped the massacre from being even worse. Jeffrey hadn't expected it, but the senator mentioned in her speech how instrumental his abilities were in keeping her alive.

Tamara stepped out onto the balcony and leaned on the rail beside him. "I thought you were still on the phone. It looked important."

He snorted. "Yeah, I guess."

"What's wrong?"

Jeffrey sighed. "Since the senator's speech, I've had several elected officials offer me jobs on their security detail. One was even a congressman."

She squealed and hugged him. "That's great! For you, I mean. I don't want to lose you. Maybe we could get the senator to pay you really well, so you'll stay on."

"I'm turning them all down."

Tamara's jaw dropped. "What? Don't you still want a career in politics?"

"That's right—politics. I want to do the work of making things better, not follow around the people who do the work." He turned and looked back out at the street. "It bugged me that the senator wanted me to keep my ability quiet, but really, I should've been grateful. Because once people know you have a power, it's all they see. None of those job offers tonight were because of my degree in political science or my experience as your intern. They heard I have a power they can exploit, and that's all that matters."

"Is that a horrible thing?"

"Yeah, Tamara, it is." He shook his head. "I could've gone to Hero Academy, like those kids we met today, but I didn't want that life. Once people know you're a para, though, it's what they expect. You have to be a hero—the costumed, code-named, rush-into-danger sort of hero, not the kind who pushes through legislation making life better for everyone."

"There's plenty of paras who do things other than hero-ing. Sure, they want you for your power now, but wait until they get a look at what else you can do."

He looked her in the eye. "Yeah, sure, the ones like me, who can hide. Take WyldWing, though. Her wings pop out, everyone says *oh, you should go to Hero Academy*, and once you're there, your path is set. She's . . . what, fourteen or fifteen? Sure, she could decide to do something else, but how many schoolteachers have you seen with wings? How many attorneys have horns or hooves? How many elected officials are known paras, let alone obvious ones?"

Tamara squirmed. "Okay, I get your point. So, don't let anyone pigeonhole you. Stay here and work with us. Make the world better for the next generation of paras, so future Chloe Wylds can be whatever the hell they want to be."

"After all this," he gestured down at the sidewalk memorials, "do you really think we stand a chance against hate?"

"I do, Jeffrey. I really do."

Chloe blew out the fifteen candles on her cake in one huge breath. Her parents, Charlie and his parents, Zeke, Gabe, and Sam Abara sang Happy Birthday around the patio table.

"Thanks for holding the party for me, Wyld." Charlie grinned at her. He'd left the hospital, with a sling and strict instructions to keep his feet on the ground, just in time for the ceremony. Lindsay and her mom had driven over for it, but they'd already headed back to Montana.

Chloe said she was sad Lindsay couldn't stay, but in truth, she felt relieved. She was exhausted from worrying about both her and Charlie. Seeing the haunted expressions on Zeke and Gabe's faces was almost too much to bear.

"I've got some big news," Charlie announced, then dragged out the moment of anticipation when all eyes turned to him. "One of the doctors suggested a new name for me, and I've decided I like it. So, say good-bye to Meta Moth," he paused, "and hello to Divebomber."

Everyone cheered and applauded. Chloe thought the new name was *meh* but a definite improvement. At least people would know what it meant.

Once they all had their cake and ice cream, Phil asked Zeke if he planned to join Chloe and Charlie at the Academy. With the Bruderschaft leadership dead instead of standing trial, they wouldn't need to witness protection program after all.

"Oh, um . . . no, I'm not interested in being a hero."

"I tried to talk him into it," Gabe said, "because seriously, who doesn't want that?"

Chloe didn't respond. She wasn't at all sure she wanted it right now.

"So, what is your plan?" Heather asked.

"I'm gonna go down to Missouri and see my ma. Then . . ." He took a deep breath. "The social workers connected some of us from the compound with a church group that helps people escape from hate groups and cults and stuff. They travel around the country talking to people about the real stuff from the Bible, the parts about love and acceptance. They got tutors and counselors to help us re-learn the stuff we was taught wrong, too."

"Naomi's going, too," Gabe said. "So, I'm guessing there'll be lots of—" He cleared his throat. "Love and acceptance going on."

Zeke blushed while everyone laughed.

"So if you don't want to be a hero, do you know what you want to do, down the road?" Abara asked Zeke.

"I want to work with animals. Like on a ranch. There's lots of them down where my ma lives, and my pa says he's gonna settle down there, too." He shrugged. "Plus, I can always sign up for the Champions if I change my mind, right?"

"For sure!" Charlie said. "What about you, Gabe?"

"Mrs. Wyld's helping me get emancipated from my parents so I can move back in with Aunt Kim." Through Heather, he'd learned his aunt had tried to get someone to conduct a welfare check on him. The restraining order, different state jurisdictions, and local law enforcement's general reluctance to interact with a radical hate group had made for hurdles she couldn't clear. "I might travel around with Zeke and the others next summer, and then college. I'm thinking maybe I'll go into law. Maybe even parahuman law. You know, help protect the rights of the people protecting the rest of us."

Heather smiled. "That's a noble goal."

Even though it was her party, Chloe wished everyone would leave, already. She'd had few quiet moments since the parade. Between visiting Charlie at the hospital, giving statements to police, and talking to mom-approved media outlets, she needed some down-time. Charlie would head back to Nevada in the morning, and that, too, would be a relief.

She wanted to get out of Coeur d'Alene and back to school, where things could feel normal again. Her hometown was broken. Then again, she wasn't sure even Hero Academy would be better—her roommate and boyfriend were broken, too. So was she, she supposed. At least at school, she'd have classes and training to focus on.

After everyone left, Chloe climbed the stairs to her bedroom. Everything about it seemed wrong. It was a little girl's room. It didn't fit.

She took down her gymnastics medals and put them in a shoebox that she tucked up onto the high closet shelf. Next, she removed the Mustang Sally poster above the bed and the newspaper clippings about Sally and her other favorite heroes. Like she'd told Alex Peters, they really weren't like rock stars and actors; each one had faced horrors and had nightmares like she now did. Each one had been in life-and-death situations and their continued life, she now understood, meant they had killed. Chloe wondered how long it would be until she joined the club her closest friends now belonged to.

That wasn't the stuff of baseball cards and magazine covers. Or, at least, it shouldn't be.

Her walls cleared, she moved her stuffed animals from atop the bed to underneath, then cleared some trinkets from the desk and bookcase and shoved them in a drawer.

When it was done, she looked around. It didn't look like her room anymore, and that was okay. Chloe no longer knew who she was.

She felt like she should check on Lindsay and send Charlie a good-night message. She didn't want to, though, and that brought on guilt.

Her phone chimed, but the new message wasn't from Lindsay or Charlie. It was from Corvid.

You doing ok?

She blinked back tears. What could she say? *Yes* was a lie. But was she ready to open up to someone she didn't know very well?

Another message came in. *You're like me. I saw that in you at school. You try to stay strong all the time, take care of everyone. Makes it hard at times like this.*

She burst out sobbing, letting go for the first time since the parade. *It really does,* she messaged, the words hazy through tears. *How do you deal?*

You gotta lean on the people around you. Reach out to someone who gets it. Even when you think you shouldn't cuz other people got it worse right now.

She chuckled a little at that because of how much she related. *How'd you know that's what I was feeling?*

I'm there too. Dude, Charlie got shot. Those boys from the compound saw all those people they knew die. I just flew around a little, so why I got a right to feel sorry for myself?

Wow, that sounds familiar.

Like I said, we're a lot alike. Stay in touch, Speed. I know we weren't close at HA, but I got your back, k?

Chloe's shoulders relaxed for the first time in . . . she had no idea how long. *Thanks, Corvid. I got yours, too.*

Heather tapped at the door and she opened it. "Whoa, redecorating, are you?"

Chloe glanced back at the now-bare walls. "Oh, yeah. Seemed like it was time."

"I wanted to check on you before I went to bed. How you doing, Fly Girl?"

She paused before answering. Over the past few days, she'd told countless people countless times that she'd be okay. This time, though, she almost believed it.

ABOUT THE AUTHOR

Adrienne Dellwo is a novelist and award-winning indie filmmaker from Washington state. She's ecstatic to be playing in the Just Cause sandbox and looks forward to many more stories in that universe. In other arenas, she has two books out in an urban fantasy series—*Through the Veil* and *Traveler Lost*—and is working on the third. She also writes horror and traditional fantasy.

Adrienne's had short stories published by Local Hero Press, Alliteration Ink, Siren's Call and others, has one published poem, and has seen two of her stage plays performed. (Three, if you count one from third grade.)